HOUSE OF THE SHRIEKING WOMAN

PRAISE FOR HOUSE OF THE SHRIEKING WOMAN

"Ramirez's second Sarah Greene Mystery builds on *The Girl in the Mirror* by expanding the world of his spunky sleuth. This mystery strikes a great balance between quirky and thrilling and between modern and timeless, and it's easy to read, enjoyable, and thought-provoking."

— BOOKLIFE REVIEWS

"*House of the Shrieking Woman* is a solid psychological drama that steps away from the norm and carries a real small-town vibe. Claustrophobic and surreal, it spins from creepy to thoughtful with a stark and memorable narrative."

— INDIEREADER

"Pitting her nascent investigative skills against a sinister power that thrives in places of pain and suffering, the main character makes this quick thriller hard to put down. Ramirez is a master of building tension when the story most calls for it, making *House of the Shrieking Woman* a thrillingly dark slice of suspense."

— SELF-PUBLISHING REVIEW

BOOKS BY STEVEN RAMIREZ

LITERARY FICTION

Let's Get Lost

HELLBORN SERIES

Tell Me When I'm Dead

Dead Is All You Get

Even The Dead Will Bleed

HARD TO KILL SERIES

Brandon's Last Words

Faithless

SARAH GREENE MYSTERIES

The Girl in the Mirror

House of the Shrieking Woman

The Blood She Wore

OTHER BOOKS

Chainsaw Honeymoon

Come As You Are: A Short Novel and Nine Stories

Come As You Are: A Novella

Glass Highway

Los Angeles, CA

stevenramirez.com

Publisher's Note: This is a work of fiction. Names, characters, places, and incidents are a product of the author's imagination. Any opinions expressed belong to the characters and should not be confused with those of the author. Locales and public names are sometimes used for atmospheric purposes. Any resemblance to actual people, living or dead, or businesses, companies, events, institutions, or locales is coincidental.

House of the Shrieking Woman / Sarah Greene Mysteries Book Two / Steven Ramirez.—1st ed.

Paperback: 978-1-949108-06-4

EPUB: 978-1-949108-04-0

Kindle: 978-1-949108-05-7

Library of Congress Control Number: 2020900028

Edited by Natasha Hanova

Cover design by Damonza

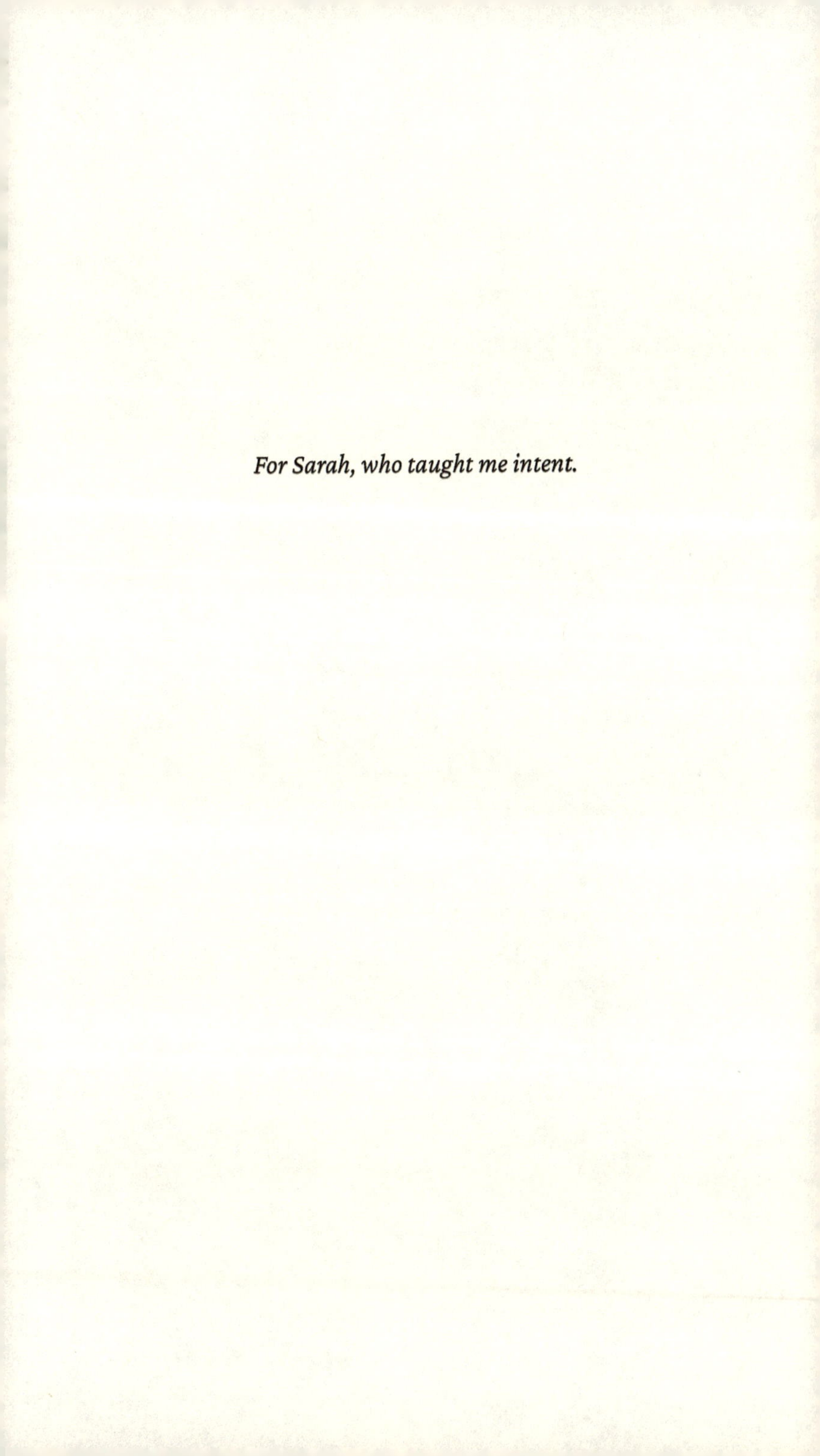

For Sarah, who taught me intent.

HOUSE OF THE SHRIEKING WOMAN

A Sarah Greene Supernatural Mystery

STEVEN RAMIREZ

glass highway

The blouse was pale, the colour of ivory, and as I watched, incredulous, three small drops of crimson seemed to spring from nowhere to the surface of the silk, and then, like ink on blotting-paper, rapidly to spread. I tugged down the blouse's collar and saw beneath it, on her bare skin, a scratch, quite deep, evidently freshly made, still rising, still beading red. She dropped her gaze.

'My little girl,' she murmured. 'She's so eager for me to join her. I'm afraid she...isn't always kind.'

— SARAH WATERS, THE LITTLE
STRANGER

CONTENTS

HOUSE OF THE
SHRIEKING WOMAN

ONE

January 2011. Laurel Diamanté looked out the window of her four-hundred-dollar-a-week hotel room off Pioneer Square. *It's an off day.* Normally at this time of year, the pelting rain would drive the homeless deeper into the dark recesses and under-explored burrows of Seattle, occasionally creating a comical juxtaposition of awkwardness during one of the city's famed underground tours.

But today was different. The sky was dense, an unrelenting gray blanket that covered the city to keep in the cold. No, it was a good day, she decided as she gathered her things and left her dingy quarters for the last time.

The elevator was out of service again. The hotness at the back of her neck made her curse as she headed for the emergency exit. Down, down she went, struggling to keep her purse strap from sliding off the smooth shoulder of her waterproof raincoat as she carried the neatly wrapped present in both hands. Fortunately, it was only two flights.

When she emerged, the usual malingerers were infesting the lobby. Unbathed old men mostly, single and immune to the foul weather that seeped in whenever anyone entered the building. Could they be of some use? No —too weak. Or drunk. There were plenty of other suitable candidates. Taking a last look at the forlorn, toothless denizens, she turned sharply and headed for the front desk to pay her bill.

"Four hundred even," the man with the lopsided haircut said. "Did you take anything from the honor bar?"

"No." She counted out four crisp one-hundred-dollar bills. "I don't drink, and I don't eat snacks."

"Okay." He handed her a receipt and a card with a website address. "If you wouldn't mind, could you fill out a survey online? Even better, how about posting a Yelp review?"

"Sure thing."

She needed to get gas before heading to the office. The man at the front desk said goodbye, but she ignored him and walked briskly toward the door, which led to the parking structure. She spotted an ashtray stand next to the doorway and deposited the card on top of a pile of yellowed, soggy butts.

One of Laurel's tires was low. As she unlocked her car door, she hoped it wasn't punctured. She would check it at the gas station. The heat radiating from her neck had transformed into a familiar, dull throbbing at her temples as she set the present on the passenger seat beside her purse and climbed in. Her bags were already in the trunk, along with everything else she needed. Nothing left to do now but get on the road.

It wasn't long before she'd gassed up her car and checked the tire pressure. Nothing was wrong with the car. A woman dressed in activewear had gotten into her vehicle as she pulled out. She shot in front of Laurel, causing her to slam on her brakes. The other woman stopped too. Infuriated, Laurel got out and marched up to the driver's side window.

"It was rude, I know," the woman said. When she saw the strange, threatening look on Laurel's face, she fumbled for the switch to raise her window.

"A person could get killed driving like that." Though her accuser smiled, her eyes were merciless.

"I... I didn't mean to..."

"Uh-huh. You should be more careful."

"Yes," the other woman said in a meek voice.

"Have a nice day."

As Laurel stepped back, the flustered woman put her car in gear and shot out of the gas station, barely missing a homeless man with a gimpy leg.

"Lucky for you I have other business," she said.

The day had gone quickly, and Laurel looked forward to getting things underway. Her friend of six months was quitting the Catholic social services agency, Mary's Gift, and they were going out to celebrate. Laurel had given her the present at lunch, a porcelain figure of a cocker spaniel. Her friend loved dogs but was allergic.

The plan was for Laurel to follow her friend to her house in Beacon Hill and drive them to dinner. When they left a little after five, the sky was already black, and it was raining hard. Though it seemed to rain constantly in Seattle, people had never learned how to drive safely. There was always some idiot who thought he could speed down Pike Street toward the fish market. The unexpected steepness of the grade would get the best of him, though, and there would be the inevitable fatal accident. She planned to be extra careful.

"I'm starving," her friend said as they got onto the I-90 toward Bellevue.

"Me too."

"I really appreciate you driving. But did we really have to go so far for dinner?"

"Oh, it's not far. And I think you're going to love the restaurant. So, what are your plans once you get to Phoenix?"

"I might take off a few months before looking for work."

"I'll miss you. And I understand—it's this stupid weather."

As if to underscore the remark, the sky lit up with tentacles of white crackling lightning. The inevitable thunder followed.

"I was thinking maybe I should go to Arizona too," Laurel said.

"That would be lovely! I was just getting to know you."

It took only fifteen minutes to get across the floating bridge. Laurel had already checked the directions and made her way easily to downtown Bellevue. On Bellevue Way NE, she spotted the building and, luckily, found parking on the street.

"This place is beautiful!" her friend said as they entered.

"I knew you'd like it."

Soon, they were seated. By the time her friend had returned from the restroom, their drinks were standing untouched on the table. Laurel raised her iced tea and toasted her friend, who'd treated herself to a martini since she wasn't driving.

"I wish you all the happiness in the world," Laurel said.

By the time the salads arrived, her friend felt unwell. She thought she should go to the restroom and splash cold water on her face. But when she tried standing, she became dizzy.

"Oh, dear," Laurel said. "Did they make the martini too strong?"

"I feel so strange."

A concerned restaurant manager came over. "Is there anything I can do?"

"My friend isn't feeling well. Can you help me get her to our car?"

The two of them pulled the other woman to her feet.

"Oh, the bill," Laurel said.

"Don't worry about it."

"Thank you."

Outside, the rain came down in sheets. Laurel and the manager helped the other woman into the car as a busboy held an impossibly large striped umbrella over them. Laurel thanked them and drove off, peering through the windshield to find her way to the I-90 south. She grabbed a fresh water bottle and handed it to her friend.

"Here, drink this. You're probably dehydrated."

"You're such a good friend," the woman said.

Within hours, Laurel had maneuvered her car down a treacherous dark road and found the small parking lot inside Mt. Rainier National Park. The rain had abated—a good sign. She parked and looked over at her friend, who was unconscious. Turning around, she reached for her purse on the backseat and removed the martini glass she'd stolen from the restaurant. In all the confusion, no one had missed it.

She got out and stood facing the public restrooms. It was quiet except for the howl of a sharp wind through the trees, and bitterly cold. She would have to work quickly. She dropped the glass and crushed it with her foot, destroying all evidence of the Ambien she'd used to incapacitate the victim.

She opened the trunk. A folded plastic tarp and a coil of yellow nylon rope lay on top of her suitcases. Next to those were a neatly folded bundle of heavy clothing and a pair of waterproof hiking boots. She laid the tarp and the rope on the ground next to the car's passenger side. Grabbing the clothes, she went into the restroom to change.

Taking her time, Laurel opened the passenger door, turned the unconscious woman until her back faced the door, and hooked her arms under the other's to drag her out. As she did so, the woman groaned. Laurel laid her on the tarp and tied it up at the feet. To make things easier for the short trip to the grave, she fashioned a noose and placed it around the victim's neck.

Now came the hard part. She would have to haul the body down the trail about a mile. She'd estimated it would take her less than an hour. Taking a quick look around her, she locked up the vehicle, draped the nylon rope over her shoulder and, like a logger, dragged the woman by the neck.

As she made her way slowly, the tarp left a noticeable trail, as if some giant snake had slithered through the forest. She looked up at the sky. Clouds were moving in again. Soon it would rain, washing away all the evidence.

"Why, Laurel?" she thought she heard the woman say.

As she struggled over rocks and mud, which in places

was inches thick, she answered the imagined question. Because it was all part of the plan—His plan. And she'd been promised a great reward—to know the unknowable. To lord it over the vermin, who did nothing more than occupy space.

To be like a god.

Laurel was sweating, despite the cold. Ignoring the vice-like pain in her head, she kept on. Eventually, she saw it up ahead—a tree trunk, its top bent completely over and back into the earth, forming the letter U. Opposite it, she knew, was a hollow.

Stopping to catch her breath, she looked around her as if someone might be spying on them. She dragged the woman's body up to the partially obscured entrance. Pausing to look at the sky, she climbed through, turned around, and pulled the body in the rest of the way.

She'd already dug the grave the previous night. The shovel lay where she'd left it. The hole was partially filled with rainwater. No matter. Only one thing left to do before disposing of the evidence. She picked up the shovel. Standing over the woman's body, she unrolled the tarp, exposing the head. Livid rope burns circumscribed her victim's aged neck, and her eyes bulged from a lack of oxygen. By all rights, she should be dead.

But she wasn't.

Her eyes searched Laurel's face for a shred of mercy.

"This is for the best," her killer said.

Straightening, she raised the shovel, and grunting, brought it down on the woman's head. Through the wet, crunching noise, she thought she heard the pathetic crea-ture mewling. Reveling in her victim's suffering, she repeated the action two more times. When she was sure her friend was dead, she went about burying the body.

As she emerged from the hollow, flushed with exertion and sweating under her heavy clothing, a wolf bayed somewhere far off. Everything was happening according to plan. Easy peasy.

Her work here was done.

TWO

Tell me about the dream," the psychologist said.

January 2018. Sarah Greene looked at her hands. They were shaking. She rubbed her right wrist. It ached where they'd installed the titanium plate to stabilize her shattered bones three months earlier. She didn't want to talk about her dreams—not to this woman, however well-meaning she was. She had only agreed to come at Joe's insistence.

He was worried about her, he said. So was her sister, Rachel. In fact, everyone she loved had practically ganged up on her, intervention style, to convince her she needed to go. That was before the holidays, which she used as an excuse to put it off. But this was January. Her anxiety and sleeplessness hadn't gotten any better. So at last, here she was, wrist aching, nerves jangly, not wanting to say anything about her terrible night in the forest.

She'd almost died.

Why was she here again? Right, to get better. *Better.* It was what people said about patients in mental institutions. Fighting the dread, which made her wrist hurt all the more, she straightened herself out of a slouch and looked at her therapist.

"It's always the same—no, different. The walls are closing in. Those hands—thousands of them—are trying to grab me. Only this time, I can see his face. He's the only one who isn't shrieking in pain."

"Peter Moody?"

"Yes."

She bit her lip until she tasted blood. She hated hearing his name. Saying it out loud was like giving him power.

"When I wake up, I'm drenched. And I feel like I can't breathe." When the tears came, she didn't fight them. "That monster took away my happiness and made me into *this*. I mean, look at me!"

Dr. Roxanne Marsh sat back in her comfortable-looking royal blue wingback chair with the light blue piping running along the edges and around the seat cushion. She was a widow and favored knit pants with cardigans and chocolate-brown loafers. She could have easily been ninety.

"Peter Moody is dead," she said. Her tone was firm but kind. "He can't control you unless you allow him to."

Sarah used a tissue to blow her nose. "I know, but it doesn't change anything. He's still in my head."

"What did you call it, your Wall of Souls dream?"

"I've been having it since I was fifteen."

The therapist referred to her yellow legal pad. "Ah, after your friend died."

"Alyssa."

"Mm. But you don't have it all the time?"

"I didn't use to. Usually, it precedes Alyssa's appearance. This must all sound very—"

"Everything is relevant."

Sarah couldn't tell where the kindly old woman with

the silver pageboy cut stood on the whole paranormal thing. Was she a fan? Or was she simply humoring her patient to get her to open up about what was really bothering her? A bad childhood? Or a drug problem? She squirmed on the love seat, whose colors matched those of the wingback chair.

"Are you taking the Prazosin?" Dr. Marsh said.

Sarah had forgotten all about her medication. She felt like a child who'd lied about having cleaned her room. And it didn't help that the woman, who insisted on being called Roxanne, had an English accent. When Mary Poppins turned ninety, would she prefer chocolate brown loafers?

"No, I... I don't like how I feel. It makes me too tired. And nauseous."

The therapist wrote something down. "There are other drugs. Check with your doctor."

Sarah's English bone china teacup sat untouched on the small rosewood side table. The room wasn't like an office at all. It was pleasant, and the wallpaper reminded her of a dayroom she'd seen once in *Architectural Digest*. Through the window, thorns like snake teeth jutted out of barren rose bushes. But there were no blooms. In January, everything was asleep. Or dead.

Dr. Marsh got up slowly, and placing her notepad and pen on the chair, sat next to her patient. Sarah was forced to admit she looked like a caring woman—someone who must have been through a lot herself. Sarah wondered if she'd ever had children. *Will I ever make it to ninety?*

"My dear," the English woman said, "you've been through something quite extraordinary."

Sarah avoided the blue-gray eyes, which were as clear as crystal. "I almost died."

"But now, you're here with me in this safe place. I can

see you're quite intelligent. You know in your heart, none of what happened was your fault."

"My fault?"

"And you're also smart enough to know..." The therapist took both her hands, careful not to squeeze the injured one. "You are a strong woman. And in time, with my help, you will heal."

That did it. Hot tears poured down Sarah's cheeks. Reddening, she wanted to shrink into nothingness, like the blurry, unstable image on an old-fashioned TV when you ripped the plug from the wall. But she answered, barely able to get out the words.

"Roxanne, I was so scared. He—"

"Shh. I know, dear. But he's well and truly gone."

Gone maybe. But not forgotten.

Reaching back, the therapist picked up a box of tissues. When she handed it to Sarah, she looked up, as if something had just occurred to her.

"You know, I'm glad you stopped the medication," she said and got to her feet. Then, looking at the side table, "Oh. I'm afraid your tea's gone cold."

She took the cup and left the room. A sense of calm settled over Sarah. She was safe here and was glad she'd agreed to come. Roxanne returned with a fresh cup and handed it to her patient.

"Drink up," she said, settling into the blue chair. "It's chamomile, with a kiss of honey."

Though she preferred coffee, Sarah sipped the beverage. "It's nice. Thank you."

"Now, I'd like you to try something for me, and when we meet again next week, you can tell me how it went. Okay?"

"Sure."

"Yoga."

Sarah scrunched her nose. "Really?"

"It might help you relax. I'm not what you would call religious. But I know this—what you're going through is of a spiritual nature. Yoga is the great equalizer, no matter your faith."

"Have you been talking to Father Donnelly behind my back?"

The therapist's laugh was light and cheerful. "He's your priest? No, I have not. But anyone with a brain can see the problem. Well, that's enough for today, I think."

The women rose and headed out of the office to the waiting room, where Joe Greene sat, staring at his phone. When he saw them, he got to his feet and gathered his ex-wife's leather jacket and purse.

At the door, Roxanne took Sarah's hands again. The therapist's were spotted, the skin soft and shiny.

"Promise you'll try yoga straight away."

"Okay, I will. Thanks for everything."

As Sarah headed out the door, Joe extended his hand. "Thank you for agreeing to see her."

"You're welcome." She waited until her patient had gone outside. Then, "She's lovely, Joe. And I trust you'll do everything you can to see her through this?"

Something in the way she'd said those words disconcerted him. It was almost as if she knew something—something bad.

"All right," he said, unsure of what he was signing up for.

"Good. There isn't a moment to lose."

From the doorway, she watched as he helped Sarah into his truck. In the sky behind them, gray clouds gathered over the city like slow-moving giants.

"I do hope it rains," Dr. Marsh said.

"I appreciate you coming with me," Sarah said.

They were on the 154, leaving Santa Barbara and heading north toward Dos Santos. She glanced at the Apple watch he'd given her for Christmas. It wasn't even eleven yet.

"No problem. You like her, right?"

"Yeah. Although I'm supposed to try yoga for my PTSD now."

"Instead of the meds? I seem to recall you going down this road before."

"Yeah. I do like her, though."

Recognizing the tenor of her own voice, she wondered if she was lying. No, she decided—she felt relieved, as if Roxanne had shown her a way out. She'd try yoga and put this horrible nightmare behind her.

In college, she'd taken a free yoga class the PE Department had offered to all incoming freshmen. Despite the occasional ghost phenomena invading her thoughts, she'd enjoyed it. But she hadn't loved it, and as a result, she didn't sign up for the next one.

"Early lunch?" Joe said.

"Sure, why not?"

Walking up to the entrance of The Cracked Pot, Sarah hesitated. Would they stare at her? Apparently, the whole town knew what had happened at Devil's Bluff, thanks to her friend's story in the *Dos Santos Weekly* last fall. And though three months had passed, she had the sense people thought she might be—what was the word?—*unstable*.

When they were inside, she headed for a booth in the back. No sooner had they sat when Carter Wittgenstein appeared carrying two cups of freshly brewed Guatemalan Antigua coffee. The girl's signature choppy bob looked a little shaggier. And she'd added metallic purple highlights to her almost jet-black hair. Sarah thought they were very becoming.

"I had a feeling I'd see you guys." Carter touched Sarah's arm. "How're you doing, Special Agent Starling?"

"I've gone off my meds," her friend said.

"I'll warn the staff. So, late breakfast? Lunch?"

Sarah had been coming to The Cracked Pot for so long, she'd memorized the menu. She considered for a moment.

"Blueberry pancakes."

The girl never wrote anything down and waited for Joe to order.

"And I'll have...the same."

"I'm warning you," Carter said as she walked away. "You're both getting a crap ton of bacon. My treat."

He sipped his coffee. "So, I assume seeing Dr. Marsh was a good idea after all?"

"It was. Speaking of which, you never told me how you found her."

"Oh, thought I had. Your dad recommended her."

"Eddie? Wow, I didn't see that coming. I wonder how he knows her. I'll have to ask him about it."

She reached across the table and took his hand. "Thanks for, you know, insisting. I, um... I guess I didn't realize how badly the incident affected me. Oh, crap."

"What?"

"I'm such a yutz. I never thought to ask how all this has been affecting you."

He hesitated. "I... Well, I'm not having any nightmares. I guess the new project helps me forget."

"I wish I could. How's the renovation coming, by the way? No hidden rooms with cursed objects, I hope?"

"No, thank God. Just a routine job."

"Can I ask you something? Does it bother you at all having to stay with me?"

"What? No, it's fine."

"Are you sure? Because I don't want you to think I'm trying to get my ex-husband back. But at night—"

He kissed her hand. "Come on. We've known each other too long. I like us being together—always have. Hey, maybe you can break your leg next time."

She was about to respond when Carter returned with two oversize plates of pancakes. Another server was right behind her, carrying a platter of thick-cut bacon.

"I'll be back with more coffee," the girl said. "Oh, I forgot the syrup."

"Take your time."

Sarah tried her food, then watched Joe eat his instead. She couldn't stop thinking about Devil's Bluff. If he hadn't shown up when he did—Lou and him—she would've fallen to her death for sure, just like Peter Moody aka Michael Peterson. *But he did come, Sarah.*

Carter watched them from across the room, a curious expression on her face. The moment they made eye contact, the girl pivoted and marched into the kitchen. Okay, it wasn't Sarah's imagination. Something was up.

"Joe?" she said. "Do you think we'll ever find a buyer for Casa Abrigo? I mean, it's been ages."

He set down his fork and wiped his mouth with his napkin.

Uh-oh, I'm right. Is it something bad? Please, God. Don't let it be something bad. Did the property burn down in some kind of holy fire? Stop it, Sarah, and let the man talk.

"I was waiting for the right time to tell you. We sold Casa Abrigo. We'll be in escrow by the end of the week."

The news took her breath away. "I-I can't believe it. But who would want to... I mean, it's beautiful and all. But after what happened? Everybody in town knows the story. What, did you sucker some out-of-town rich guy into buying the place?"

"You never know. Feel up to taking a ride?"

"To Casa Abrigo? Oh, I don't know..."

"This is a good thing, I promise."

She stared at the scar on her wrist. The dark, irregular line seemed to spell out a warning.

He put away his phone and got out his keys. "Fr. Donnelly has already blessed the house, remember?"

She tried finding the deception in his eyes. "What are you up to?"

"Nothing," he said, looking guilty as hell. "Finish your bacon so we can go."

Though she hadn't wanted ever to set foot on the property again, Sarah felt she needed to trust Joe. Getting past her dread of this place was part of her therapy, she told herself. Even though being here again made her feel weak, as she had when fighting for her life on the cursed cliff. *Trust Joe.*

He pulled into the newly paved driveway and parked. For a moment, she wondered why there weren't any trucks outside and had to remind herself the house was finished.

She gazed up at the roof, looking for ravens. Then she got out.

A vehicle, which resembled her friend's MINI Cooper, sat parked down the street. Though nervous, she had to admit the house looked beautiful. The landscaping was complete with newly planted trees. The rich green lawn and the freshly painted exterior gave the impression of an expensive Spanish-style home you might see in neighboring Montecito.

She expected to sense the evil presence resulting in her near-death experience. She was certain it was waiting for her inside, unseen and ready to take her. But as she touched the door handle, she felt nothing other than the sting of cold brass. *It's a house.*

Before opening the door, she turned to him. "This isn't one of those lame surprise parties?"

"Nope. Go on, open it."

As the door swung open, Carter was standing in the foyer, wearing a black-and-white striped shirt, pencil skirt, and her trademark Doc Martens.

"Well, hello there," she said.

"Okay, I'm really confused," Sarah said as her friend embraced her. "Are you two getting married?"

Joe laughed. "Meet the new proud owner of Casa Abrigo."

Carter looked at her friend hopefully. After a long silence, she said, "Well, say something. What do you think?"

Sarah felt dizzy, as if she'd passed through a portal into an alternate reality. Though someone was speaking, she couldn't make out the words and forced herself to focus.

"I came into my money recently," the girl said. "And I

thought if I'm gonna settle down in Dos Santos, I needed a house."

"Sure, but—"

"And since I fell in love with Casa Abrigo the first time I saw it—even with all the paranormal shenanigans—I thought, why not?"

Fighting the urge to run, Sarah looked past her at the flawless interior. The tile, the staircase, the lighting. It was all so beautiful. Was this really happening?

"I need a drink," Sarah said.

"Perfect timing." Joe trotted over to the kitchen.

Moments later, a cork popped. As she took in the pristine dining room, he returned with a tray of champagne flutes. He handed one to Carter, then Sarah. Taking his, he raised his glass.

"To Casa Abrigo," he said. "Officially ghost free."

Everyone clinked glasses and tasted the champagne.

"By the way," he said to Sarah, "you're drinking a Roederer Cristal 1964."

She took another sip. "From the wine cellar?"

"You bet. Look, I know we talked about splitting everything between us. But I felt our new client needed a good wine collection to go with the house."

"I hope you don't mind," the girl said to her friend.

Sarah bit down on her tears and held her close. "Now I know where to come for a tasting. Honestly, Carter, this is wonderful news. I'm so happy for you."

"I hoped you would be."

"Sorry I was a little off-kilter." She hugged the girl again. "So, when did you turn twenty-five?"

"Two weeks ago. I didn't want anyone to make a big deal out of it. You remember when I was gone a few weekends ago? I went to see my parents to sign papers and stuff. It's official. I'm rich—or well off, I guess."

"Happy belated birthday. And I owe you a present. Something for the house, I think."

"There's really no need, but thanks." Carter looked away. "It's just that... Well, after what happened... Joe and I didn't wanna, you know, upset you."

"No, I get it. Look, I know I've been a handful lately. But I'm better now. I think. So, I suppose you'll be having your band practices here?"

"Actually..."

"Uh-oh."

"The others missed San Francisco. They asked me if I wanted to come, and I told them I wanted to stay here."

"Well, I'm glad you did. But I am sad about the band. You guys sounded great. So, what are you doing about furniture? And don't say IKEA."

The girl finished her champagne and burped. "Excuse me. It'll take some time. First, I need to find an interior designer—"

"What are you talking about? You've got me."

"Really?"

"Of course. And I come cheap. Well, I do expect a decent wine now and again."

The women high-fived. Carter insisted on conducting a tour, which made Sarah even more anxious. They spent the afternoon going room by room, planning the décor. Soon, Sarah felt herself getting into the spirit—until they reached Peter Moody's room. When the girl saw the look on her friend's face, she closed the door.

"I already know what I'm doing in there."

By the time they'd returned downstairs, Sarah felt better. She stood in the spacious dining room, imagining the house filled with furniture and accessories. Gazing at one of the blank terra fresco walls, she decided on the perfect birthday present. She would purchase Carter a painting.

On the drive home, she closed her eyes, savoring the effects of the champagne.

"I'm glad you didn't tell me," she said. "I was feeling so down about everything. And a surprise like this, well. It was magical. Thanks."

"No charge. Want to pick up something for dinner?"

"Nope. I feel like cooking."

"Hey, things will be different now. How about we just, you know, enjoy life for a while?"

She touched his arm. "Sounds good."

As they made their way down San Marcos Pass Road toward the town, she thought she saw someone standing off to the side near the trees. Turning, she recognized Alyssa, barefoot. She was distraught. Sarah closed her eyes and tried pretending it was all a dream. She didn't see ghosts. It was merely pretend, like when she was little.

But she knew better. The spirit of her best friend had appeared again to deliver a dark message. Not about Casa Abrigo—Sarah was sure of it. Something new was coming, and she wasn't ready. Though Roxanne had assured her she was strong, Sarah felt as though she would shatter at any moment. And what would follow? Madness?

"You okay?"

Joe's voice startled her. Taking a breath, she looked at him and smiled serenely.

"Everything's fine," she said.

THREE

Sarah didn't understand why Carter wanted to live at Casa Abrigo. There were plenty of other nice properties. In fact, her friend could afford to purchase a vacant lot somewhere nice and build the perfect custom home. Though the house on San Marcos Pass Road was ghost free, as Joe and Fr. Brian had assured her, she had the sense that, because of Peter Moody's influence, it was and would always be cursed.

As she parked off Anacapa Street and followed the familiar path to the parish office at Our Lady of Sorrows, she made it a point to avoid looking at the field in the Notre Dame School across the street. Occasionally, she'd seen her dead fourth grade teacher, Mrs. Lech. Sadly, she recalled the woman had never taken a vacation. Was she doomed to spend the rest of eternity as a ghostly playground monitor?

Unable to resist, she sneaked a look. Nothing. Just girls in Belair Plaid skirts, white polos, and navy sweaters playing soccer as living, breathing teachers watched. When she entered the office, the parish secretary, Mrs. Ivy, was at her computer typing, a tepid cup of tea next to her keyboard.

"Hi, Sarah," she said. "Fr. Brian will be with you in a minute."

Mrs. Ivy had been at Notre Dame since Sarah was in first grade. How old was she? Sarah took a seat on the long wooden bench, which straddled the wall. She recalled how she used to volunteer in the office starting in sixth grade. Then she perused the school photos on the wall, some dating back to her time there.

When the secretary wasn't looking, she lifted a frame with an index finger. The door opened, and she saw Fr. Brian Donnelly's twinkling Irish eyes.

"Come on in," he said.

His office never changed, which was a comfort to her. There were teetering stacks of books—the priest was a voracious reader—and unruly piles of unfiled papers she assumed Mrs. Ivy would get around to at some point. And everything was graced with the scent of British Sterling. She stared at a photo of Pope John Paul II amid throngs of the faithful. *Shit, I wonder if...*

"We removed it," he said. "Ages ago."

She looked at him innocently, not wanting to admit the truth. Then, "Oh."

He laughed. "Whatever possessed you to stick your gum behind our Holy Father?"

"I didn't want to get caught."

"I see," he said, relaxed at his desk. "What can I do for you? You're not here to talk about the Joe situation?"

She blanched. Ever since the Peter Moody incident, she had insisted Joe move in, though they hadn't actually been having sex. She was too frightened to be alone and needed him close. Just not too close.

At first, Joe had agreed to sleep in the guest bedroom, which she'd finally cleared out and made habitable. But when the new nightmare came, he had gone to her as soon as she woke up screaming. That night, he'd done nothing more untoward than lie with her in bed, holding her until she fell asleep.

The next night, she asked him to stay in her bed. They hadn't had anything to drink because At the time, she was taking Prozasin for her PTSD. Then again, she and Joe had never needed alcohol as an excuse for romance. As he lay there gently stroking her hair, she kissed him. Aroused, he pulled her close, and before she knew it, he was massaging her breasts and kissing her neck.

A feeling of intense panic came over her, and for the first time ever, she pushed him away as if he were attacking her. Unsure of what to do, he returned silently to the other room, leaving her confused and alone. After a sleepless night, she'd planned to apologize, but when she went downstairs, she discovered Joe had already left for work.

"Sarah?" Fr. Donnelly said.

"I'm not here to talk about...you know."

"Okay. You're a grown woman. You know the score. So how's the therapist working out?"

"She gave me a suggestion. Yoga."

"Interesting."

"Said what I was going through was spiritual. Which is funny because she doesn't consider herself to be religious."

Fr. Brian thought a moment. "There are people who are spiritual without being aware. It's as if they have a God-given intuition, which lets them truly see. Even though they themselves may not acknowledge where the gift comes from."

"And you think Dr. Marsh—"

"Might be one of those people, yes. So, what did you come here for?"

Her eyes stung as she thought again about what had happened at Devil's Bluff. It was as fresh in her mind as ever, even though so much time had passed. The running. The pleading for him to release her. And finally, the hundreds of ravens who tore her attacker to shreds and, blinding him, sent him hurtling to his death off the dark cliff.

"What happened to Peter Moody?" she said. "The birds, I mean. Did I witness a miracle?"

The priest's eyes darkened. "Miracles are normally associated with something good—not a man's death."

"But something good did happen, Father. I was saved."

"True. Often, we don't know why things happen. We must continue to trust in God. And pray. Eventually, every-thing becomes clear, and we can see our true path."

"Practicing your homily for Sunday?" she said.

"How do you like it so far?"

"Not bad." She got up and shook his hand. "But I'd leave out the part about the ravens. You know, for the kids."

"Indeed." He leaned forward. "Listen, I'm sensing there was something else you wanted to discuss."

"I..."

She massaged her wrist, something she'd been doing since the cast came off. Though she avoided eye contact, she knew he was watching her. Reluctantly, she sat.

"That night," she said, "Peter told me something. He said someone had found me through the mirror."

"The spirit of the girl, I thought."

"No, someone else. It was the way he said it, as if it was a person—or thing—more powerful than him. He told me they wanted me dead, and Peter was just following orders."

"The ravings of a madman, perhaps?"

"No, I don't think so." Her eyes filled with tears. "I'm so frightened—I don't want to die. Not like this."

Fr. Brian rose and came around the desk. Gently, he helped her to her feet and embraced her as she wept.

"I'm praying for you, and I said a Mass. But you must try to be strong. I can't pretend to know God's mind. But I know this. He loves His children. And if you believe, He will show you the way."

She grabbed some tissues from his desk and blew her nose. "I'm such a mess."

"No. You've been hurt. You're being human. Promise me you'll try and rest. I want you to come and see me again."

"I will. Thanks for the pep talk. And the tissues."

As she made her way to her car, she thought about what the priest had said. She would have to be strong, but she wasn't sure she was up to it. A flock of crows was perched on the playground equipment of the kindergarten across the street. They reminded her of the ravens. Strangely, she hadn't noticed any at Casa Abrigo on her last visit. Was this God's way of saying things were getting better? She hoped so.

For Carter's sake.

When Sarah returned to Greene Realty, the offices were busier than normal for a January. Blanca, the assistant, was speaking Spanish to a young, eager couple. The mother held a baby boy who looked to be around one. From the conversation, Sarah understood they were new in town and were looking for a house to rent. Her sister stood outside her office with another couple. When she saw Sarah, she waved.

"Thank goodness," Rachel said. Then to the couple, "Sarah will take care of you."

She extended her hand. "Hi, I'm Sarah Greene."

"I'm Robert, and this is my fiancée, Stacey."

"Nice to meet you," she said. Then to her sister, "Thanks, Rache."

Sarah escorted the couple into her office to take down their information. Though it wasn't even two, she hadn't planned on showing any properties and wanted nothing more than to go home to rest.

"I can show you guys a few listings on my computer, but I'm afraid we'll have to wait until tomorrow to see anything in person."

The man seemed disappointed and exchanged a look with his fiancée. "We were really hoping to see something today."

"Well, we do have a condo here on Dos Santos Boulevard. It's a two-bedroom. Would you like to check it out? We can walk."

Her clients' faces lit up. "Yes," the woman said.

"Great. Let me print the listing."

In a few minutes, Sarah was leading the eager couple out by way of The Cracked Pot, where she'd bought them cappuccinos. They continued walking south toward the condo complex. Ignoring her emotional exhaustion, she played tour guide, pointing out all the trendy shops and restaurants.

She recognized an elderly couple she'd seen off and on downtown. They were getting into a 1966 Buick Skylark GS with dull beige paint and a broken taillight. A faded bumper sticker read DON'T WORRY BE HAPPY and featured a yellow smiley face. She had never paid attention to them before. Now she watched them more carefully. She assumed they were married, yet they seemed distant toward one another—almost as if the other didn't exist.

As she walked past the vehicle with her clients, something moved in the backseat. She wanted to look closer, but there was no way to do it without being obvious. As the couple drove off, she thought she saw a girl with haunted eyes staring out the rear window, her shadowed face and hands pressed against the glass.

"Is this it?" the man said to her.

When she turned, she saw the wary look on their faces. "Yes, we're here."

Later, when she returned to Greene Realty alone, Sarah headed directly for her sister's office "Rachel, you need to get your real estate license."

"What? Why?"

"So we can switch jobs. Robert and Stacey? Yeah, they're never coming back."

"They didn't like the condo?"

"They loved it." She looked away. "They didn't love me. I think I might've creeped them out."

When she wiped away a tear, her sister got up and held her.

"I can't help what I see," Sarah said. "I must've said something—I don't remember. Something about ghosts. They got very quiet. And when we were outside again, they thanked me and practically sprinted down the sidewalk."

Rachel kissed her sister's cheek. "Come on. Tapas time."

"I can't, I—"

"Don't say no."

"I promised Joe I'd cook tonight. Oh, what the hell. I'd

probably mess that up too. Do you think Katy will mind if you're a little late?"

"I'll give her a call and meet you over there."

"Okay. Thanks."

It was nearly five, and El 600 was already filling up. Sarah found a table near the window and slid in. When she was settled, she texted Joe, asking if he wanted takeout. He declined. When the server came over, she ordered two Priorats and a selection of tapas.

She watched as Rachel crossed the street and walked in. Her sister was beautiful, and it pained Sarah to see her alone. Despite her own complicated situation, she often prayed Rachel would meet someone special and remarry.

"Wow, busy," her sister said.

Sarah handed her a glass and clinked hers against it. "Here's to my next career."

"Stop. You had one little setback."

Soon, the server reappeared with the food. After saying a blessing, the women ate and talked. Sarah was beginning to think Rachel was right. Things would get better. But a voice in the back of her head warned her not to get too comfortable. She'd seen Alyssa, which meant only one thing—something terrible was coming.

"Pretty shifty of you," Sarah said, helping herself to the gambas al ajillo.

"What?"

"Not telling me about Carter purchasing Casa Abrigo."

"Not my fault—I was sworn to secrecy. By the way, I have a ton of papers for you to sign. How do you feel about it?"

"I don't know. I mean, I'm happy? Ish. I guess it's time for someone to make some good memories there."

"Agreed." Her sister stood. "Save me some shrimp."

Rachel had made it halfway to the restrooms when a loud clap rattled the window, startling Sarah. A homeless man with no teeth and swollen, crazy eyes was glaring at her. His greasy hands were pressed to the glass. And he was saying something she unintelligible, gesturing in a way that suggested he did not know sign language.

A police cruiser happened to be passing, and letting go a short siren, pulled over immediately. When the man saw the cops getting out, he grinned toothlessly and shuffled away.

Rachel returned, and taking her seat, glanced out the window. "Did something happen?"

"I think I'm going to need another drink," Sarah said.

Sarah parked her black Ford Galaxie 500 XL in the garage and walked into the house through the kitchen, where Joe was cooking something that smelled wonderful. He hadn't done this since the time she pushed him out of her bed. Eventually, they got past the fiasco, and during the day, things were fine between them. But at night...

"I had no idea you were here," she said. "Where's your truck?"

"It's getting new tires. Manny dropped me."

She sidled up to him and looked at what was cooking in the pan. She recognized olive oil, garlic, mushrooms, and onions.

"So, are you trying to be the perfect man?"

"I thought I already was."

Before she could change her mind, she turned him around and kissed him full on the lips. "You definitely are."

Gently, he pulled away and tried to look busy. *Shit, he's still mad.*

"There were chicken breasts in the freezer," he said. "I'll get the pasta going, and we'll be eating shortly. I assume you're hungry."

"Always."

She opened the refrigerator and took out an ice-cold bottle of Orvieto. Then she poured two glasses and handed one to Joe.

"Thanks. So, how was the meeting with Fr. Donnelly?"

"Fine. I asked him if he thought those ravens were a miracle. As per usual, he dodged the question. I don't know. Ever since it happened, he's been different."

"Maybe you're different."

"Sure, blame the victim."

An uncomfortable silence hung in the air. He'd finished cutting up the chicken and added it to the sizzling mixture. She ignored his comment.

"Sure you don't want to throw in some chopped Italian parsley?" She gave him an exaggerated wink.

"I knew I forgot something."

"Don't sweat it. I'll take care of it."

As they ate, she wondered how they would ever get past the awkwardness of sleeping under the same roof. As far as she knew, Joe didn't exhibit any overt resentment over the arrangement. On the other hand, he wasn't particularly affectionate either. She felt as if they were in some weird limbo. *Stay calm. Everything will be fine.*

She realized she was getting anxious and gulped her wine. She thought of the homeless man at the restaurant, remembering his devilish face.

It was probably nothing.

As Sarah lay alone in bed, she felt around for the cat. Though she knew Joe was close by, she wanted so much to feel his arms around her. *You pushed him away, remember?* It was late. Outside, a sharp wind had kicked up. She adjusted herself on her back and, her eyes closed, commanded herself to sleep.

All of a sudden, the room turned cold. *Oh, not now.* When she opened her eyes, Alyssa was standing at the foot of her bed. Sarah knew this wasn't a dream and sat up. In an instant, the ghost was standing beside her. She glanced at Joe, who was in a deep sleep.

"Don't be afraid," Alyssa said.

"I'm not."

"Something's happened. You must help."

Sarah felt her stomach tightening. Her wrist throbbed. She heard her own breathing—it was labored. Why would her friend ask this of her? She wasn't ready. In fact, she wasn't sure she'd ever be ready again. What had happened on Devil's Bluff had scared her straight. All she wanted now was to live like a normal person with normal problems.

"I can't, Alyssa, I..." She stared into the girl's liquid eyes. "Don't ask me to..."

The ghost touched her wrist, and she sensed a soothing calm. It felt like a soft, warm towel. Soon, her wrist no longer ached.

"So much pain," Alyssa said.

Sarah wasn't sure if her friend was talking about herself or about Sarah.

"Who's in pain?"

"You must help."

The ghost glanced over her shoulder. As if someone had flipped a switch, the wind outside ceased, and Alyssa was gone. Everything in the house was still, and the temperature was normal. Then the soft, familiar padding across the floor. In a moment, Gary was at the door. He trotted up to the bed and hopped on, purring.

"There you are," she said, stroking the cat's head. "So, what do you think I should do?" He meowed. "Really? You're no help."

Joe stood at the door, wearing a T-shirt and boxers. She did her best to suppress her naughty thoughts as he yawned and stretched.

"Everything okay?" he said. "I heard voices."

"I couldn't sleep."

"Want some company?" Then, raising his hands, "I promise I won't try anything."

She thought for a moment, then placed the cat on her side of the bed and opened her arms to him. He climbed into bed and laid her head on his chest.

He kissed her forehead. "Try to get some sleep."

As he stroked her hair, she felt herself letting go, drifting off. Somewhere in the dim recesses of her consciousness, she saw Alyssa hovering there, her beautiful brown hair flowing, her face peaceful.

"Goodnight, Alyssa," she said.

FOUR

Rupinder Anand took Sarah's hand and lowered it into the paraffin bath. This was Sarah's favorite part of the therapy because the hot wax seemed to draw the pain away from her. The physical therapist performed this task two more times, then wrapped the patient's wrist in a towel. Finally, using tongs, she applied a hot compress, wrapped the wrist, and stepped away.

Sarah felt the heat work its way deep into her shattered bones. Before the surgery, the surgeon had shown Joe and her X-rays from the injury. All the tiny pieces of bone floated in a viscous void. When he showed them new images taken after the surgery, they saw the plate and screws the surgeon had drilled into the bone to force everything back into place.

When Rupinder returned after ten minutes, she removed the towels, peeled off the wax, and massaged in generous amounts of soothing lotion. Heaven. Followed by hell, which consisted of the physical therapist beginning a series of exercises, moving the wrist and causing intense pain, which had lessened only slightly since Sarah had begun the treatments in December. She knew it was the only way she'd get her strength back, though, and endured the process like a silent martyr.

Rupinder was a quiet, thoughtful woman who laughed easily. Sessions lasted an hour, two times per week. Despite the punishment she inflicted, Sarah had come to enjoy her company.

"So what about your son?" she said. "Did Johns Hopkins hire him?"

"We are still waiting."

"I've been praying for him."

"Thank you."

Sarah winced from the pain. To distract herself, she picked up the pen lying on a clipboard and read what was printed on it—Sᴛ. Rɪᴛᴀ Wᴏᴍᴇɴ's Cᴇɴᴛᴇʀ.

"I am a volunteer there," the physical therapist said.

"I've heard of this place. It's over on Myrtle, right?"

"Yes."

She concentrated on a clock on the wall. The women's shelter. A feeling of uneasiness crept over her, and she thought of Alyssa. Could this be it? *Don't do it, Sarah. Normal life, remember?* She sighed, knowing in her heart what she had to do.

"Rupinder, this is going to sound...a little crazy, I guess? Did something happen at the shelter recently?"

The woman stopped what she was doing, and glancing at her watch, looked at her patient evenly. "We're done for today."

"What time is your next one?"

"Not until ten."

Sarah grabbed her purse. "Come on. I'm buying you a tea."

There was a Starbucks within walking distance of the

medical building in Santa Barbara. The women found seats near a window. Sarah insisted Rupinder settle in while she purchased the drinks. In a few minutes, they were sitting across from each other.

"It's strange your bringing this up," the physical therapist said. "How did you know?"

"Hard to explain. I felt it."

"They say you can see ghosts."

Sarah shook her head. "Really wish Carter hadn't published that story."

"I come from a small village along the Ganges. When I was a little girl, there was a man who had died. He was ancient—no one really knew how old.

"According to our tradition, his body was cremated. A week later, many people reported seeing him wandering through the village."

"Did you see him?"

"Yes. I was so frightened, I was afraid to tell my parents."

"And have you seen any ghosts since?"

"No."

Rupinder was holding something back. Sarah felt the familiar tingle in her midsection, and though she didn't think she was ready to hear this, somehow she knew she needed to.

"The women who stay at the shelter, they have all been abused," the woman said. "As a result, they have come to us with drug and alcohol problems. Some have engaged in self-harm."

"Oh, those poor things."

"We have a psychologist who works with these women, and nothing like this has happened for a long time." Rupinder took a deep breath. "A week ago, one of the staff discovered a resident called Julie attempting to swallow a knitting needle."

"Was she...upset about something?"

"No. The opposite. She seemed happy. Fortunately, an orderly took it away from her, but she was spitting up blood. The strange thing is, she was laughing."

"Drugs maybe?"

"The women are closely monitored and tested regularly. A few days later, another resident—Roberta—found a brick in the courtyard and smashed her hand with it."

"But why would she—" Sarah said.

"I was there. She tried doing it again, and I managed to take it away from her. When I did, she looked at me and said, 'I thought there would be more blood.'"

Sarah stared at her coffee but didn't drink it. "They might be depressed."

"The psychologist has interviewed them and said both seemed cheerful. It all started so suddenly. I'm afraid of what might happen next."

"Has anything at the shelter changed? I mean, like a disruption to the routine or...?"

"You are wise," the physical therapist said. "There is a woman who arrived recently from Guatemala and is here on asylum. She left her country because of domestic abuse."

"Husband?"

"During their time together, he broke her arm, her nose, and several ribs."

"My God."

"She said the police there do nothing. They always think it's the woman's fault. She must be running around with other men and deserves what she gets."

"And did he try following her here?"

Rupinder drank her tea and set it down carefully. "He is dead."

Sarah thought of Peter Moody. Sometimes, the dead had a way of coming back.

"I see," she said.

"They fished his body out of the river. His wife identified him."

Sarah continued to turn the situation over in her mind. Why would two women, seemingly in good spirits, want to harm themselves? *So much pain.*

"When the psychologist spoke to the residents," the woman said, "they denied having done anything."

"How did they explain their injuries?"

"They couldn't. I said I was there in the courtyard when Roberta injured her hand. What I didn't tell you is, there was someone else there too."

Rupinder's hand trembled as she picked up her tea. She took a long, thoughtful sip and looked into Sarah's eyes. "It was the new resident, Ana Robles."

"You think she had something to do with these accidents?"

"Not at first. But when the orderly said she'd also been in the room with Julie, I wondered, can it be true?"

Sarah took a sip of her tepid coffee. She didn't need this —not now. She still had difficulty sleeping. And there were the dreams. Then again, hadn't she been the one to initiate it? After turning it over in her mind, she decided.

"You said the Guatemalan woman's name is Ana?" she said.

"Ana Robles."

"I'd like to meet her. Look, I'm no expert. I was thinking when she left her country, she might've—"

"Brought something with her?"

"Exactly. I'm not sure if I can help, but I'd like to try."

"Thank you, Sarah. I will text you the name and phone number of the director. I'm sure she will be grateful." She got to her feet. "And thanks for the tea. I must get back and prepare for my next patient."

"Bye, Rupinder."

Sarah watched as the woman left the store and disappeared down the sidewalk. In a few minutes, a text appeared on her phone. It read *Heidi Lewis*, followed by a phone number. She wondered again about the wisdom of pursuing this. Groaning, she dialed her phone. It connected on the second ring.

"Lou? It's Sarah," she said. "I need to see you right away."

When Sarah walked into the Dos Santos police station, the first person she saw was Officer Tim Whatley. His sandy hair was shorter, and he had the beginnings of a mustache, which was at odds with his boyish face. *Really, Tim?*

"Hey, Sarah," he said. "I didn't expect to see you here today."

"Can you let me through? The chief is expecting me."

"Sure. Follow me."

He used his card key to open the door, which led to the interior of the station. As she followed, people side-eyed her, some whispering. *Get a life.* When they reached Lou's office, Tim poked his head in.

"Chief? You have a visitor."

Lou was poring over a case file. When he saw her, he got to his feet, knocking over his coffee cup. The small amount of liquid in the cup spilled onto some papers and went unnoticed.

"Sarah," he said, coming around his desk. Then to Tim, "Thanks."

The officer lingered a moment, then disappeared down the corridor.

"I appreciate you seeing me, Lou," she said.

"No problem. Have a seat." Both his visitor chairs were piled with mug shot books and other case files.

"Crime on the rise again?" she said.

"We have an audit coming up. Hang on, let me clear a spot."

He freed up a chair and motioned for her to sit. Then he closed his office door and returned to his desk. Seeing the spill, he shook his head and looked for something to wipe up the mess. She spotted a roll of paper towels in a corner and retrieved it for him.

"Thanks," he said. "See what a mess I am without you?"

"No shit. I have a good cleaning service I can recommend. I understand they're also good with crime scenes. And this one definitely qualifies."

Distracted, he sopped up the coffee and apparently hadn't heard her. He picked up a DVD in a plastic sleeve and set it aside.

"Isn't that the disc you got from the *Dubious* people?" she said. "I thought it was police evidence."

"Yeah, well, the Peter Moody case is solved, so I really have no use for it. Want it?"

She remembered the image of the dead girl floating in the cemetery, and hesitated. *What the hell? Might come in useful later.*

"Sure." She took it and slipped it into her purse.

Lou leaned back and folded his hands on his stomach. "So, what's new? How's the wrist?"

"It hurts. Which sort of leads me to why I'm here."

She recounted her meeting with Rupinder. Lou listened attentively and waited for her to finish. Then he cleared his throat.

"Sarah, I realize you're trying to help. And I applaud you for it. But are you sure you want to get involved? You've had it pretty rough."

Though she knew he was right, she bristled. "Lou, I'm not an invalid. And as far as any aftereffects, I really am trying to get back to normal."

"And by *normal*, you mean poking around in the dark looking for ghosts."

"That hasn't been established yet. Look, it could be nothing. But so far, two women have harmed themselves for no good reason. I think it's worth looking into."

He placed his hands on his desk. "Well, it's a free country. And I suppose you're bringing Carter along?"

"I was hoping to. And I may be trying to get back to normal, but that doesn't mean I'm ready to fly solo."

"Okay. Be sure to report back to me with anything you might find. I like to know what's going on in my town, physical or otherwise."

"Great. Thanks, Lou."

The police chief followed her to the door. He placed a tentative hand on her shoulder.

"Does Joe know you're doing this?"

"I haven't told him yet."

"Just be careful, okay?"

"Always."

Sarah left Lou's office and noticed Tim standing against a wall, muttering into his phone. When she waved, he glanced at her and, blushing, walked briskly down the hall.

"Okay, that guy is getting squirrellier by the minute," she said.

Sitting alone in a booth at The Cracked Pot, Sarah sipped her cappuccino when Carter appeared carrying a demi-tasse. She'd finished her shift and wore casual clothes. Taking a seat across from Sarah, she sipped her espresso.

"So tell me already," the girl said.

"You feel up to visiting the women's shelter?"

"I don't know. Why?"

"'There's something strange in the neighborhood.'"

"Oh, boy. Are you sure you—"

Growling, Sarah pretended to throttle an invisible throat. "I swear, if one more person asks me if I'm okay, I'm seriously going to lose my shit."

"Sorr-ee. So, what do you think's going on?"

After Sarah had run everything down, her friend agreed immediately.

"When can we go?" Carter said.

"How about now?"

"You must really wanna do this."

"I don't. But I feel like I'm going to remain a hot mess until I get back in the saddle."

"Speaking of which, how are things with Joe?"

"Carter!"

"Well?"

"I don't know. It's a process."

"So, still no sex."

"You know, you've become pretty salty since you came into all that money."

"Just trying to lighten the mood. Hey, you never really told me what you thought about me buying the house. I mean, Casa Abrigo. Scene of the crime and all."

"To be honest, I was worried. *Am* worried. But I have to admit, the whole time we were there, I didn't sense anything malevolent. I mean, the house is blessed, right? So, I guess you're safe."

She reached across the table and took her friend's hand. "And it is a beautiful house. Congratulations."

"Thanks. Oh, did Joe tell you? Before I made my decision, he let me spend the night there in my sleeping bag."

"Alone? But why would you do that?"

"I asked myself the same question. I think it's because I needed to know everything would be okay. Also, I'm trying to get back on the horse too. I know nothing actually happened to me—physically—but seeing you hurt, well, I guess it did something to me."

"Oh, Carter. I didn't realize. Wow, I am really blowing it. I didn't think about how those events may have affected Joe, either. I'm a horrible friend."

"It's okay."

Sarah slid out of the booth. "Come on. I want to make it over there before it gets dark. And no camping overnight."

"Didn't even cross my mind. Although..."

"You are definitely a bad influence on me," she said.

Sarah parked on Myrtle Street and gazed at the modest stone and glass building, which rose five stories and seemed to dominate the other commercial buildings. Joe had renovated a place not too far from here. Visiting it one time, she had passed St. Rita Women's Center, never dreaming she would have any reason to go inside.

She and Carter got out and walked up to the entrance. The lawn was neatly manicured, and there were low, rectangular jasmine shrubs on either side.

They walked into a small lobby filled with Craftsman furniture, artsy lamps, and framed photographs of past events featuring happy women with careworn faces. As they stood in the center gazing, Sarah felt an almost imperceptible coldness. It was as if something were hovering nearby, though everything appeared normal.

"Do you feel it?" she said.

As the girl was about to respond, a young woman who looked to be in her early twenties appeared from an office and approached them. She had pale hair down to her shoulders, wireframe glasses, and wore a skirt and an animal print sweater featuring baby koalas.

"Hi, I'm Nellie Watson," she said, extending her hand.

Sarah reciprocated. "Sarah Greene. And this is my friend, Carter Wittgenstein."

"Pleased to meet you both."

"I believe Heidi is expecting us?" Sarah said. She caught Nellie blushing as she took Carter's hand.

"Yes. I can take you back to her office."

As they followed, Carter said, "So, do you work here full time?"

Nellie laughed. "Actually, it's research. I'm in grad school, trying to complete my doctorate."

They stopped in front of a small, neatly appointed office.

"Heidi is meeting with our psychologist," Nellie said. "But you're welcome to wait in her office."

"Okay, thanks," Sarah said. As the young researcher walked away, Sarah looked at her friend. "Thinking of volunteering?"

"What? No."

They were about to step inside when Sarah heard voices. A woman of medium height was shaking hands with... *Roxanne Marsh*? As the elderly psychologist departed in the opposite direction, the other woman walked toward them, extending her hand.

"Hello. I'm Heidi Lewis."

Sarah took her hand. "Sarah Greene. And this is Carter Wittgenstein."

The director motioned her guests inside.

"So, Dr. Marsh works here?" Sarah said as they sat.

"She's more of a consultant. Do you know her?"

"As a matter of fact."

Heidi sat with her elbows on the desk, her hands in a praying position under her chin. She was attractive—fifties —and wore her auburn hair in a flip, giving her a more youthful appearance. Sarah liked her immediately.

"So," the director said. "Lou Fiore has vouched for the two of you, and that's good enough for me."

Sarah exhaled. "Wow, I didn't realize you'd spoken to him."

"I contacted him right after you and I talked on the phone. You must understand. Everything we do here for our residents is based on trust. They've been hurt both physically and emotionally.

"And what they hope to find here is someone who they can put their faith in without reservation. It's the only way they can feel safe."

The girl leaned forward. "Can I ask how long has the shelter been here?"

"We celebrated twenty years last May. I've been in charge at St.Rita's since it opened." She turned to Sarah. "I am aware of what happened to you. I suppose everyone in town is, thanks to Carter's article."

"Oh, you read it," the girl said.

"Very well written. Kudos. Anyway, I only mention it because the experience might come in handy, should you speak to any of the women. Empathy goes a long way around here."

Sarah felt defensive and looked away. "I'm not here because of that."

"No, I don't expect you are. So, why are you here?"

"Carter and I thought we might be able to help."

"And so did Rupinder, apparently."

"I hope you don't mind her telling me what happened. Actually, I instigated it."

"Not at all."

"When we walked into the building just now, we both sensed something—something malevolent."

"Really?" Heidi absently rubbed her wedding ring.

"Are you having problems?"

"Well, nothing recently, thank God. But the residents are on edge, I'm afraid. The women who had those—what shall we call them? Accidents?—are their friends."

"Rupinder said these incidents started around the time a woman arrived from Guatemala. Is that right?"

"You don't think Ana had anything to do with them?"

"Can we meet her?" the girl said.

The director hesitated. "It might be tricky. Ana is... Let's say she's very withdrawn. We haven't been able to gain her trust yet. In fact, she didn't speak at all for the first week. And Roxanne has had no luck with her either."

"A language barrier?"

"I thought so at first. But no, I'm told she speaks fluent Spanish and very little English."

"I understand she suffered physical abuse by her late husband?" Carter said.

"Yes. Unfortunately, her bones didn't set properly, and one arm is nearly useless. The thing is, ladies, Ana is not unusual. If she were, this place would not exist."

"Heidi, you said you've been here twenty years?" Sarah said. "Can I ask what you did before?"

"I was a doctor. I used to see female patients who came to me with various injuries, always claiming they were accidents of one sort or another. But I knew better. I wanted to do more to help these women. And when the right opportunity came along, I leapt at it. I'm not only the director, but I am on the board."

"I see you're married."

Heidi observed her left hand. "Yes, but not in the way you think. Are you Catholic, Sarah?"

"Yes."

"Then you must know about consecrated virgins."

The girl's mouth fell open. "What does that even mean?"

The director looked at her with kindness. "I am a bride of Christ."

"But how—"

"Think of it as someone who is a nun but doesn't wear a habit or live in a convent."

"I've read about this," Sarah said. "But I never thought I would actually meet someone who—"

"There are fewer than three hundred of us in the US."

"So was there, like, a wedding ceremony?" Carter said.

"Oh, yes. But no groom."

She took down a framed photograph and handed it to the girl. She marveled at Heidi wearing a beautiful white wedding dress and lying prostrate on the altar, her head down in prayer. Carter handed the photo to Sarah, who took it with reverence.

"As you can see, it's a pretty big deal," the director said. She stood. "Come on. Let me give you the tour."

As they made their way down the hallway, they passed offices with staff all at their computers. Some were on the phone, and it sounded like they were fundraising. Continuing on, Sarah's friend saw Nellie working diligently at her computer, and lingered.

"This is the dining room," Heidi said.

The area was large and inviting, with bright lighting and colorful murals on the wall. None of the pictures Sarah had seen so far featured children—only women of various ages. A group of residents was in the kitchen. They were cooking and chatting. One woman, thin and pale, was standing at a cutting board, chopping vigorously and saying something to the others. Whatever it was, made the rest of them laugh.

"That's Marcy. She imagines herself a standup comic."

"What's for dinner?" Carter said.

"Spaghetti."

A tiny woman was setting places with flatware and paper napkins. She had straight, waist-length, dark brown hair held back by a white plastic headband and wore a long-sleeve white sweater and a turquoise skirt. She was solemn, hardly making a sound in her black flats.

When Sarah saw the difficulty she was having with her left arm, she realized it must be Ana.

"Marcy!" someone said.

A scream turned Sarah's blood to ice. She and Carter followed the director into the kitchen. Marcy stood over the sink, her arm down the running garbage disposal. Heidi switched off the device. When she saw an orderly approaching, she said, "Call 911!"

The director gently pulled the woman's arm out. It caught on something, and she had to work to remove it. The other women crowded around, some whimpering. When Marcy's arm was free, she raised the mangled hand dripping blood. Staring at it in wonder, she giggled like a schoolgirl.

"Oh, Marcy," Heidi said.

As the director bandaged Marcy's hand, Sarah returned to the dining room. Ana stood facing the wall as if paralyzed. Lifting her head, the tiny woman let out an ear-piercing shriek and fell on the floor in a dead faint. Sarah started toward her, but her friend grabbed her arm.

"Look!" she said.

Carter pointed at an enormous man with long, stringy dark hair and red eyes. Rage rolled off him in a tidal wave of foul, negative energy.

He stared at the now motionless Ana lying on the floor and moved toward her deliberately. Then he glared at the women, aware they could see him. Letting go a deafening wail that rattled the windows, he pressed against the wall, where he melted into nothingness. Sarah turned to her friend, her eyes wide.

"He wants to kill them," Carter said, barely able to get the words out. "All of them."

FIVE

Sarah and Carter sat in silence in the conference room, their coffees untouched. Lou was winding up his interview with the director. Then he shook out his writing hand with a grimace.

"If you don't mind, Heidi," he said, "I'd like to continue here with my team."

"No problem." Still shaken, she got to her feet. "The room is yours for the afternoon." She left without saying anything else.

From where the girl was sitting, she could see Nellie in her office across the hallway. When they made eye contact, Carter looked away. The police chief had been standing and took a seat, blocking her view.

Lou had finished his coffee long ago, and from what Sarah observed, he desperately wanted another cup. He pondered the two full cups sitting in front of him.

"Go ahead," she said, sliding hers over. "You need it more than me."

"Thanks." He accepted the lukewarm drink and drained the cup. "That's better."

He opened his notebook and went through the pages of what he'd recorded, grunting occasionally and muttering, something he did a lot while concentrating, she noticed. Finally, he set the notebook aside, folded his hands, and looked at the women.

"You guys need anything?"

The women side-eyed each other. Then Sarah said, "I'm pretty sure they don't permit alcohol on the premises."

"Right. Okay. So, I've interviewed each of the residents who were in the kitchen with Marcy Lund. Everyone of them told the same story. She was chopping onions when she stopped, walked over to the sink, turned on the garbage disposal, and shoved her hand in."

"Did she say anything?" the girl said.

"No. Technically, this isn't a police matter, but the director insisted I come by." He looked at his empty coffee cup. "Also, I knew you two were here and…"

"You thought something might've happened to us?" Sarah said.

"Yes."

"We're both very touched. Now, do you want to hear about what we saw?"

"Absolutely."

"There's a ghost. And not Casper, either."

Carter joined in. "This thing is huge. And he's angry as hell."

"Do I want to know how you know that?" Lou said.

"Like Sarah said, we saw him. Also, we both felt his rage. It's hard to explain. We think he's connected to Ana Robles."

"How do you know?"

"Because he was drawn to her," the girl said. "I think he wanted to harm her."

"And the other women," Sarah said. "Oh, and there's something else. He knows Carter and I can see him."

"Oh, boy. So you two are in danger, right?"

"I'm going to say yes."

"So, police protection…"

"Would be pretty much useless," the girl said. "Unless you happen to have a ghost trap."

"You mean, like in *Ghostbusters*? I wish."

He stood, and without asking took Carter's cup and finished her coffee for her.

"Look, my job is to protect the citizens of Dos Santos. I can't have some insane boogeyman running around here. Tell me what I can do."

Sarah rubbed her temples. "I don't know. I guess we could use your help. Until we can find a way to deal with a vengeful spirit, everyone here is in danger."

The director walked in. "Pardon me for interrupting. Chief Fiore, I wanted you to know Marcy is in stable condition. They were able to save the hand, but she lost three fingers."

"Where'd they take her?"

"Cottage."

"Thanks, Heidi. What about Ana?"

"We've given her a sedative. She's resting now."

"Any idea what's wrong with her?"

"That's the curious thing," the director said. "Do you remember those other incidents I told you about? The same thing happened both times. Ana screamed horribly and fainted."

He glanced at Sarah and Carter. "Was she anywhere near the victims?"

"Yes."

"I need to interview her at some point. Also, I'd like the name and phone number of her caseworker."

"No problem," Heidi said. "As for Ana, let's try tomorrow when she's feeling better."

Sarah had decided to buy Carter a drink to thank her for her help at the shelter. The women sat at the bar of a new place in Dos Santos called Rich. The name was meant to be ironic. It was a small hipster establishment filled with black-and-white photographs from the Great Depression by Dorothea Lange, Walker Evans, Marion Post Wolcott, and others. She'd heard somewhere they served a mean espresso.

As Sarah nursed her Super Tuscan, her friend waited for the bartender to finish pulling her Guinness from the tap. When he placed it in front of her, the women clinked glasses without enthusiasm.

"I don't need to tell you," Sarah said. "I'm really scared. Remind me again why I'm doing this?"

"Because you're a good person. And talk about scared. When I saw that...thing glaring at us, I seriously thought I would lose my shit. What is it, a ghost?"

"If it is, it's damn angry."

"We don't need to do this. I mean, I'm an amateur. And you're..."

"Recovering, I know. I didn't tell you this, but I saw Alyssa the other day. Actually, twice."

"That can't be good."

"The first time was right after Joe and I left your house."

"Wait a second." Carter grabbed her friend's arm,

almost knocking over her beer. "Was it about my house? Should I be worried?"

Sarah slouched. Though she wanted to console the girl, she didn't want to lie to her. Her friend waited.

"I don't know. But I got the feeling it wasn't about Casa Abrigo."

"Are you telling me the truth?"

Sarah looked into Carter's eyes. "I promise never to lie to you. I think Alyssa was there for something else."

The girl drained half her glass. "Okay, I believe you. What about the second time?"

"It was in my bedroom. She told me several things. But what I remember most was 'so much pain.' She's counting on me."

"Well, do you still wanna investigate?"

Sarah closed her eyes. And when she did, she saw the teenager she'd discovered in the mirror. Though Sarah had been frightened when the ghost first appeared, she had an overwhelming sense of empathy—even love. Was it because her best friend was also dead? And now, that same feeling included the women at the shelter. She opened her eyes and looked at Carter.

"I want to help those women," she said.

"Especially Ana. She's so tiny."

"Like a doll, am I right? Though I'm afraid whatever it is might eventually kill her."

Wistfully, the girl turned to find a group of young women a few stools away laughing over something on one of their phones.

"I think it's a given," she said.

Sarah took a sip of her wine and set the glass down firmly, determination in her eyes.

"Okay. The reason we figured everything out the last time was that we did some serious research."

"Yeah," Carter said. "We even went to Kansas, for shit's sake."

"So, what do we know about Ana?"

"Just that she's from Guatemala."

"Right. And I don't think we're flying down there anytime soon. There has to be another way to learn about her."

The girl waggled her eyebrows. "Well, we could try asking her."

"Didn't Heidi say she was shy and hardly spoke?"

"It's worth a shot." Carter toyed with her glass. "Hey, I know. Let's talk to the caseworker and see what they know."

"Good idea. I'll run it by Lou."

The girl frowned into her beer. "There is a problem, of course. How do we keep the whatever-it-is from coming after us?"

"I think I might know a way. Can I ask? You told me once your family was Catholic way back when. Were you ever baptized?"

Carter seemed surprised. "No. And where exactly are you going with this?"

"Never mind. I thought it might help. No worries—I think we can pull this off."

"Okay. I guess?"

"Don't worry, my dear," Sarah said. "It won't hurt a bit."

When Sarah arrived home, she saw Joe's truck parked on the street and sporting new tires. Leaving her car in the driveway, she trotted up to the front door and let herself in. Gary was nowhere in sight.

"Honey, I'm home!"

No answer and no cooking smells. She walked into the kitchen. No pots on the stove. The cat was drinking water. When he was finished, he looked up at her with squishy eyes and meowed.

"Hey, buddy. You wouldn't happen to know where the big guy is?"

She set her purse down and took off her watch. When she reached into her bag to get her phone, she found the disc Lou had given her. The door to the garage opened, and Joe walked in, his hands filthy.

"Oh, hey," he said. "So, how's Carter doing?"

"She's really excited about the house. Um, what exactly were you doing out there?"

"Want to see?"

She followed him out and marveled at the workbench he'd built. Underneath was a red tool chest on wheels.

"Wow, impressive."

"I thought it would be good if you had your own setup. You know, in case you ever want to change your oil here instead of going over to your dad's."

"And abandon my free mechanic? Never. But it was very sweet of you to do this. Thank you."

"My pleasure. What are we doing about dinner?"

"Takeout, I guess. I really don't feel like cooking."

"Me neither. How does Papa Pepito's sound?"

"Great," she said. "Can you call them while I change?"

She returned to the kitchen, wondering if his gesture might be an olive branch. Whatever it was, it made her happy. She grabbed her phone from the counter. The screen showed a new voicemail. Ignoring it, she ran into her bedroom, quickly disrobed, and jumped into the shower.

When Sarah returned to the kitchen, Joe was pouring two glasses of a new Barolo he'd bought at a local wine shop. Sitting on a barstool, she was about to raise her glass when she remembered the voicemail. As she listened to it, she made a face.

"What is it?" he said.

She put the phone down and took a huge swallow of wine. "You remember Harlan Covington, right?"

"The wealthy lawyer from Santa Barbara? Sure."

"That was his housekeeper. It seems he wants to see me."

"Really? When?"

"First thing tomorrow morning. At his house."

"Did he say why?"

"No, but he said it was urgent. What does the pompous ass need with me?"

"No idea. You don't have to go, you know."

"You sound like Carter. My curiosity has gotten the better of me. I'll go. I mean, seriously, what can he do to me?"

"Are you kidding? He's a lawyer."

The doorbell rang. Joe answered it and returned with a large pizza. As they ate, she told him all about what had happened at the women's shelter, which seemed to upset him.

"Look," he said. "I know you're trying to do the right thing here. But I don't like the idea of you getting involved. And the same goes for Carter too. After what happened the last time—"

"We're fine. And if you saw Ana, you would want to help her too. She's adorable."

"But what if something evil tries to attack you?"

"I plan to protect myself—and my trusty sidekick."

"How exactly?"

"I'm still figuring it out."

"I don't know. I mean, you're starting to get back to—"

"Normal? Face it, this *is* normal for me. Sometimes, I pray it isn't. Carter and I will be fine."

After they'd cleaned up the dishes, she reached up to a cabinet and brought down the bottle of Talisker. It was nearly empty.

"Well, this sucks all kinds of ass."

He stopped what he was doing. "Oh."

"Okay, why aren't you as upset as me? You love this stuff too."

"It's no big deal. Really."

He turned on the dishwasher and strolled out the front door, whistling.

"Where's he going?" she said to Gary.

When he returned, he was carrying a brown paper bag.

"So, we're reduced to drinking Night Train?" she said.

Ignoring her, he removed a bottle from the bag, making her cackle. It was a shiny new bottle of Talisker.

"I thought I'd better stock up," he said, "since you're using this to treat your PTSD now."

"Shut up and get the glasses."

"Yes, ma'am."

As they sat on the living room sofa enjoying the scotch, Sarah fired up some jazz on her phone. When the smoky tenor sax broke into "Three O'Clock in the Morning," Joe sat up.

"Cannonball Adderley?"

She shook her head. "Pathetic. It's Dexter Gordon."

"One of these days…"

She snuggled close to her ex-husband and lay her head against his shoulder. "I could get used to this."

"Yeah?"

"Mm-hmm." Straightening up, she faced him. "There's something I want to say."

"Only if it's good news—and doesn't involve ghosts."

"Deal. You know how these past three months—God, has it been three months?—we haven't been, um, intimate?"

"I am aware."

"It's not because of Catholic guilt. I know technically it's a sin, but screw that. You know how things have been with me. Duh, of course you know—you were there. I think I might be…snapping out of it."

"And what is *it* exactly?"

She punched his arm. "Come on. Are you actually going to make me spell it out?" Then, on his silent smirk,, "Fine. I want you. There, I said it."

"Was that so hard?"

He set their glasses on the Italian coffee table. Then he reached toward her and took her hand. When she was on her feet, he swooped her up, and throwing her over his shoulder in a firefighter's lift, carried her into the bedroom.

"I think we might've set the women's movement back a few hundred years."

"Mm."

"For the record, I'm not complaining," she said.

SIX

Sarah wore a languid smile as she made her way north on Hot Springs Road in her Galaxie. The previous night, Joe had made love to her the way he always did. Strong, but never hurtful. Passionate and filled with the deep love he had for her. Although it was a sin to have sex with someone she was no longer married to, there was no going back. Not now. Maybe never. She prayed God would understand.

As she passed one expensive property after the next, she imagined representing a rich seller here and coming away with an impossibly fat commission. Montecito was one of the wealthiest communities in the US and home to more than a few celebrities. In a way, Harlan Covington living here irked her. The truth was he was wealthy. Where else would he live?

Good thing the roads were dry. Joe purchasing new tires reminded her she needed to do the same for her car. Coming out of nowhere, a red Lamborghini shot out from a side road directly in front of her. She hit her brakes, nearly skidding into a light pole.

Fishtailing, the Lambo accelerated away. She growled under her breath. Eventually, she found the driveway she was looking for and turned off. Around fifty feet ahead, she arrived at a set of wrought iron gates supported by huge gray pillars, each with a security camera on top.

She drove up close to the column on her left and pressed the intercom button. Instantly, a motor snapped on and whirred as the gates slowly opened.

She continued up the paved road. The house, a huge, gray stone mansion, which looked like something out of *Condé Nast Traveler*, loomed before her. The circular driveway was pale brick, and a half-circle of Leyland cypress hedges bordered the entire area. Though the property was elegant, she thought it was dreary.

She parked and walked up to the front door. Before she could ring the bell, the door opened, revealing a middle-aged woman wearing a St. John Collection black suit and low heels. Her gray hair was tied back in a bun.

"Ms. Greene?"

She extended her hand. "Sarah's fine."

"I'm Mary Mallery, Mr. Covington's housekeeper."

Housekeeper? Dressed like that?

The women shook hands. Mary led the guest into the foyer, which featured an incredibly high ceiling. The house was silent, except for the clacking of their heels on the black-and-white checkerboard tile floor and the steady ticking of an unseen grandfather clock as the housekeeper led her toward the library. Mary left her at the door and turned to leave.

"It's all right," she said. "He's expecting you."

As she walked away, Sarah wasn't sure what to do and knocked softly. When she got no reply, she opened the door and went in.

The lawyer sat on a blood-red Chesterfield sofa, a large book lying open on his lap. He wore a dark three-piece suit and expensive shoes, which were very shiny. Laying the book aside, he rose and crossed the room, his hand extended.

As she shook his hand, she recognized the onyx-and-silver ring with the strange etching on the face. He'd worn it the last time they met. She was having difficulty understanding why this man was being so gracious, but played along.

"I'm so pleased you're here, Sarah—oh, may I call you Sarah?"

"Of course. But why did you—"

"Won't you have a seat?"

He gestured to one of the matching Chesterfield chairs that stood near the roaring fireplace. Faintly, she smelled the fragrant wood as it burned and wondered what it was. As if reading her mind, he pointed at the fire.

"Taxus baccata. Better known as the yew tree. I have the wood flown in specially from Sardinia."

"It smells wonderful," she said.

He settled into the chair opposite her. "I was reading Mark. Do you know chapter nine, when Jesus casts the demon out of the boy?"

"It's about faith, isn't it?"

"But more importantly, the power of prayer."

A maid appeared, carrying a tray with two bone china mugs. She couldn't have been more than twenty. Without making eye contact, she handed a mug to the guest and the other to her employer.

"Thank you, Elsa," Covington said.

She left the room, closing the door behind her.

Sarah sniffed the drink and took a sip. "This is magnificent."

"It's Ethiopian."

"I'm going to suggest they get some of this at The Cracked Pot," she said, trying to lighten the mood.

His face darkened. "Unfortunately, they would have a difficult time locating a supplier."

"Ahh."

"I'll get right to the point."

His entire manner had changed. Now, she saw the cold—and to be honest, frightening—man she and Lou had first met at his offices in Santa Barbara. For no reason at all, she imagined him ordering the guards to escort her to the tower.

"I understand you paid a visit to St. Rita Women's Center," he said. "May I ask why?"

Her cup clanked against her saucer. Discreetly, she checked for cracks as she set it on the side table. It was none of this man's business what she did with her free time. She started to cross her arms but folded her hands on her lap instead. His gaze never left her, and she shifted uncomfortably.

"I'd like to ask *you* a question," she said. "And excuse my directness. But how is this any of your business?" *Good one, Sarah. Prepare to die.*

Rather than be offended, he sat there, studying her the way an entomologist looks at a bug on a pin block. Though she wanted to leave, she had an overwhelming desire to find out what this meddling attorney was up to.

He set aside his coffee and rose. Then he paced slowly. She imagined him using this visual technique in the courtroom, although she wasn't at all sure he'd ever been a trial lawyer.

"Apparently, you and that other girl—"

"Carter Wittgenstein. You met her, remember?"

"My sources tell me the two of you have decided to investigate a series of strange occurrences. And you think they're tied to one of the residents."

He turned to her sharply, disconcerting her.

"Both of you seem to feel these events are of a para-normal nature. Of course, Chief Fiore has found no physical evidence to support a crime, which I think must make your theory all the more attractive. Any time you'd like to disagree, feel free."

His voice had taken on a sharp, authoritative tone. Nonplussed, she realized this three-piece suit despot had succeeded in getting her off-balance—a feeling she detested. She tried thinking how to answer. Should she be open with him? Clearly, he knew everything. Doing her best to keep her anger in check, she answered him.

"Mr. Covington—"

"Call me Harlan." He faced the fireplace, giving her his profile. *How Victorian.*

"Look, I don't know how you learned about all this."

"I'm on the board of directors."

"Oh. Still, I don't think you should be concerned about what Carter and I—"

He turned to his right and faced her dead on, his eyes betraying nothing.

"I want you to listen to me very carefully," he said. He wasn't angry, but there was a tone of concern in his voice. "You and your friend—"

"Carter."

"You're both in grave danger. And I would advise you to stop what you're doing immediately. There are things..." He turned away again and stared at the fire. "I don't want to see you getting hurt."

He seemed ancient, and Sarah felt something for the lawyer she never thought she would—empathy. It seemed that, like her, he carried a terrible burden. A knowledge of something dark and otherworldly. She rose and touched the sleeve of his suit jacket.

"Harlan, you don't know me. I am not afraid. For reasons known only to God, I can see things—things that would probably scare the life out of most people. Several weeks ago, I almost died because of a man who was possessed by the spirit of your former client, Peter Moody.

"The only reason I'm even alive is because of a miracle. This is going to sound crazy, but it's true. A flock of ravens saved me. Fr. Brian doesn't think it was a miracle, but I do."

Unexpectedly, he took her hands. His were warm. As he spoke, his eyes glistened in the firelight.

"It wasn't a miracle," he said. "It was I who saved you."

Harlan's words repeated in Sarah's head like a portentous echo as she accompanied him to the garden. They walked along a well-maintained gravel path bordered by hedgerows. Everything was barren. The bleakness of winter reminded her of her own emptiness, constantly filled with confusion. And it made her question her resolve to continue with the case. If he was the one who'd saved her, did it mean she was powerless to help anyone on her own?

She'd never imagined that in her adult life she would chase ghosts. Though as kids, she and Alyssa had always enjoyed pretending. But things had changed in high school.

When she turned fourteen, she dreamed of a husband who was tall and a house filled with children. Now here she was, childless, with this strange old man—discussing magical ravens.

He showed her the ring. She studied the familiar figure of an old man, slightly bent and holding a staff.

"The first time you saw this, I worried we would get to this place."

"I don't understand," she said.

He gestured toward a stone bench, which faced south and offered an impressive view of the city below.

"The figure on your ring," she said. "Who is he?"

"The founder of our order, Abramo Levy. I am a Guardian."

"You mean, like a guardian angel?" She hadn't meant the question to be funny.

"Not an angel. We are a group of men and women—how many is unknown—who are sworn to fight evil."

"You mean, like superheroes?"

"Brian warned me about your sense of humor. But this is no laughing matter. What I said about you being in danger is true."

She had so many questions—she didn't know where to begin. *Be patient, Sarah.*

"Dos Santos is a place filled with evil," he said. "It all began with its founder, John Dos Santos. By all accounts, he was a good man. But then, he went to France to fight the Germans in WWI. Something happened to him over there, and he came back different."

"Shell shock maybe?"

"He was corrupt—filled with greed and lust. And now, it's as if the town itself attracts evil. I believe it's why Peter Moody gave himself to Satan."

"And how did you become involved with the family?"

"When Gerald Moody contacted the bank about a loan, they put him in touch with me. You see, I am—"

"On the board of directors?"

"My job was to handle the family's legal affairs. But over the years, as I learned more about these unfortunate people—and about Peter—I got more involved. Eventually, I became a trusted friend."

"So, all this time, you knew about the man who attacked me, and about Peter's sister?"

"Yes."

Her eyes widened in fear. "The ravens. You sent them to kill Peter's sister?" She rose, and gaping at him, considered running away.

"It doesn't work that way. There are sacred rituals. The rite I performed was a plea for justice. Whether the punishment was carried out was not up to me."

"But earlier, you said you saved me."

"The rituals can work both ways. I can also plead to save someone's life. In your case, I had no way of knowing whether the rite I performed would work. You could've as easily fallen to your death. I prayed fervently for your deliverance."

She studied her surroundings. Birds chirped among the naked trees. Why in the world were they so happy in such a dead place?

"I guess it helps to be a lawyer when you're pleading your case," she said. "This is so much to take in. Does Fr. Brian know? About who you are, I mean."

"Yes. You have a great friend in him. He made me promise to protect you."

Suddenly unsteady, he sat on a nearby bench with his

head down. Unsure of what to do, she waited. Using a handkerchief, he wiped his brow and stood.

She touched his arm. "Are you okay?"

"We should head back," he said. "I hope you can stay for lunch."

Sarah sat to the right of Harlan at the head of the long dining room table that seated twelve. The maid she'd seen earlier—Elsa?—placed a field greens salad before each of them and refilled Sarah's glass of sparkling water.

"What about Carter?" she said.

He had taken a bite of salad. She waited while he chewed and swallowed.

"Did Fr. Brian ask you to protect her too?"

"No," he said. "My job is to make sure no harm comes to *you*."

"Does Fr. Brian have some kind of authority over you?"

He chuckled. "Brian is a dear friend. He asked me as a personal favor."

"So, I guess you guys—the Guardians—report to the head honcho in Rome?"

"I can't give you any details about our organization. But no. We are an independent order."

"So, have you met any of the others?"

"We are not permitted to contact one another directly. It's for our protection. Satan has many friends in high places."

"Well, then how to you know what to do? I mean, there must be a plan or..."

"There is. But again, I can't really talk about how we do

things. Suffice it say we have been around since the seventeenth century, and so far, no one has complained."

"Well, those going to hell might have a few choice words."

When they finished their salads, the maid returned with their entrée, flaky halibut accompanied by brilliantly colored steamed vegetables.

"This looks wonderful," she said.

"Everything we are eating today is organic. My health has deteriorated, and I'm doing everything I can to stay fit."

"If I may ask, how serious?"

"Recently, I was diagnosed with metastatic prostate cancer, which has spread to my bones. One of the hazards of old age, I'm afraid."

"I'm so sorry."

"Nothing to be sorry about. You have questions, correct?"

"Yes. What can you tell me about the women's shelter?"

"I take it you're not backing down?"

"Fr. Brian must have also told you I have a stubborn streak."

"So I'm learning." He forked a steamed carrot. "Shortly after Ana arrived at the shelter, a black stain smelling of sulfur appeared on a wall in her room."

"Isn't sulfur..."

"The smell is often associated with the demonic."

"Oh, boy."

"Which is the reason I warned you. You saw what Peter Moody could do to you. Can you imagine if a demon had the opportunity?"

"If I'd been better prepared..."

"Possibly. But these are dangerous forces."

Something broke in the kitchen, startling her. A

moment later, the maid appeared at the door, looking flushed.

"Sir, I dropped a plate."

"Not to worry, Elsa."

Sarah mulled over the question she was dying to ask. When she'd gathered her nerve, she spoke. "Peter told me something. He said if I hadn't discovered the mirror, *he* wouldn't have known about me."

"Go on."

"I've been seeing this black entity from time to time. It looks kind of like a cloud or smoke. Carter saw it too. And the second time, it spoke to her."

"What did it say?"

"'She's mine.'"

"Meaning you?"

"Yes."

He rubbed the bridge of his nose. "I call it The Darkness. It's a malevolent thing that's been gaining power as time goes on. So far, it has confined itself to Dos Santos."

"Can't you destroy it?"

"Not until I understand its nature. I suspect it has something to do with John Dos Santos. Sometimes after we depart this earth, a residual energy remains. Those who have chosen the path of evil often leave powerful traces of themselves. And like poison left in the ground, it's deadly."

"And you think this darkness sees me as a threat?"

"Perhaps. Peter may have done you a favor by warning you. If you see it again, I would encourage you not to engage it."

"You don't have to tell me twice," she said.

After lunch, Harlan walked Sarah to the front door. Having spent several hours with him, she came away with a new understanding. And respect. Here was a man who neither drank nor smoked. And he was celibate—a requirement for Guardians, apparently. He was single-minded—devoted to ridding the world of the evil that had befallen it. *How is that even possible?*

"Thank you again for inviting me," she said. "It was enlightening."

"I'm glad we got to spend time together. And remember, no one can know about me and my work."

"I understand. But what about Carter?"

"Can she be trusted?"

"I trust her with my life."

"Quite an endorsement. Don't say anything to her yet. When the time is right, I will meet with you both."

"Okay, fair enough. There is one other thing. You know how you agreed to protect me as a favor to Fr. Brian? Look, I realize I have no right to ask. But can't you do the same for Carter? She's working closely with me, and I don't want anything to happen to her."

He remained silent.

"Isn't there some kind of force field you can put around us?"

"Unfortunately, those things only exist in the movies. Prayer is your best defense."

She showed him her medal. "And St. Michael."

He examined the object. "Wait here a moment."

He left her in the foyer and returned to the library. After a time, he reappeared carrying something. He handed her a black leather bracelet with a familiar metal disc embedded in the top. In the center was a cross formed by the initials CSSML and NDSMD. The cross was surrounded by a circle, each quadrant containing a single letter. C-S-P-B.

"It's a St. Benedict medal," she said. "I've seen these for sale online."

"You won't find one like this anywhere. It was made at a monastery in Norcia. The medal is pure silver. Do you remember your Latin?"

She scrunched her nose. "I remember memorizing the initials in fifth grade for an art project. Let's see. CSPB. *Crux Sancti Patris Benedicti.* 'The Cross of Our Holy Father Benedict.'"

"Impressive. And the rest?"

"Nope, that's all I got."

He took the bracelet and pointed at the cross. "CSSML. *Crux Sacra Sit Mihi Lux.* 'May the holy cross be my light.' NDSMD. *Nunquam draco sit mihi dux.* 'May the dragon never be my overlord.'"

"'Let the devil not be my leader,'" she said. "I remember."

"Is Carter Catholic?"

"No."

"This bracelet is blessed and may help. St. Benedict is the patron saint of exorcists. Give it to your friend and tell her it holds great power, but only if she believes."

"I will. Thank you so much."

Carefully, she placed the bracelet in her purse. Then, she stared at him, her mouth hanging open.

"It was you who blocked me when I visited the cemetery that one time," she said. "It's why I got nothing when I touched Peter Moody's headstone."

"I did it to protect you."

She hugged the old man and felt him tense, then relax as he patted her shoulder.

"God may have set you on this path, Sarah," he said. "And it's not for me to stand in your way. But you must be vigilant. If, in fact, it is a demon you're dealing with, it could lead you to the precipice."

"Harlan, you know before, when I told you I wasn't scared? I only said it because I didn't feel comfortable telling you the truth. I'm terrified."

"Remember to pray. I have a private investigator working to find out about Ana Robles's past. He's in Guatemala, looking for family members."

"Wow, you guys don't mess around."

"We do not. Now, if you'll excuse me, I really must get back to work."

"Me too. Bye."

As soon as she'd stepped outside, he closed the door. She was worried she might let something slip the next time she spoke to Carter. *Shit, and what about Joe?*

Driving back to Dos Santos, she checked her watch. It was almost three, and she was scheduled to meet Rachel at the office. Afterward, she was having dinner with her sister, her niece, and her father. Staying quiet about a thing like this wouldn't be easy.

Who's the patron saint of keeping a secret anyway?

SEVEN

Charlie Beeks finished his eggs and plantains and sat back in the rustic chair with the faded floral seat cushion. The restaurant's terrace faced south toward a smoking volcano on the other side of Lago Atitlán, the deepest lake in Central America.

As he drank his coffee, he thought about the past week. He believed he had clearly understood how to find the town where Ana grew up. But due to a mix-up in birth records, he'd followed a false trail and ended up in Villa Nueva, almost three hundred kilometers from where he needed to be.

Working with Guatemalan officials who he bribed, he determined that Ana's mother lived in a small town to the west, Nahualá. He could've gone there directly but felt he needed to rest. So, he made a detour to the lake and spent the night. Waking up refreshed, he felt ready to continue the journey.

He signed the restaurant check and returned to his room. He stopped to admire the simplicity of the white-washed walls and ceiling with the exposed wood beams.

Grabbing his bags, he walked down a flight of stairs to the front desk.

Opening his wallet, he saw the business card with HARLAN COVINGTON printed in a thin, elegant black font. He thought back to when he was first introduced to the attorney. Two weeks ago, he had received an anonymous letter instructing him to contact the lawyer in Santa Barbara regarding an urgent matter.

They'd met at Harlan's home in Montecito. The attorney never mentioned the letter or the person who had sent it. He merely told the ex-cop he needed his help. Which was strange because, technically, Charlie was retired. He'd been a private investigator for nearly twenty years. His health wasn't what it used to be, and he'd looked forward to spending whatever remaining time he had in San Diego.

But Harlan Covington wasn't a man you said no to, and after listening to the details of the case, Charlie felt compelled to take it on. Besides, the pay was generous. The lawyer had already arranged everything, including the brand-new black Land Rover the PI drove through the unpredictable roads of a country where poverty and beauty coexisted like fingers intertwined, as they had for thousands of years.

After putting his bags in the car, Charlie took a walk along the narrow, faded wood-plank path that bordered Lago Atitlán. On his left stood a wall with tall grass growing high above it. And on his right, the deep blue lake filled with bass and freshwater crab, which may or may not have been safe to eat owing to the pollution. When he reached the entrance to the forest, he lingered for a moment, enjoying the tranquility, then turned around and headed back.

As he climbed into his vehicle, he wondered whether the temperature would reach seventy-five, as it had most other days. Though his knees were hurting, he liked the climate and wished he had time to explore the country as a tourist.

He got on the road and headed north on the SOL-4. Eventually, he would reach CA-1, the Pan-American Highway. The entire trip would take less than two hours. Harlan had arranged for him to meet the translator at a Catholic church in Nahualá. As he made his way through the green, rugged beauty of the countryside, he prayed the Rosary.

He would need all the grace he could get to complete his mission.

Charlie parked on the street in front of the Catholic church. A few raindrops fell on the windshield. As he got out, he saw the thunderheads. The church was called La Iglesia de Jesucristo de los Santos de los Ultimos Días. *Los Ultimos Días*—the last days. Lately, he had been thinking a lot about his last days. How would he account for himself when the time came? Had he lived a good life? As a PI, not everything he'd done over the years was noble. He reminded himself that although he had certainly lied when the occasion called for it, he'd never cheated anyone. And more importantly, he had never taken a life.

The church's architecture was beautiful in its simplicity —white with orange trim and twin bell towers. A vendor selling granizadas stood at the base of the steps with his cart. The PI had tried a "hailstorm" when he arrived in the country. The concoction of ice, sweet syrup, and condensed milk was superior to any American snow cone. He got out and stretched. A few tourists were making their way inside, phones in hand to take pictures.

He stretched once more and walked up the steps to the main doors. Like the exterior, the inside was white and orange. On the dark wood ceiling hung silver chandeliers, which ran the length of the roof to the altar, accentuated by a series of white ceiling drapes trimmed in silver. Was the décor meant to suggest heaven?

He made his way toward the altar. A nun in a gray habit was praying alone in a pew toward the front. As quietly as possible, he moved in next to her and knelt.

"Sister Elizabeth?" he said, keeping his voice to a whisper.

She regarded him. "Yes?"

Her eyes were kind. He guessed she might have been in her mid-forties.

"I'm Charlie Beeks. Supposed to meet you here."

"I need to get my bag."

She crossed herself and rose. He did the same.

When they walked outside, it was raining.

"My car's over there," he said.

He helped her in and placed her small roller bag in the trunk with his things. Soon, they were on the road. The windshield wipers were beating furiously, and he had to drive slower than normal.

"You're with the Sisters of Mary, right?"

"Yes. I teach English at our Girlstown in Guatemala City."

"I see. What do you know about the case?"

Google Maps chattered intermittently in the background, irritating him. When he spoke to someone, he liked giving his full attention. But without the app, he'd never find Maria Lopez's house.

"Not much. I was told you needed my help. Though I'm somewhat familiar with the area, I've never met the family. Watch out!"

Just in time, he saw the two boys on the scooter as they shot in front of him from an unmarked side road. Laughing and not wearing helmets, one of them shouted an apology and continued on.

"I was about to curse," he said, "when I remembered who I'm with."

She laughed. "I almost did too. Can I ask you something, Mr. Beeks?"

"Call me Charlie."

"Why me?"

Seeing her large, questioning eyes, he wondered how to answer. He wasn't at all clear on why Harlan had selected him for the job.

"I don't know much—my employer arranged everything."

"And why is Mr. Covington looking for Maria Lopez?"

"It has to do with her daughter, Ana."

"Is she in trouble?" she said.

"Hard to say. All I know is I was sent down here to locate her family and learn about her past. Which reminds me. Is it true most people here speak K'iche'?"

"Yes, but they also know Spanish. I speak both, but I think for our purposes, Spanish will suffice."

"You're the doctor."

When he turned the wheel to the right, she noticed the wide gold band on his ring finger.

"Is your wife worried about you being so far away?"

"Well, she was always a worrier. She passed five years ago."

"My condolences. Any children?"

"No."

He tried to hide the sadness in his voice. His wife had longed for children. But he was always too busy with police business. Later, as a PI, his work often took him from one end of the country to the other. Sometimes, out of the country. There came a point when she stopped bringing it up.

When eventually they did try, she ended up miscarrying. Rather than try again, she went back to school and got a teaching credential. Soon, she found a position at a Catholic school and devoted the rest of her life to "her kids." When she died, he felt he hardly knew her.

They drove slowly through the wet, unmaintained streets filled with potholes, past shops and restaurants toward the edge of town. Charlie told Sister Elizabeth everything he knew about the case, which wasn't much. When he'd finished, she said nothing. For a time, they rode in silence.

"There's a lot of superstition here," she said at last. "People often go to shamans when a family member is sick. Some still pray to the nature gods."

"Old habits die hard."

"The Church has made great progress, but..."

"Witch doctors are big business?"

"Yes."

Google Maps advised him to turn on an ascending cobblestone street made impossibly narrow by the cars and motorcycles parked along one side. Rather than risk getting stuck, he circled back and found a small dirt lot next to the world's tiniest gas station. Before getting out, he grabbed his black leather messenger bag. The exhaust fumes from all the passing vehicles were intense, and he covered his mouth and nose with a handkerchief.

When the nun saw the gas station proprietor, she walked over and spoke to him in K'iche' to make sure it was okay for them to park there. But before he could answer, the PI handed the small man with the shiny, expectant eyes twenty American dollars. He grinned through large teeth shot with gold and said something Charlie assumed was *thank you.*

The PI pointed. "I think Maria's house is at the top of the street."

Worried about his knees giving out, he was about to start up the hill when she touched his arm.

"Wait. We can't just show up empty-handed."

"What?"

Glancing around, she walked over to the little man again. After a few brief words, Charlie saw the proprietor point somewhere.

"Come on," she said.

"Where to?"

"You'll see."

Soon, they were trudging up the hilly street, each carrying plastic bags filled with meat, produce, and dry goods.

"How long have you been in Guatemala?" he said.

"Nineteen—no, twenty—years. Can't believe it's been so long. Before that, I was in the Philippines."

"Well, I'm pleased to have your company. My Spanish is pretty rough, and I don't want to miss a thing this woman says."

"I wonder how long it's been since she saw her daughter."

"My records indicate Ana entered the US fairly recently."

At the top of the street stood a decrepit, grayish cinderblock building perched precariously on what looked like a cracked foundation. He wondered what would happen in an earthquake, then dismissed the thought.

Children's voices were laughing somewhere nearby as they approached the dark-stained wooden front door of a residence facing the street. The scent of fried food made him realize he was hungry again.

He knocked once, and they were met by a short woman who looked to be in her twenties, with the smooth, dark hair and brown eyes of the Mayan people who had lived in this part of the world for thousands of years. She wore jeans, Nikes, and a printed T-shirt featuring the silkscreen image of someone named Rebecca Lane.

"Buenas tardes," Sister Elizabeth said.

She introduced the PI and herself. When she'd finished explaining that they were hoping to speak to Maria Lopez, the girl invited them in.

Inside, the cement block walls had been plastered over and painted white. A large rug covered the concrete floor, and toys lay everywhere. It looked to him as if they kept the home as clean as possible. He was glad he had come prepared to make a cash payment to the woman. He was sure they would put it to good use.

A few minutes later, the girl returned, followed by another woman who appeared to be in her fifties. When they saw her, the visitors handed the grocery bags to the girl, who took them into the kitchen. Maria was diminutive, wearing a long plaid skirt and an orange blouse. Around her neck hung a gold crucifix on a chain. He addressed her, knowing his companion would translate everything he said.

"Señora Lopez?" Charlie said. "I'm here about your daughter, Ana."

* * *

Sitting at his desk in the library, the elderly lawyer stared at the computer monitor, waiting for the Skype session to begin. The internet connections in Guatemala were spotty in small towns, and he worried the PI wouldn't be able to get through. Eventually, Charlie and Sister Elizabeth appeared, a little too far away from the webcam.

"Can you hear me okay?" the PI said.

"Fine. Hello, Sister. I'm Harlan Covington. I want to thank you for helping with our investigation." Then to Charlie, "What've you got for me?"

"We spoke to Ana's mother. At first, she was reluctant. But Sister Elizabeth seems to have a way with people. She assured Maria we were only trying to help her daughter."

"Did you get through all the questions?"

The PI glanced at the nun. "For the most part. We would ask a question, and often Maria would start to remember things. And we'd be off on another topic."

The lawyer gripped his pen, and he realized his impatience was getting the better of him. Taking a breath, he spoke in a modulated voice.

"I want to know everything," he said.

"When Ana was eight, she got very sick. Maria wanted to take her to the hospital for tests, but her brother insisted on contacting the local shaman.

"They call themselves Ajq'ij," Sister Elizabeth said. "It means spiritual guide."

Harlan was perplexed. "I thought the family was Catholic."

"Maria is," Charlie said. "And deeply religious. But, as far as the rest of the family, there's a deep attachment to the old ways."

"So, this guy—"

"The shaman is a woman," she said. "Was. She died recently. She told Maria her daughter was suffering from el susto. Roughly, it translates to 'the fright' and is of a supernatural origin."

"The evil eye," the lawyer said.

"Mr. Covington, I don't think the shaman did anything wrong. Apparently, Ana was already suffering when she went there. In any event, the healing ceremony the woman performed didn't work. Ana remained sick off and on for years."

"Symptoms?"

"Bad dreams. Calling out in the night. Others in the family reported hearing animal noises—cows lowing and the like. Eventually, things got worse. By the time she was fifteen, Ana was considered wild. And she suffered from terrible headaches."

"Meaning?"

"Her mother said she was boy crazy. That same year, her father disappeared."

"What do you mean? He ran away?"

"No one knows. According to Maria, he vanished."

"What about Tomás Morales? When did Ana meet him?"

"When she turned twenty," the PI said. "Her uncle introduced her to him. Tomás was a Christian pastor and told Maria he was interested in helping her daughter."

The lawyer wrote something down. "How did Ana's mother feel about it?"

"Maria is no fool," the nun said. "Men who claim to

want to help young girls are plentiful. She insisted Tomás marry her daughter if he was serious. He agreed."

"I see. And they were married for two years, correct?

"Yes," Charlie said. "They moved to Cobán, which is in the north."

"And where Tomás died."

"Correct. He drowned in the Pasión river. Sister and I are headed to Cobán tomorrow."

Harlan had hoped there was more. Why, for instance, had the father disappeared? And how had it affected Ana?

"Does Ana's mother have any idea what might have been wrong with her daughter?" he said.

The PI referred to his notes. "After the shaman failed, she did end up taking Ana for medical tests. But they never found anything conclusive."

"And what about Tomás? Does she have any opinions about him?"

"She claims her daughter contacted her through a neighbor, who lent the girl her phone. Ana told her mother Tomás beat her and that she wanted to come home."

"And did she?"

"Apparently, she tried. But her husband wouldn't let her. So, her uncle arranged for her to travel to the US to seek asylum."

"Do you think he was the one who killed Tomás?"

The PI hesitated. "It's possible. But he was never charged."

"Okay," the lawyer said. "Let me know what else you find out. Oh, and did you give Maria the cash?"

"I did. She was very grateful and asked us to thank you."

"Take care, Charlie. Thank you again, Sister."

"You're welcome. Mr. Covington. I sense this case has

little to do with domestic abuse and more to do with something else. Am I correct?"

"You're very insightful. Let's say this investigation is of a spiritual nature."

"I see. Thank you."

Harlan ended the session and closed his eyes. It was after seven, and he hadn't yet eaten. Mary would have made sure a plate was waiting for him in the refrigerator. He thought again about Ana. Then he tried reconciling the "boy-crazy" girl Maria Lopez had portrayed against the quiet domestic abuse victim staying at the women's shelter.

Ana was hiding something—he could feel it.

EIGHT

Was it Sarah's imagination, or was her father staring at her? He'd always had an uncanny ability to see into her soul, and she wondered whether he was doing it now. They sat in the kitchen of her childhood home. Katy laughed over something that happened in Science class involving smoke bombs while Rachel served Mexican meatloaf—one of her daughter's favorites.

"Eddie, how are things at the college?" Sarah said.

"Same as always. Except for the lockdown today."

"What?"

"It was nothing, some troubled kid. He didn't even have a weapon." He took a swallow of beer. "Forget I mentioned it."

"Did the police come?" Katy said.

"Of course." Her grandfather sounded impatient. "And they took the boy away, and we all went back to our happy lives. On a brighter note, two of my students are failing."

Sarah nudged her niece. "How will this country ever survive with two fewer sociologists? Am I right?"

"Oh, Sarah, I forgot to mention," Rachel said. "Someone approached me at the grocery store yesterday, asking where they could find a good realtor. I told them I didn't know but would put them in touch with you."

Katy nearly squirted milk out of her nose.

"Thanks, sis. By the way, you're getting a tarantula for your birthday."

"Seriously, though, they seemed interested. I'm sure they'll call you."

"I appreciate it, Rache." *Let's see if I can mess this up.* "I still say you should think about getting your license."

"Oh, no. We are not switching jobs."

"I'm being serious. You already know all about contracts. And we need an extra agent now that business has picked up."

Her sister blushed. "But me selling something?"

"Why not?" her dad said.

"Well, for starters, I'm a back-of-house kind of gal. I don't enjoy being out there with the public."

"Mom, what about the speech you gave at City Hall?" Katy said.

"Okay, it was a town meeting—three years ago—and it wasn't a speech. I simply expressed my opinion about helping the homeless by not confiscating all their stuff."

"I remember," Sarah said, raising an index finger. *"This will not stand, man."*

"I'm pretty sure you're confusing this with *The Big Lebowski.*"

"I knew I heard it somewhere," Sarah said, winking at her niece.

"I think it's a great idea," Eddie said. "Don't sell yourself short."

Rachel dropped her fork on the floor.

"Hey, what's wrong?" her sister said. "He was only trying to compliment you."

Rachel refilled her daughter's glass with milk. Then she leaned over and whispered to Sarah.

"That's what you-know-who said the night he nearly scared me to death," she said.

It was drizzling as the sisters said goodbye at the front door.

"I shouldn't be so sensitive," Rachel said. "It wasn't like the freak attacked me."

"Well, as my therapist likes to remind me, he's dead. Hey, are we still on for yoga?"

"Are you kidding? I'm so looking forward to kicking your butt at Dhanurasana."

"I think I liked you better when you were a back-of-the-house wallflower." Sarah kissed her sister's cheek.

"Fine, I'll think about getting my license," Rachel said. "But it doesn't mean—"

"We'll see."

As her sister walked off, Rachel called to her. "Not making any promises!"

Sarah smirked. "Night, sis."

Heading home, Sarah decided to take a detour and drove to St. Rita's. The street was quiet, and it was raining. She parked her Galaxie directly across from the building. The lights were on inside on the first floor. But the upper floors where the women slept were dark. *What am I, on a stakeout?*

There was a police cruiser parked farther away on the

street. As rivulets of water poured down the windshield, it was impossible to see who was behind the wheel. A moment later, the headlights came on, and the vehicle pulled out. As it passed her, she thought she recognized Tim. When he turned his head toward her, she wiggled down into the seat. *Great, now I'm acting like a criminal.*

She was about to start her car when she happened to look up. Someone had opened a window on one of the upper floors. The pale curtains billowed. A figure stood there, but she couldn't make out who it was. She lowered her window and took out her phone. As the icy rain splashed her face and hands, she used her phone's camera to zoom in. Though the image was grainy, she saw Ana dressed in plain cotton pajamas. And there was someone else.

A behemoth of a man stood behind her, bathed in an ethereal mist. As Sarah continued to observe them, he looked at her, his eyes on fire.

Shaken by the ghostly presence earlier, Sarah walked into her kitchen through the garage and found Joe sitting on a barstool drinking scotch, his face grim. The bottle of Talisker stood next to his glass.

"Who died?" she said, setting down her purse and keys.

"It's my dad."

"Me and my big mouth. Is he—"

"He's in intensive care. It was a stroke."

"Do they know how bad it is?"

"Not yet. Listen." He took her hand. "Mom called earlier and wanted me to fly out."

"You have to go."

"I already booked a red-eye, but I don't like leaving you alone."

"Joseph Nathan Greene, you do not—I repeat, *not*—need to worry about me. Go be with your family."

"Are you sure?"

"Read my lips."

"I'd rather kiss them."

"Well, then?"

He took her in his arms and kissed her. Then he pulled away and checked the time.

"I guess that's going to have to last me," she said. "So, do you need a ride to the airport?"

"No, I'll use Uber. I should pack."

"Have you eaten?"

"I'll grab something at the airport." He headed for the guest bedroom. "Manny is in charge of the new renovation till I get back."

When the Uber driver arrived, she followed him to the front door. "When do you think you'll be back?"

"I'm hoping I don't have to stay more than a week. It depends on what they find. I think Dad's chances are better if the stroke was ischemic."

"As opposed to...?"

"Hemorrhagic, which is caused by a ruptured blood vessel."

"You really should've gone to medical school like you planned."

"Why?"

"Because then I could tell everyone my ex-husband is a doctor, silly."

"I'm making a mental note to find you a doctor you can divorce."

She kissed and hugged him, wishing he would stay. "Take all the time you need in New York. And give my love to your parents. I'll be here, praying."

"Try and stay out of trouble while I'm away."

"You're no fun."

"I mean it, Sarah. I'm—"

"Worried about me, I know. I will." She shooed him. "Go."

Sarah stood in the doorway, watching Joe get into the white Honda Accord and drive off in the rain. It was only after the taillights had disappeared around the corner that she realized how much she would miss him.

The only good thing to come out of this was that she didn't have to lie to him about the women's shelter. She thought about the old days when they were married. Home every night. Making dinner together, then relaxing in front of the TV. *Idiot! Why did I have to screw it all up?*

She didn't want to be alone and checked her watch. Not even nine. Returning to the kitchen, she grabbed her phone and punched in a number.

"Carter?" she said. "You busy?"

The Cracked Pot was unusually crowded for a weeknight. Sarah and Carter sat in a booth next to the front windows. Outside, the rain came down in intermittent showers, making the street shiny in the orange glow of the streetlights.

Each of them had a mug of coffee, with a single piece of French silk pie sitting between them. The girl admired the black leather bracelet she wore on her right wrist and proudly modeled it for her friend.

"This is so me," she said.

Sarah laughed. "I'll be sure to let Harlan know."

"But St. Benedict? I don't understand why he wanted me to have it."

"As a board member, he already knew we were investigating the women's shelter. And don't forget, he's a devout Catholic. I guess he was being a little…"

"Fatherly?"

"I never thought of Harlan Covington as the fatherly type."

"Is it blessed?" Carter said.

"You bet. He mentioned the monks in Norcia made it, so I did a little digging."

"Surprise, surprise."

Sarah grabbed her phone and showed her a photo from a website. "Monastero di San Benedetto in Monte."

"The Monastery of St. Benedict on the Mountain," the girl said.

"Wow, I wasn't aware you knew Italian."

"I get by." She studied the medal. "I'm never taking this off, by the way."

Sarah picked up her fork and tried the dessert. "This is so decadent."

Carter joined her. "Mm. Let's make this a sugar night— calories be damned."

"I like your style, sista."

Their server brought two more desserts. As they ate, the women talked about the new house and the kind of furniture Carter might be interested in. It was hard for Sarah to believe her friend was in a position to purchase such an expensive home.

Originally, Joe had planned to set the asking price at 1.2 million. But because the buyer was Carter—and at his business partner's insistence—he'd agreed to let it go for $990,000, leaving them a modest profit. Sarah had already promised to take her friend to an interior design store she liked on State Street. Despite her initial reservations, she was genuinely happy for the girl.

It was after eleven when they walked outside. The air was chilly, and the sky clear. Sarah saw the ascending moon and thought of Devil's Bluff, which weakened her knees. She shrugged off the feeling. Carter's MINI Cooper was parked behind Sarah's Galaxie.

"So, what's your day like tomorrow?" the girl said.

"I've got to show some properties. What time are you off work?"

"Four."

"Okay. I'll call Heidi to see if we can drop by. I'll pick you up, okay?"

"Great. Do you think the situation with Joe's dad is serious?"

"He'll call me as soon as he knows."

"Are you sure you'll be okay? You know, being alone?"

"I've had enough of feeling sorry for myself. I'll be fine. Besides, I have Gary."

When Sarah got home, she found the cat on the kitchen counter, prowling around for something to hunt. As soon as they made eye contact, he tried hopping off, but she caught him in midair and held him like a baby.

"You know what, dude? I'm not even mad."

Meowing, Gary tried wriggling out of her arms, and she placed him on the floor. The Talisker was still out. She took down a whiskey glass, and pouring a drink, clinked the bottle. Her feline companion trotted off.

"Looks like it's going to be another Long Dark Tea-Time of the Soul," she said.

Sarah awoke drenched in sweat. She sat up and forced herself to breathe slowly to calm herself. After a few moments, she relaxed. It hadn't been the nightmare she expected. This was something new, and it terrified her. It wasn't long before the afterimages came.

It had started with the noises. First, the creaking of the hardwood floor coming from outside her bedroom. Then a kind of shuffling, as if someone were approaching her door. As the menacing thing got closer, the noise stopped.

She sat up in bed, staring at the closed bedroom door. Had someone broken in? In horror movies, the doorknob always turns slowly, building on the audience's fear of the unknown waiting on the other side. But that's not what happened.

The door burst open with a deafening crack, revealing a man shrouded in darkness. He entered the room, limping with determination toward her. He was short and dark, with straight hair. Though he looked like a priest, she knew he wasn't. He grabbed her injured wrist, sending a shooting pain up her arm, and she cried out. Then, gripping her even tighter, he spoke. His eyes were filled with agony, but it was his voice—it was the sound of pebbles in a rock crusher.

"Ella aparenta ser una mansa paloma, pero no lo es."

When the last of the images vanished, she held herself and sobbed. Nearby, Gary purred, which calmed her as she stared fixedly at the ceiling. Then she felt her wrist—it was hot. She turned on the light and examined it. The area around her scar was bright red and formed a pattern. It looked just like...

"Human fingers," Sarah said.

NINE

Sarah's eyes were closed as she listened to her yoga instructor. She tried not to fall asleep. The previous night had been awful, and eventually she'd given up and binged *Santa Clarita Diet* until early morning rather than spend any more time analyzing her dream. Not bothering to shower, she drove straight to the studio and waited in the car for Rachel.

It was a little after seven, and ten women had shown up. She and her sister had chosen spots in the last row. The instructor was a woman of around forty. Her long hair was pinned up, and she wore no makeup. She began with the easy pose, Sukhasana. Together, the class inhaled and exhaled while slowly rolling their shoulders. Next, they moved their heads forward and back and side to side. So far, so good.

Gomukhasana—cow face pose. As Sarah put her arm behind her back, she felt the tension in her muscles and wished she'd gotten in a run. Rachel easily moved through the motions. God bless her for attending a beginner's session. It wasn't long before something in the corner of Sarah's eye glimmered.

Adho Mukha Svanasana—downward-facing dog. A sharp pain lanced her wrist as her forehead touched the mat. She felt self-conscious with her backside up so high, then remembered that everyone else was doing it too. A warm memory came to her. Her sister as a toddler, asleep in her crib with her little butt in the air. She glanced up as something darted playfully past the instructor. Unaware of it, the woman continued with the lesson.

The last time Sarah had tried yoga, something similar happened. Now, there were faint voices, which sounded like children *Evil children?* They were close. As the class proceeded to Utthita Balasana—extended child's pose— several tiny figures danced across the floor and vanished into a wall. Neither Rachel nor any of the other women reacted. *Oh, come on.*

A hand rested on Sarah's shoulder. When she turned, she discovered a scary-looking child with shiny white eyes and made of coal dust. It grinned at her. Getting to her feet as quietly as possible, she got her things and waited outside. In a few minutes, the door opened, and her sister emerged, carrying her mat.

She touched her sister's arm. "Bad experience?"

"Not too bad. Just some creepy children doing a dance number from *Hamilton.*"

"Hey, what about martial arts?"

"I'm going to ignore that. Want to grab breakfast?"

"Sure. I'll meet you at The Cracked Pot." Then, as Rachel walked away, "I was being serious."

As Sarah got into her car, her watch vibrated. It was Joe. She took her phone from her purse and answered.

"Hey, you," she said.

"Is this a good time?"

"Sure. How's your dad?"

"Still in intensive care. I'm going over there again later."

"So, was the stroke—what did you call it?"

"Ischemic. And yes, it was."

"How's your mom?"

"Pretty shaken up. Um, I might be here longer than I thought. Someone needs to look after her."

She wanted to tell him how much she missed him. Instead, she said, "You're a good son."

"My sister is coming as soon as she and Aaron can figure out what to do with the kids. Hey, I had a thought. Why don't you fly out this weekend? I know my mother would be thrilled to see you. We could come home together."

"Oh, I would love to." She scrunched her nose. "But I can't. I'm in the middle of—"

"Don't tell me. This has something to do with the call you got from Harlan Covington."

"Well, in my defense, Lou's up to his eyeballs with an audit. And Carter and I are trying to help out at the St. Rita's."

"Okay, no problem. Guess I'll see you in a week or so."

"Joe? I love you."

Silence. Then, "Love you too."

As he disconnected, she felt a rift growing between them. What was the matter with her? She should've accepted his offer. What difference would a couple of days make? Angry at herself, she started her car.

When she walked into The Cracked Pot, she didn't see

Rachel anywhere. The place was almost empty, which was unusual. She spotted a booth next to the window and slid in. Almost immediately, a male server came by.

"Coffee," she said. "The strongest you have. Also, there'll be two of us."

He wrote down the order on his pad and left. Soon, he returned with a steaming mug. She gazed out the window. Lou's police SUV pulled up, with her sister in the front seat. *What the...* Rachel got out and approached the front door as the police chief drove off. Was it her imagination, or did this chick look flushed? She did her best not to say anything as her sister slid into the booth.

"So, you're getting rides from cops now?" Sarah said.

"It's nothing. My car died on the way over."

The server reappeared with another mug of coffee and a second menu. After they'd placed their orders, Rachel continued, as if obligated to explain.

"When the tow truck arrived, Lou spotted me and offered to give me a ride. You're taking me home to change, by the way."

"Hmm."

"What *hmm*?"

"Just hmm."

"Why are you making a big deal out of nothing?"

"Here's a better question—why didn't you call me?"

"I don't know." She was blushing. "When Lou showed up, I...I figured I'd see you soon enough, that's all."

"So, what about your car?"

"The mechanic is looking at it. Hey, too bad yoga didn't work out."

"Nice segue. Guess it's back to copious amounts of alcohol to deal with the stress."

"God, I hope not."

"Actually, I'm going to focus more on running. Hey, Rache? Can I tell you about this dream I had?"

"Does it involve Joe? Because…"

"No, it's nothing like that."

Sarah told her sister about Ana and the women's shelter. After she'd finished describing her dream, Rachel took another bite of her omelet and wrote on her napkin.

"Mansa?" she said. "It means gentle. And of course, paloma is dove."

"Right. His exact words were, *Ella aparenta ser una mansa paloma, pero no lo es.*"

Rachel read off her napkin. "She appears to be a gentle dove, but she's not."

"What I can't figure out is who he was talking about."

"I don't know, but it sounds to me like he's saying she's tougher than she looks. So who do you think he is?"

"No idea. Okay, this might be a stretch, but maybe he was talking about Ana."

"The woman at the shelter? Her husband died, right?"

"Yes. Okay, if it was his ghost, is he saying, after all the abuse, she's tougher than she looks?"

"Well, aren't most women?"

Sarah clinked mugs with her sister, but she wasn't satisfied. Why would the ghost of a dead man make an appearance just to tell her his wife was tougher than she looked? Ignoring her food, she got out her phone and keyed in something.

"I can't believe I didn't look this up before," she said. This has nothing to do with Ana being tough."

"But that's how it translates."

"Yeah, if you're being literal. It's a Guatemalan saying. *Ella aparenta ser una mansa paloma, pero no lo es.*" She looked at Rachel, her mouth open. "She's not what she seems."

"Then the ghost was trying to say..."

"It was a warning," Sarah said.

Joe stood staring at the thousands of headstones and monuments, holding a bouquet of wildflowers. There wasn't anyone else around. A biting wind stung his face, and he jammed his free hand into his coat pocket. Though he was tall, the vastness of the slate sky made him feel like a pinpoint on a map. Why had he come here? He hadn't thought about the little girl in years.

The traffic on the Van Wyck Expressway was loud and constant. He shrugged deeper into his coat as he walked among the graves, some of them dating back to the 1800s. He didn't remember exactly where she was buried, but he was determined to find her. Referring again to the directions the assistant in the office had given him, he continued walking east. As he reached a familiar path, he saw a flock of crows passing, cawing angrily.

There. As quietly as possible, he approached the small, plain headstone. The graves surrounding it looked better maintained, many with fresh flowers. This one was barren, and suddenly, he was overcome with emotion. Crouching, he laid down the flowers. Then he wept bitterly, and touching the stone, and read the words.

LEAH TALMAN. BELOVED DAUGHTER. 1989—1999.

"Forgive me," he said.

Lou made his way across the lobby. The place was unusually quiet. Nothing like the stereotypical hospital scenes in the movies. Santa Barbara Cottage Hospital was a sprawling, Spanish-style complex surrounded by trees and grass. It wasn't the kind of facility you'd expect poor people to end up in. Then again, the women's shelter was well funded and probably had some kind of arrangement with the hospital.

As he got into the elevator, he thought again of his chance encounter with Sarah's sister. He had known Rachel Zamora about as long as he had Sarah and had always thought of her as attractive and pleasant. Though he liked her, he certainly entertained no romantic notions. Then, this morning happened. She'd been so sweet and self-deprecating as she talked about her life as a single mom. It was charming.

When the elevator doors opened, he struggled to put Rachel out of his mind. He walked up to the nurses' station, where he found a nurse at the computer.

"Hi, I'm Police Chief Fiore from Dos Santos. I need to speak to a patient who was admitted yesterday. Marcy Lund."

"Can I see some ID?" she said.

He showed her his badge and waited for her to look up the information. Then she gave him the room number. As he walked in, he saw an elderly woman visiting with the patient. She sat next to the bed and held Marcy's good hand.

"Excuse me," he said as they looked at him. "I'm here to interview Marcy."

"Chief Fiore?" the old woman said. "I'm Roxanne Marsh."

As she started to get up, he motioned for her to remain seated. "It's okay, I can stand." They shook hands. "Pleased to meet you."

"Heidi asked me to stop by. I'm a psychologist contracted by St. Rita's."

"I see." Then to the patient, "Can I ask you a few questions?"

"Okay."

Marcy's right hand was bandaged. All he saw was her thumb and another finger. And nothing but a rounded lump in between.

"Ms. Lund, can you tell me what happened yesterday?"

"I've told everyone already. I was helping to prepare dinner, and the next thing I know…" She held up her hand.

"So, you don't remember walking over to the sink?"

"No! When they told me what I'd done, I couldn't believe it. Why would I…?" She stared at the hand with the missing fingers, tears springing. "Why would I do this to myself?"

He referred to the file he was carrying. "I've been over your records. And it says that in 2013, you were taken to the emergency room twice with deep cuts on both arms."

Imploringly, the woman looked at Roxanne, who patted her hand. "I used to be a different person. But since I've been at the shelter, I've changed, thanks to Dr. Marsh." Then to the psychologist, "Tell him."

Roxanne cleared her throat. "She's made wonderful progress. Which is why this was so unexpected."

"I see," he said. Then to the patient, "And you say you don't remember anything?"

"No, except... It's hard to explain. I remember hearing it in my head."

"What?"

"Singing," Marcy said.

Roxanne warmed her hands around the paper cup filled with hot tea. Lou had already finished his coffee and was making notes. The hospital cafeteria was deserted, except for the workers and a few doctors and nurses.

"So, you've already had sessions with the other two women?" he said.

"And generally, it's the same story—they have no memory of what they did."

"What about the singing?"

"They didn't mention anything. Chief, I've been treating these women for months. Though each came to the shelter with emotional problems, they've learned to become happy and well adjusted. So, this is as much a mystery to me as it is to you."

"Have you met with Ana Robles?"

"I did. Several times when she first came to the shelter. I'm afraid she's a closed book. I haven't spoken to her since."

"I keep looking for evidence that a crime was committed. But so far, I've found nothing. I plan to interview her myself. After I complete my investigation, I'm afraid you and the director will have to sort through it."

"And Sarah Greene." Noticing his surprised look, she smiled. "I'm told she's involved."

He hesitated. "Yes, she is. I hope you don't mind."

"I don't. But I'm worried about her well-being. She's had a terrible shock."

"She's tough. I'm sure she can handle it."

"Women put on a brave front because we have to," the psychologist said.

He thought about the night at Devil's Bluff, when he and Joe saved Sarah from falling to her death. He scooted his chair out and stood.

"Thanks for everything, Roxanne."

"Call me anytime. You will be careful when you speak to Ana, won't you? I'm afraid the abuse she's suffered has made her quite guarded."

"How so?"

"She doesn't mix well with the others. Whenever I tried speaking to her, she refused to open up to me. I sense there's a deep hurt. I don't want someone who is untrained to—"

"Step in it?" he said.

"Well, yes."

"I'll be careful. And thanks for the warning."

As he left the hospital, Lou wondered how good Sarah's Spanish was.

TEN

Carter had managed to find an open parking spot at the rear of the building on State Street and made her way across the dark lot to a hipster bar called Renown. Nervous, she was not at all sure she should do this—yet she felt she had to. Besides, after all the band drama, she wasn't seeking a relationship—just some company with someone her own age.

"It's just drinks," she said.

Inside, the place was warm and filled with women and men who looked to be in their mid-twenties and early thirties. She marveled at the interior. Used brick walls and solid, antique-style tables and chairs made of dark wood. The black grid sconces gave off a warm yellow light. The bar stood in the center, against a wall, a perfect half-circle. Inside, sharply dressed bartenders scooted past one another, filling drink orders. One had just plopped a freshly manufactured ice ball into a whiskey glass.

Pushing past a group of men, she made her way to the bar. She couldn't help noticing them eyeing her. She'd gotten those looks most of her life since she was eleven.

Later in her teens, there were the comments—and worse. As a result, she'd gone through a phase where she wore nothing but loose-fitting jeans and dark hoodies. Now, at twenty-five, she took it in stride. Fronting a band had helped.

She spotted Nellie sitting at the bar, nursing a sweet-looking drink and scrolling on her phone. When she saw Carter, she blushed. A man and a woman were sitting next to her, and there was an empty barstool next to the man.

"I don't know why I suggested this place," Nellie said. "It's always like this."

Carter scanned the room. "Wanna see if we can find a table?"

"Good luck."

The woman next to them had overheard and tugged at her date's sleeve. Then to the two young women, "It's okay, we'll slide down."

"Thanks," Carter said.

As she settled in, a bartender hurried over. After setting down a fresh cocktail napkin, addressed her. "What'll you have?"

"Guinness."

She pointed at the other girl's drink. "Looks good. What is it?"

"Pomegranate margarita. I sort of got hooked on these in college." She picked at her napkin, leaving tiny paper shreds around the glass.

"You okay?"

Nellie stopped. "It was a bit of a crazy day today."

"Did something happen?"

"Forget it. Hey, I was admiring your bracelet—it's so unusual."

"St. Benedict." Carter showed it off.

"Are you Catholic?"

"A friend gave it me. I just like wearing it."

"Fashion statement, huh?"

"I guess."

The bartender placed a tulip pub glass of dark beer with a perfect head in front of her.

"I meant to ask," Nellie said. "Are you a cop?"

Carter laughed. She felt relaxed and realized she liked this girl. And she was glad she'd suggested meeting up. Tucking her short hair behind her ear, she tried her beer.

"I'm not, actually. I work at a restaurant."

"Oh? Which one?"

"The Cracked Pot on Dos Santos Road?"

"I love that place. I go there sometimes, but I don't think I've ever seen you."

"My shifts seem to be all over the place lately. So, tell me about your research. I take it you've been working with those women for a while?"

"I have. And I've really come to care about them. Which is why this whole thing has been so distressing."

"How'd you get involved?"

"I'm a grad student at UCSB in the Cognition, Perception, and Cognitive Neuroscience program."

"Sounds impressive."

"We study how humans perceive, remember, think, learn, and act on the world. At least, that's what it says in the course catalog." She laughed.

"And where does St. Rita's fit in?"

"I think Heidi has some kind of connection with the school. Our department head approached her to see if we could work with the residents as part of our research. Nothing invasive. Observation mostly, and a few tests.

"Me, I'm really interested in how the brain functions

under different conditions. Lately, I've focused my research on brain imaging."

"Maybe I should volunteer. Although I'm not sure you guys would like what you find."

"Okay, you've just piqued my scientific curiosity."

Carter braced herself. She hadn't meant to go down this road. "So, you've met Sarah, right? She and I are, well, we're sort of...psychic."

"Really? That's incredible."

"Incredible, not so much. It's more of a burden than anything. I guess she and I have come to terms with it, each in our own way."

"So, have either of you ever been tested?"

"Well, I can't speak for Sarah, but I haven't. And anyway, I'm not sure I'd want to. I mean, it's not like we're, you know, trying to make a living at this."

"Right." Nellie was thoughtful. "So, are you and she..."

Carter laughed again. "We're good friends. She's madly in love with her ex-husband. But that's a whole other story."

"And you?" Nellie said, moving bits of her napkin around the bar with her finger.

"Me? I just came off the worst relationship ever—bass player. Never again, let me tell you."

"Was he mean?"

"The bass player is a she. And no, she wasn't. At the end of the day, Lindsay and I were incompatible, though we did try to make it work. She wants to be this famous musician. You know, like Tina Weymouth.

"She's really talented, by the way. I sang with the band off and on for years when I lived in the Bay Area. But for me, it was a lark. I never wanted to go professional. So, what about you?"

"There isn't anyone right now. Relationships are hard for me. I guess it's a middle-child thing. And last year, I lost my dad."

"Oh, how awful."

"And with school and work... And then, there's my mother. There's this whole denial thing going on. She has high hopes that someday I'll snap out of it and marry Dr. Handsome."

"I should introduce her to my mom. They'd get along famously."

Carter hadn't realized she'd finished her beer and flagged down the nearest bartender.

"Another Guinness?" he said.

"Yeah." She turned to Nellie. "And a pomegranate margarita."

The other girl smiled. "Thanks."

Tentatively, she touched Carter's finger. When she didn't pull away, Nellie ran her forefinger down the length of it, then retreated.

Later, in the backseat of the MINI Cooper, Carter made out with Nellie. Their bodies pressed together, they couldn't get enough of each other. She hadn't even heard her phone vibrating. Breathlessly, Nellie tried to speak as the girl with the choppy bob covered her neck in kisses.

"I don't live far," she said.

Sarah set down her phone and stared at Gary. Either Carter was asleep or out having a good time.

"Am I the only one stuck at home with a stupid cat?" she said.

Gary meowed, which meant he was looking for someone to scratch behind his ear. She obliged. Though it was after ten, she didn't want to go to bed. After speaking to Lou, she wasn't sure she was ready to talk to Ana. She actually feared the Guatemalan woman. And although the police chief would drive the inquiry, Sarah would be in the middle. She needed her friend for moral support.

She picked up the cat and went to her bedroom to change. As she brushed her teeth, she thought about Joe. She was unhappy over their last phone conversation. Was he angry with her? It was probably his dad being ill. *Maybe I'll surprise him by showing up. No, too rom-com.*

As she lay in bed, the cat purring next to her, she closed her eyes and prayed she would sleep without interruption. *No nightmares, please. Thank you.*

When Carter awoke, she found Nellie curled up in a ball next to her, snuggled warmly under the blankets. Her bedroom was a jumble. There were piles of books, maga-zines, and research papers everywhere. On the windowsill stood a multicolored collection of potted plants, some in the throes of dying, others thriving. A laptop connected to a monitor sat on a desk in a cute cubby. And large color photographs of what looked like brain images were taped around the walls like sci-fi family portraits.

She climbed out of bed and went to the bathroom. When she returned, Nellie was sitting up, brushing the hair from her face and looking disconcerted. Carter slipped under the covers and took her hand.

"You think this was a mistake," she said.

"Not at all. It's just... It's stupid, never mind."

"What?" She ran her fingers through Nellie's fine blonde hair.

"This is usually the part where the other girl says, 'I'll call you.'"

"Oh."

"And I'm really not into hook-ups. You know what I mean?"

"Can I tell you something? Neither am I. Look, I can't promise anything. My life is... Well, it's kind of unusual." She showed Nellie the bracelet. "This is way more than a fashion statement."

"Does it have to do with what you and Sarah are investigating?"

"Yeah. It has everything to do with it. But I like you. I mean, I really like you."

"I'm glad. I like you too."

"So, let's see where this goes, okay? But only if you want to."

Taking Carter's face in her hands, Nellie kissed her. "I'm making us breakfast."

Amused, Carter watched as she practically leapt out of bed and scavenged for clothes. She threw on her sweater and jumped her way into her skinny jeans. As she left the room, Carter's phone buzzed. It was Sarah.

"Morning," she said, yawning. "What? Well, I guess I can, sure. Okay, see you there."

She got dressed and, her shoulders sagging, left to tell Nellie she had to leave. There was singing coming from the kitchen.

"Perfect," she said. "She's in a good mood."

"I went to see her."

Joe sat in the waiting room at the hospital. It was a small, closed space—claustrophobic. His mother, Evelyn, sat next to him. She wore her coat, even though the room was stifling. Other people were present, waiting for news about family members coming out of surgery. Some read magazines or their phones. Others swapped embarrassing stories and laughed.

She took his hand. Though still attractive, she'd aged since the last time he saw her. The toll the years had taken was evident in the lines on her face. His father had been sick off and on for a very long time, though no one had ever said anything to Joe. He wondered if his sister knew.

"What did you say?" She'd tightened her grip on his hand, and when she realized it, she let go.

"I've been thinking a lot about her lately—about that day," he said.

"Why?"

"I don't know." He wanted to disappear.

She moved closer. "It was an accident. She ran in front of you."

"The ball was the warning. I should've—"

"Oh, you poor thing. Having to carry this around with you all these years."

"And what about you?"

"Me? I'm fine."

"Did you ever tell Dad the truth?"

She was silent for a time. Then, "No, I never did. And besides, what good would it do?"

"Don't you think he'd want to know that his wife—"

"Let's not talk about it anymore."

She patted his hand. That was what mothers did when it was time to stop. They'd take the thing secretly tearing them apart and return it to its special box, where it would remain in some dusty corner until they stumbled on it again.

"How's Sarah?" she said.

"She's okay. Wrist is healing."

"It's not what I meant."

"I guess she's fine for the most part. But there are days when..."

The door opened, and a nurse entered the room and approached them.

"Mrs. Greene?" she said. "Dr. Shapiro can see you now."

They followed her into the corridor and down the hall to intensive care. There were three patients in there, all hooked up to breathing tubes. Except David Greene. He was unconscious, a CVC attached to his right arm. A blue blood pressure cuff was wrapped around his upper left arm, and there was a saturation monitor clipped to his left thumb. He was asleep.

Evelyn approached the bed, and blinking back tears, stroked her husband's arm. A doctor who looked to be in his mid-fifties entered quietly.

"So, what's the latest, Dr. Shapiro?" Joe said.

There was a sharpness to his voice he hadn't intended. He remembered how he'd planned to become a doctor. In another life, it might've been him standing in a room like this, meeting with the distraught family.

"Let's talk outside," the other man said in a low voice.

They walked farther down the corridor until they reached an area with a couch and a lamp. The doctor gestured for them to sit.

"We got the results of the MRI." He opened the large envelope he was carrying and removed several color photos. "I'm afraid it doesn't look promising. As you know, we have him on a tissue plasminogen activator to dissolve the clot, but the damage has already been done."

"Is he conscious?" Joe said.

"We've seen him come in and out of consciousness. The nurses are keeping a sharp eye on him. So far, he can't communicate. We've tried getting him to eat, but he either can't, or he refuses. Mrs. Greene, do I have your permission to insert a nasogastric tube?"

"Yes, of course."

"Then I need you to sign this."

He handed her a form, a pen, and the envelope for her to write on. She was about to sign when Joe took the form from her and read it carefully. Satisfied, he handed it back. When she'd finished, Dr. Shapiro gathered everything and got to his feet.

"I'll call if anything changes," he said. "And I wish I had better news."

She cried. Joe waited for the doctor to leave, then helped her to her feet.

"Come on, Mom," he said. "You need to rest."

Sarah sat with Lou and Carter in the conference room at St. Rita Women's Center. Several bottles of water stood in the middle of the table. The police chief grabbed one and took a long swallow. She looked at her friend, whose hands were folded in her lap. Before going to the shelter, she'd decided to remain neutral toward Ana. They were there to gather information, she reminded herself. And she was simply translating.

The door opened, and Heidi appeared with Ana. He gestured for the resident to take a seat. She slipped into one of the large leather chairs, which made her look even tinier. She didn't make eye contact with anyone.

"Try not to be too long," the director said to Lou. "Ana has an art class at eleven, and she really loves it."

"Sure, no prob."

After Heidi left, he smiled at the shy resident, trying not to stare at her deformed arm.

"Would you like a water?" he said.

Sarah translated. "¿Quiere algo para tomar?"

When she declined, he opened his notebook. As he spoke each sentence, he waited for Sarah to translate.

"As you know, we're investigating the recent accidents. Have you noticed anything unusual since you arrived?" No response. "Are you friends with the women who hurt themselves?"

Still nothing. He carried on. After several minutes of questioning, he hadn't made any progress. Whether out of fear or discomfort, she was clearly stonewalling.

"Do you mind if I try?" Sarah said.

He seemed relieved. "Be my guest."

"Ana, ¿tiene miedo de lo que esta pasando?" Then to the others, "I'm asking if she's afraid of what's happened here."

"No. Porque tengo un protector."

"She says she has a protector."

The police chief leaned in. "Ask her who."

"Quien es?"

The diminutive woman looked down for a moment, two slender fingers toying with the top button of her shirt. When she looked up again, her eyes were hooded.

"No one," she said.

Sarah's friend rested her hands on the table. When Ana saw the St. Benedict medal, she made a mewling noise and got to her feet, knocking over the chair. The temperature in the room plummeted as she pressed herself against the wall, glaring at the leather bracelet.

"What's happening?" Lou said, his voice rising. Why is it so cold in here?"

Sarah ignored him. Then, "Ana, ¿a qué le teme?"

She wrung her hands and panted like a dog. The other women rose at the same time. When Carter made a move toward her, Sarah raised her arm to keep her back.

"She's terrified of your medal." Taking a breath, she approached Ana. Then she took her hand.

Sarah felt herself being pulled into a tunnel of swirling black smoke. She had no sense of direction as the force dragged her farther in. Wailing voices and the sounds of lowing animals surrounded her.

Now, she stood in a dark void. The atmosphere was stifling. A sickly light illuminated her surroundings, and she saw the interior of a rude shack made of wood and a cement floor. A rough wooden table stood in the center of the room. Ana lay there on her back, shackled at the hands and feet by heavy iron chains. She was naked, her small, delicate body drenched in sweat and blood. Somewhere, wild birds screeched.

A sudden noise. She forced herself to turn around. As soon as she did, she saw him—the short, dark man with the straight hair. He faced his prisoner, holding what looked like a heavy cane. Sarah tried speaking but could only manage a single word.

"Why?"

Sarah was in the conference room again, and the

Guatemalan woman was gone. Vaguely, she felt a hand on her shoulder. It was Carter. She and the police chief looked at her expectantly.

"What did you see?" her friend said.

Her eyes filled with tears, she shook her head and pressed the back of her hand to her mouth. "He-he kept her chained up like an animal. And he beat her. God, it was horrible."

She sank into a chair, her hands trembling from the adrenalin. Then she wiped her eyes, and feeling Ana's rage, turned to Lou.

"I'm glad he's dead," she said.

ELEVEN

"Are you okay?" Carter said.

She and Sarah stood on the sidewalk in front of St. Rita's. Rubbing her wrist, her friend looked off somewhere. The girl didn't know what she'd experienced, but she had also felt the room turn icy—and so had Lou. And there was something else. Carter had seen the formless black entity hovering in a corner of the conference room like a wraith.

"I'll be all right," Sarah said.

"When we were in there, I—"

"Listen, I need a minute. What I saw made me angry. I see why Heidi cares so much about this place. These women need protection."

The girl lit a cigarette and took a nervous drag. "Kids too, right?"

Sarah hadn't seen the troubled expression on her friend's face as she walked to her Galaxie. "What time do you have to be at work?"

"I'm on at five today." Carter glanced at her phone. "Wanna get something to eat?"

"Sure. Come on, I'll drive."

The girl had finished the cigarette already. Crushing it, she nudged it over the curb. As they were about to drive off, she noticed Nellie walking toward the building entrance.

"Hang on a sec," Carter said and got out. Then to her new friend, "Hey."

"I didn't expect to see you."

"Yeah, we met with Ana today."

"Oh? How'd it go?"

"Not so good."

"I'm scheduled to meet with her. Maybe I can find out something."

"What exactly will you be doing?"

"Interviewing her. Also, our team developed a series of tests. The subject does everything on the computer. Later, we evaluate the results."

Carter took her arm. "Listen, you need to be careful with Ana."

"What do you mean?"

"Just be careful, okay?" She glanced over her shoulder. "Sarah's waiting. Hey, about this morning. I didn't mean to run out on you."

"It's all right, I understand. So, are you busy later?"

"I have work, and I get off kind of late. But if you feel like dropping in, dessert's on me."

"Thanks, I might."

They lingered awkwardly. Carter kissed her and got into the car.

"Nellie seems nice," Sarah said as they drove away.

"She's part of a research project involving the residents. But I'm worried about her." Then on her friend's expression, "She's planning to test Ana."

"Oh, shit."

"I know."

"Let's pray it all goes well."

Before the girl realized it, they were on the 154 headed for Santa Barbara. "Where exactly are we having lunch?"

"I thought we might stop at the interior design store I was telling you about."

"Are you sure?"

"Yeah. I really need something to distract me."

"So, did you wanna talk about—"

"Maybe later." Sarah switched on the radio.

As they cruised easily through light traffic, the sounds of Stan Kenton and His Orchestra filled the interior. She let her mind wander and thought of Harlan. Why hadn't the attorney invited both of them over to let Carter in on his secret? She wanted so much to tell her friend, but she'd made a promise.

They spent nearly two hours looking at furniture and fabrics. An eager sales rep had tried to help, but Sarah waved him off. Since Carter hadn't mentioned her price range, she focused on the good stuff.

"This sofa costs more than I make in a year," the girl said.

"It's Italian. And besides, you can't put a price on quality."

"Actually, you can."

"Okay, let's try Henredon. You want this stuff to last, right?"

By the time they were done, Carter had decided on Henredon for most of the rooms. She'd work on accessories as time went on—maybe Italian. She couldn't wait to move in and had already thought about throwing a party, which made her want to invite Nellie.

The women were starving as they walked next door to a pizza and sandwich place.

"Here okay?" Sarah said. "Looks like they have an espresso machine."

"Sold."

When their personal pizzas arrived, Sarah said a blessing and took a bite of hers. "This is incredible. How come I didn't know about this place?"

"Right? The crust is perfect."

After a few minutes, Sarah set aside her food and looked at the girl. "I know you want to talk about what happened. And I do too. I was pretty upset before."

"I get it. That place kind of makes me sad too."

"But let's get dessert first."

Sarah finished her espresso in one gulp. "Wow, I think I'm turning into Lou Fiore." She used her fork to break off a section of the cannoli they were sharing.

"So, the guy in your vision," Carter said. "You think he was Ana's husband?"

"I'm positive. He was also the man in my dream."

"And he kept his wife chained up?"

"Uh-huh. I saw the place—it was like I was there. Somewhere in a forest, I think."

"Do you know how long she was there?"

"No, but I sensed it may have been weeks. And it wasn't just the one time. I got the feeling he took her there regularly."

The girl toyed with the dessert. "So, why was she so afraid of my medal?"

"I was hoping there would be a different explanation. But the only thing I came up with is..."

Sarah recalled Harlan's words. *You saw what Peter Moody*

could do to you. Can you imagine if a demon had the opportunity?

"Ana may actually be possessed," she said. "It would explain her aversion to your bracelet and the creature we saw."

"But you have a St. Michael medal around your neck. Why didn't she react to it?"

"I'm wearing a sweater, so she wouldn't have been able to see it."

"I thought that was the whole point. If it is a demon, it would sense the object, right? Which leads me to think it's psychological. Ana thinks she's evil and only reacts when she sees something religious."

"So, mental illness and not demonic possession? And how do you know so much about this?"

"I don't. In college, I attended a lecture by a visiting Benedictine priest."

"I'm surprised Berkeley let him in."

"The Graduate Theological Union invited him. And in case you're wondering, I was all about the extra credit. Anyway, his talk was on the existence of God in a fallen world. Inevitably, someone asked him about exorcism. You know, did he think it worked because people believed, or were they truly possessed?"

"And?"

"He said when the Church investigates, in the majority of cases, the person suffers from some kind of mental illness. And out of those, many crave attention."

"So, you think Ana wants to be noticed? Don't forget her husband busted up her bones. No one needs that kind of attention."

Carter thought a moment. "Good point. I think we have

to accept that demonic possession is a possibility, though. What if her husband was trying to save her?"

"Or he only thought he was." Sarah looked at her watch. "I need to get back. Thanks for hanging out."

"Are you kidding? Thank you."

Outside, Sarah had started her car when her friend touched her arm.

"You know the lecture I told you about?" Carter said. "I remember some random girl stood up—she was really angry. She said the fact that evil exists in the world at all is proof there's no God."

Sarah shook her head. "And did he go off on her?"

"He quoted St. Augustine. Before his conversion, he said, *I sought whence evil comes and there was no solution.* The priest told us the only way to conquer evil was to have faith in a living God."

And what are your thoughts on the subject?"

"If you'd asked me six months ago, I would've agreed with the angry atheist. How can a God who is all good let all those horrible things happen? But after everything you went through—and now, this thing with Ana—well..."

"What?" Sarah said.

"I think it's the opposite. If there's evil—and we know there is—then God must exist. Otherwise, nothing makes sense."

"You'd make an outstanding Catholic."

"If only I was a joiner. Hey, there's something I need to tell you."

"Is it bad?"

"Uh-huh. I saw you-know-what in the conference room earlier."

"Oh, no. Harlan calls it *The Darkness.*"

"Actually, I'm surprised you didn't see it."

"I can only handle one spook at a time."

"I'm not sure if it's connected to Ana, but I think it's attracted to her."

"I was thinking. Regardless of whether Ana is possessed, we might need to involve a priest."

"Fr. Brian?"

"He can request an exorcist to evaluate her."

Sarah was about to pull into traffic when she got a call. Seeing it was the police chief, she answered it.

"Hi, Lou," she said, her voice chipper.

"Are you busy?"

"Well, Carter and I were leaving Santa Barbara. Hang on, I'll put you on speaker."

"Can you guys hear me?"

"We can," the girl said.

"I realize this is short notice, but can you two meet me at Our Lady of Sorrows? I arranged a meeting with Ana's caseworker, and—"

"On our way."

"Don't have an accident."

"You have nothing to worry about. I have a perfect driving record."

She pulled out of the parking space. Another car shot past, its horn blaring, causing her to slam on her brakes.

"What happened?" the cop said.

She glanced at her friend, whose face had gone pale. "Nothing. Where are we meeting?"

"The parish office."

After ending the call, she carefully pulled into traffic.

"That was way too close," Carter said.

There wasn't time to find street parking, so Sarah turned into the parish office parking lot and pulled in next to Lou's SUV. He got out of his vehicle, and the three of them walked in.

"Hi, Mrs. Ivy," Sarah said.

"You're late. The caseworker is waiting for you in the conference room."

Sarah led the way. A woman of around sixty sat at the conference table. Her hair was not quite in place, and she didn't acknowledge the others as she typed on her laptop.

"Grace Zielinski?" the police chief said.

"One sec." She closed the lid of her laptop. Grabbing the paper cup next to her, she finished her coffee. "Too many emails."

She didn't stand, and when Sarah reached out her hand, she declined to take it.

"I have to be back in LA for a court appearance. Never a dull moment."

The others took their seats.

"So what can I do for you?" she said. "I understand we're here to talk about Ana Robles?"

"We're trying to get some background on her," Lou said. "I requested her case file, but I was told we'd have to meet with you in person first."

"Right. Well, it's the Archdiocese's rules. I understand something happened at St. Rita's?"

"Unfortunately, there's been a series of accidents."

"What sort of accidents?"

"Several women intentionally hurt themselves," Sarah said.

Carter nodded. "The last one ended up in the hospital."

"Oh my. Was Ana hurt?"

"No."

"Then why—"

"We're not sure what happened," Sarah said. "The circumstances are a little..."

"Bizarre," the girl said.

Grace narrowed her eyes. "Not sure I understand."

Sarah cleared her throat. *Here goes nothing.* "We think something paranormal may be occurring. And we also think Ana is at the center of it."

The caseworker sat back and folded her hands in judgment. "I see. Have you spoken to a priest?"

"Fr. Brian is aware," the police chief said.

"Why are the police involved?"

"Heidi asked me to look into it as a favor. I've brought Sarah and Carter in because they... Well, they're more in tune with this sort of thing."

Grace looked at the other women sharply. "So, you two are mediums?"

Before responding, Sarah breathed through her nose. Then, "No."

"We don't do this for money," the girl said. "We're gifted."

The caseworker had cooled to the point of becoming hostile. Sarah began to think the meeting was a mistake.

"Well, I don't know about ghosts and goblins," she said. "I deal in real life. What I do know is that Ana is the victim of repeated domestic abuse. She has the physical scars to prove it."

Lou broke in. "We didn't mean to imply—"

"If I'd known this was why you wanted to see me, I could've saved myself a trip."

Stiffly, she got up and packed up her things as the others looked at each other, flummoxed.

"If you'll excuse me, I need to get going," she said. "There's no telling what traffic will be like."

The others rose, disappointed. As Grace got out her car keys and headed for the door, Sarah reached out and was about to touch her arm when the caseworker glared at her hand.

"Grace, wait," she said. "Look, I get that you're worried we're trying to pin something on this woman. But we're not. We're trying to get to the truth of what happened. And to prevent any further incidents at the shelter. Did Ana ever have any kind of psychological tests?"

"Of course. Before we can allow these women to stay at our shelters, we have to make sure they won't be a danger to the other residents."

"I know this is asking a lot, but can't you let the chief see the file?"

"I can get an administrative subpoena," Lou said.

The caseworker eyed the three of them. She placed her laptop bag on the table and dug around until she found a manila folder containing a sheaf of documents. Biting her lip, she handed him the case file.

"You'll have to forgive me," she said. "Most officials I deal with are trying to find ways to blame these poor creatures for seeking a better life, where they can be safe and free of violence. You'll find everything in there, including Dr. Curtis's report. Now, I really must go."

Sarah closed the door and turned to the others. "Okay, is it me? Or this that woman a beeyotch?"

"Probably overworked," the police chief said.

The women waited as he went through the file, which contained official-looking documents written in Spanish, presumably from Guatemala. There was also a copy of a birth certificate and a psychiatric report, which had been conducted by a doctor in Los Angeles. Setting aside the other papers, he read it.

Sarah and Carter went through the other documents when they came across several snapshots of Ana and other family members. Sarah grabbed a photo and showed it to her friend. Ana and another man were in a clearing in the forest. Both were dressed as if for a wedding. A female shaman wearing a colorful headdress stood behind them. Her hypnotic eyes chilled Sarah.

"It's him—the man from my vision."

"Ana's husband?"

Lou reached over and examined the picture. "He's hardly taller than she is. If this is her husband, then who's the huge dude you guys saw at the shelter?"

The women stared at each other and nodded.

"What?" he said. "Do you know who he is?"

"I don't think what we saw is a who," Carter said.

Sarah got up. "Let's see if Fr. Brian is around."

He watched as they left without him. "Sure, don't tell me what's going on." Then to himself, "I'm only the friggin' chief of police."

Fr. Brian Donnelly listened patiently as Sarah and Carter made their case. He looked at them, his clear blue eyes challenging them.

"It sounds like you two have been busy," he said. "Exorcism is a serious business. And there's a process. You don't call up a guy and schedule an appointment like it's a root canal."

Sarah nodded. "We're well aware. But based on the evidence—"

"*Evidence?* From the Church's point of view, you have nothing. Oh sure, you saw what you think is a demon."

She felt herself getting angry. "We know what we saw. Okay, we're not sure if it's demonic. But so far, it's putting on a pretty good show."

"Of course, I'm no expert in this area," the priest said. "But there are signs. The first is an aversion to things sacred. A crucifix, for example. And other sacramentals such as holy water."

"Ana was terrified of my St. Benedict medal," the girl said, showing him her wrist.

Leaning over, he examined it. "Very nice. Okay, has Ana ever exhibited extraordinary strength?"

"Not that we know of," Sarah said.

"How about foaming at the mouth?"

"No."

"Speaking in a language she isn't familiar with."

The women shook their heads.

The priest glanced at his watch. "Knowledge of hidden things. Has Ana ever told you or anyone else things she couldn't possibly know? Personal details about your lives, for example?"

"Okay, you win," Sarah said.

"I'm not trying to win. This is a very serious business. Clearly, there is something going on. What, I'm not sure of."

"But you believe we saw something," Carter said.

"I do. Look, if you want my honest opinion, I think something supernatural might be happening. But I'm not convinced it's demonic."

Outside, Sarah dialed Lou and put the call on speaker, explaining what they'd learned.

He reacted immediately. "So no exorcism, then."

"Whatever's haunting the shelter is harming those women. There must be another way to stop it."

The girl scoffed. "Without a priest?"

"This is all about Ana. It would be better for everyone if she left the shelter."

"Not my call," the police chief said.

Carter stared at her bracelet. "And besides, where would she go?"

Sarah groaned. "How did I ever let myself get mixed up in all this? What about the psychiatrist's report?"

"Ana is a classic domestic abuse victim suffering from PTSD."

"You think it's worth meeting with him?"

"I don't see why. Unless he's planning to change his diagnosis."

She was getting more frustrated by the minute. Soon, she'd have to tell Harlan what they learned. Maybe the PI had discovered in Guatemala.

"By the way," Lou said, "I've assigned Tim to check on St. Rita's from time to time."

She rolled her eyes. "Why him?"

"Actually, it was his idea. And we're short staffed, so."

"Mm. Okay, thanks."

Sarah ended the call, recalling when she'd seen the young police officer parked outside the shelter the other night. And what about all those other times at the station? He was always hanging around, especially when she was there. A crush? No, something else.

"We'd better keep an eye on Tim Whatley," she said.

TWELVE

They walked up the steps of Iglesia Evangélica de Palabra Viva, a small Christian church in Cobán. Inside, the senior pastor, James Sloane, waited for them. The PI stepped forward to shake his hand.

"Thanks for meeting with us. I'm Charlie Beeks, and this is Sister Elizabeth Valenti."

"Nice to meet you both. Let's go into my office."

He led them to the rear and out a side door to a separate building decorated with a well-cultivated evergreen shrub, whose scent reminded the PI of the holiday cookies his wife used to bake for her school.

"What kind of plant is that?" he said.

The clergyman took in its fragrance. "It's an allspice tree. Very common in this part of the world."

Inside, there were offices with people working quietly.

"Would either of you like coffee?" the clergyman said.

"I'd love a cup of tea," the nun said.

Charlie shook his head. "Nothing for me."

When they were settled, he opened his messenger bag and removed his notebook.

"As you know, we're trying to get some information on Tomás Morales. We understand he was a pastor here?"

Rev. Sloane lowered his head. "He was. But there were unfortunate circumstances, which forced me to remove him. Since he's deceased, I suppose I can talk about it."

Sister Elizabeth set down her cup. "Can you tell us if he had family here?"

"He was an orphan." The clergyman's expression changed, revealing a deep sadness. "I watched Tomás grow up. He was a good boy and well liked by everyone."

"Was he ever in trouble?" the PI said.

"No, the opposite. Whenever fights would break out, Tomás was always the one to step in and convince the other boys to make peace. He was a natural-born leader.

"When he turned eighteen, he informed me he wanted to become a pastor to help people in an official capacity. I spoke to my superiors, and we obtained a scholarship for him to attend divinity school."

"Did he complete his studies?"

"Yes. In fact, his professors loved him. He asked to be assigned here, and they let him."

"How long did he serve?"

"Barely a year." Rev. Sloane chuckled. "To be honest, I was looking forward to retiring one day and thought Tomás would replace me."

Charlie twiddled his pen in his hand. Then, "Did you know Ana Robles?"

The senior pastor's face darkened. "Yes. And I wish I never did." He looked at the nun with a pained expression. "It sounds un-Christian, Sister, but if you'd met her, you might sympathize. Look, I'm no psychiatrist, but I'm convinced the woman bewitched Tomás."

"What exactly do you mean?" she said.

"I mean, after meeting her, he changed. The beliefs and customs of this country make our work rather difficult. I'm sure you would agree.

"People are content to hear The Word, but they don't always understand it. Old traditions run deep, and superstition gets mixed up with the Good News we are trying to bring.

"After spending time with Ana, Tomás talked about evil spirits and curses. He was convinced God had appointed him to help her.

"I tried explaining to him that what she needed was a doctor. But he was insistent. Before long, he was neglecting his duties and spent all his time with the woman."

"It was her uncle who introduced them, correct?" the PI said.

"That's right."

"I understand they got married?"

"In a manner of speaking. He wanted me to perform the ceremony. I thought the whole business was wrong. So, he sought out a shaman, who joined the couple in a pagan ceremony in the forest. I had no choice but to report it,. He was subsequently defrocked."

Charlie made some notes. "Did you stay in touch with Tomás?"

"For a time. He called me occasionally, telling me how sick Ana was and how he had tried everything to make her well. Again, I encouraged him to seek medical assistance. But he insisted he could cure her."

"Did he say what he did?" the nun said.

"Mostly prayer. Later, he got it into his head that she was a prisoner of a powerful demon. He claimed it spoke to him."

"How long did this go on?" the PI said.

"For almost their entire marriage."

"And when did you learn he was dead?"

The clergyman wiped his eyes. "The police let me know they'd discovered his body in the river."

"Did they suspect Ana?"

"No. There were no signs of violence, and they concluded he'd drowned."

Charlie cleared his throat. "Reverend, we have reason to believe that Tomás abused his wife physically."

"I've heard those stories, Mr. Beeks. And if you had met Tomás—knew him the way I did—you'd find them impossible to believe. He was a sweet, caring soul and would never have hurt anyone."

"Do you believe he took his own life?"

"Honestly, I don't know anymore. Before meeting Ana, I would've said no. I suppose failing to help her might've sent him into a state of deep despair."

The PI looked at Sister Elizabeth, debating whether to ask the question they'd discussed beforehand. She touched his arm to encourage him.

"Rev. Sloane," he said. "This may sound bizarre, but my employer insisted I ask. While Ana lived here, did anyone you know harm themselves deliberately?"

The clergyman's eyes widened, and he turned pale. "But how..."

"So, something did happen."

"It was during the last year before she left the country. Several women in our congregation." He took a minute. "This is difficult. They, um... They disfigured themselves in various ways. I still have trouble believing it happened."

"May I ask what they did?" the nun said.

"One woman took a carving knife to her face. Another

chopped off three fingers of one hand. And a third tore out an eye."

"And nothing else has happened since?"

"No. It was as if some kind of hysteria had spread among the community. Others came to me later, saying they'd been badly tempted to try something. But either someone intervened, or they prayed for strength and were spared."

"Were any men affected?"

"Not that I know of. Do you think Ana was responsible?"

"I don't know," Charlie said, getting to his feet. "Thanks for everything. Oh, do you have the address where Tomás and Ana lived?"

He turned to his computer and typed something. A moment later, the nearby printer spat out a page, which the senior pastor handed to the PI.

"Tell me," he said when they'd reached the door. "The mutilations. It's happening again, isn't it?"

"I'm afraid so," Charlie said, and they left.

Charlie and Sister Elizabeth stood before an aging apartment building. The smell of cooking wafted through the windows, and somewhere, a girl sang.

> *Vamos a la mar, tum, tum.*
> *A comer pescado, tum, tum.*
> *Boca colorada, tum, tum.*
> *Fritito y asado, tum, tum...*

He didn't feel well—all the walking hurt his knees. But he had to go on because Harlan was counting on him. As screaming children with no shoes raced past, he stumbled on a step. His companion grabbed his arm to steady him.

"All right?" she said.

"Knees aren't what they used to be."

She rolled her eyes. "Tell me about it."

On the first floor, they made their way to the manager's apartment and knocked. After a moment, the door opened, and a small girl with large, dark eyes and missing front teeth stared up at them.

"¿Está tu padre en casa?" the nun said.

Saying nothing, the child ran away and shouted. "¡Apá!"

In another moment, a gruff-looking, muscular man with a substantial mustache stood before them.

"Sr. Acosta? Permítame presentarnos…"

"It's fine, Sister. I speak English."

After the introductions, the manager escorted them into a small sitting room. There were toys everywhere, making it difficult to navigate.

"Excuse the mess," the man said. "My daughter has a very active imagination, which requires the use of the entire apartment. What can I do for you?"

"Your accent," the nun said. "You're not Guatemalan?"

"No, Mexican. I moved down here twenty years ago and married a chapina."

"Oh? Can I ask what brought you to this country?"

He grinned. "In my youth, I was very active politically, and I got tired of being harassed by la juda."

"I assume you mean the police," the PI said. "Sister and I are looking for information on one of your former tenants, Tomás Morales. Can you tell us anything about him?"

The manager looked around the room. "Hijo de la chingada." Then to the nun, "My apologies, Sister. But for this, I need a drink."

He went into the kitchen and returned with a tray holding a bottle of mescal and three shot glasses.

"Join me. My wife doesn't like it when I drink alone."

"Sure," Charlie said, nodding encouragingly to the nun.

When each had a glass, the manager quickly drained his and refilled it. "Not sure what I can tell you, patrón," he said. "Morales always paid his rent on time."

"You never heard any fighting or arguments?" Sister Elizabeth said.

"What married couple doesn't fight? Come to think of it, they had some real problems. Se fue de Guatemala a Guata-peor."

She stifled a laugh with her hand. Then to the PI, "He said things went from bad to worse."

"How so?" Charlie said to the manager.

"Morales would often go out in the middle of the night and not return until the next morning. The two of them started to be gone a lot—sometimes for days at a time. On more than one occasion, the girl returned with...various injuries."

"Did you call the police?"

"I told you before, I can't afford to get mixed up with the authorities." The manager avoided making eye contact with the nun.

"Any idea where they might've gone?"

"I asked him once, and he said he had a small house north of here."

"Did you ever speak with Ana?"

"No, but my wife did." The manager's daughter appeared and, her hands behind her back, twisted back and forth. "Hablale a tu mamá."

The girl vanished. After a moment, the manager's wife came in and sat, smoothing her long skirt. Like most Guatemalan women, she was small and dark.

Without hesitation, she told the others about Ana. As she spoke, it became clear to the PI that this woman had tried to befriend her. More than once, she helped the girl get medical attention for her injuries. As she spoke in rapid Spanish, Sister Elizabeth translated.

"She would complain to me all the time," the nun said. "About how her husband beat her. She said she was afraid. I always worried the next time they went away, she wouldn't come back. But it was him who didn't return finally."

"Your husband said they had another place. Do you know where it is?"

The woman left the room. A moment later, she reappeared, holding a crumpled piece of paper, which she handed to him.

"Thanks."

"Ana gave it to me. I think she wanted someone to know where she was going."

To be polite, Charlie sipped the mescal and set down the glass. Sister Elizabeth did the same.

"My goodness," she said, fanning herself. "That's got a kick."

The manager laughed and walked them to the door.

"One more thing," the PI said. "Did your wife ever seem upset or...not herself after speaking with Ana?"

Sr. Acosta considered the question. "I'm not sure what you mean."

The nun extended her hand. "You have a beautiful family," she said. "God bless you."

Confused, he shook her hand. "Que le vaya bien."

Charlie and the nun sat in an outdoor café on the main street. He looked out on the busy street. Though he'd initially been hungry, the fumes from the passing vehicles had soured his stomach. Instead of trying his pupusas, he drank bottled water.

It was almost noon, and people were filling up the restaurant. Women in colorful clothes passed, holding small children by the hand. Laborers and office workers jostled each other on the broken sidewalk, some on phones, probably late for something.

"For whatever reason," she said, "his wife was immune."

"Thanks for intervening. I was about to ask him if she'd tried mutilating herself."

"I know. Men can be so...direct sometimes."

"'The better part of valor is discretion', eh?" he said.

"You know your Shakespeare."

"Look, I can arrange transportation for you to return home. No use you going out into the forest."

She swallowed her food and wiped her mouth with a paper napkin. "What if you run into the locals and need help translating? Besides, I love a good mystery. And I'd like to see this through."

"Okay, Sister. I guess I can't argue with that."

Soon, they were on the road again. The apartment manager's wife hadn't actually given them an address but had provided detailed directions. Google Maps would be of little use in these parts, and he had to rely on his driving companion to navigate.

They traveled to the north side of Parque Nacional Las

Victorias, where they entered the forest. The roads hadn't been good to begin with. Soon, they were on an uneven dirt path filled with large potholes and loose rocks from the last rains. Once again, he was grateful Harlan Covington had provided a sturdy vehicle.

Up ahead, among the wild orchids, there was what looked like an ancient stone relief. He stopped the car. They both got out and approached the object.

It stood several feet high and, though worn smooth by centuries of rain and wind, clearly depicted a naked woman and a large rabbit.

"This is the moon goddess Ix Chel," she said. "Mayan goddess of fertility." Her tone was matter of fact. "Looks like we turn right up here."

They got back into the Land Rover, and the PI carefully maneuvered past the carving. After a mile or so, they reached a clearing where a simple wooden shack with a tin roof stood, almost hidden. He parked and got out.

Stretching, he gazed at the primitive structure. Among the stands of Caribbean pine, there were colorful bunches of wild orchids. The air was fragrant with sweet-scented lycaste. The sounds of thousands of birds singing and screeching filled the air. Every so often, something moved swiftly through the tree branches. Probably monkeys.

She studied her surroundings as Charlie got out his phone and took several photos of the shack. When he walked toward it, she followed.

The closer she got, the more a feeling of dread consumed her, and she had to stop and get her bearings. It wasn't anything visible, a feeling. As they approached the door, a large, bright green snake slithered past them.

"Careful," she said. "It's a pit viper—very poisonous."

"I'm reminded of Genesis." He'd tried and failed to sound jocular.

They waited for the creature to pass. He reached out a tentative hand and pushed the door open. The nun almost gagged from the smell of plant rot.

"I'll go first," he said.

She covered her nose and mouth as she entered the foul place. The dirt floor was littered with used paper towels and empty water bottles. She bent down and picked up a crumpled towel. When she saw the dried blood, she released it and wiped her hand on her habit.

In the center stood a rough wooden table with shackles and chains. The surface was stained with old blood. She approached the table and picked up one of the heavy iron chains. As if feeling the pain of what had happened here, she let out a strangled cry.

"That smell!" she said. "What is it?"

He approached the table, and leaning over, took a whiff. When he straightened up, he looked at her, his face grim.

"Dried semen, I think," he said.

As she stood off to the side, he took more pictures. She hadn't bothered looking up. When she crossed the floor, something moved. By the time she recognized the danger, it was too late.

She grabbed his hand and brought him and herself low to the ground as hundreds of bats making clicking noises swirled like a dark whirlpool. Eventually, they made it to the door and fled into the forest.

"Were you bitten?" he said.

Catching her breath, she stood. "I don't think so."

As if drawn there, she walked to the other side of the table and reached for something on the ground—a black notebook.

When she examined it, she found pages of handwritten prayers and notes, which resembled the ravings of a madman. Some looked as if they'd been written in blood. The text was adorned with drawings of crucifixes. And faces —strange and demonic. One of them was of an angry man with long, stringy hair and blood-red eyes. With trembling hands, she handed him the notebook.

"Something evil happened here," Sister Elizabeth said.

THIRTEEN

Sarah arrived with Carter in the Galaxie. She was relieved they were finally getting this over with. Her friend would learn the truth about Harlan, and the three of them could work together to bring the case to a conclusion without any secrets.

The pathway lights bordering the driveway glowed like still fairies in the early darkness. Before she'd had a chance to contact him, she'd gotten the call at her office and had to drop everything. Not wanting Rachel to worry, she told her sister she was meeting with a potential client.

Carter had lied to her boss, telling him she was sick. She felt horrible about it, even though she had more than enough money now to live comfortably without ever working another day. The truth was, she hated deceit.

"You're being mysterious," she said as they got out of the car.

"I don't mean to be, but I'm following Harlan's instructions."

"Fair enough. Do I have time for a cigarette?"

Sarah looked at her watch. "You're fine. We're early anyway."

They stared at the distant lights of Santa Barbara as the girl smoked thoughtfully. Though Sarah abhorred the smell, she didn't say anything because she loved her.

"Does the smoke bother you?" Carter said.

"A little."

Nodding, she dropped the cigarette and crushed it with the toe of her boot, something her friend had seen her do often.

"I should really quit anyway."

Taking in the beautifully landscaped surroundings, she picked up the butt and tucked it in the pocket of her black leather jacket. They approached the door, and Sarah rang the bell. The sound of heels on tile, then the door opened.

"Hi, Mary."

"Hello, Sarah." Then to the girl, "I'm Mary Mallery."

"Carter Wittgenstein," she said, extending her hand.

"Mr. Covington is waiting for you in the dining room."

As she led them through, the girl marveled at the architecture and furnishings.

"Give you any ideas for your place?" Sarah said.

"Oh, yeah."

The attorney was at the head of the table, looking at his phone. Three places had been set for dinner. On the table stood a tasteful winter flower arrangement. Sarah recognized peony, Leucadendron galpinii, and silver brunia. On the sideboard, there were three open bottles of wine—two red and one white. When he saw the guests, he stood. Everyone exchanged greetings, and he shook Carter's hand warmly.

"I see you're wearing the bracelet," he said.

"Thank you so much. I love it."

"I'm glad." He gestured. "Let's take our seats and get started. Can I offer anyone some wine? Sarah, they tell me you're a fan of all things Italian."

"Have you been talking to my sister?"

"We have a Sangiovese and a Gavi I'm told is quite nice."

"Red for me, thank you."

"Carter?"

"I'll try the Gavi."

Harlan poured two glasses and set them down.

"You're not having any?" the girl said.

He took his seat. "I don't drink."

Sarah tried her wine—exquisite. "How's yours?" she said to her friend.

"I'm definitely getting some for my wine cellar."

The maid entered with a tray of salads and served the guests first. Sarah recalled how nervous Elsa had been during her last visit. Tonight, she seemed calm and efficient.

As the attorney led them in a blessing, Carter lowered her eyes, unsure of what to do with her hands.

"Sarah tells me you purchased Casa Abrigo," he said to her.

"I'm really hoping to bring some positive energy to the house. Have you seen it recently?"

"No."

"Well, Sarah and Joe did an amazing job. I have pictures on my phone."

"Perhaps later. Permit me to send you a case of the Gavi as a housewarming gift."

"Aw, you really don't need to—"

"It would be my pleasure."

"Thank you so much."

Soon, Elsa returned with the main course, beef brisket with new potatoes and fresh asparagus.

"I have to say, you have the best food," Sarah said.

"You can thank Mary. She found me a wonderful cook."

During the rest of the dinner, they talked about everything except St. Rita's. Harlan was particularly interested in Carter and asked her lots of questions about where she grew up, what she studied in school, and what her views were on The Almighty. To Sarah, it sounded more like a job interview than polite dinner conversation.

"It's kind of funny you bring God up," she said. "I was telling Sarah, after the—" Then to her friend, "What are we calling it? An adventure? Anyway, I've been thinking a lot more about Him. When I was a kid, we never discussed religion. It was always, *if there really is a God, then...*"

"I was raised Catholic. Even so, I came to Him late. In my youth, I was a very different man."

"How so?" Sarah said.

"Let's just say I took advantage of everything life had to offer. Which brings me to the reason I've invited you here, Carter."

She felt a pit in her stomach and laid down her dessert fork. "What?"

"Why don't we go into the library?" he said.

It was almost nine when Harlan opened the door and gestured for the women to enter. Inside, Sarah saw the familiar furniture, books, and objets d'art. And something new. A large TV screen on a stand next to the wall, with a tall black speaker on either side and an expensive-looking video conference camera attached to the top.

He walked over to his desk, where Mary was already sitting in front of a laptop. He leaned over her and pointed at the screen. Carter looked at her friend with mild panic.

"Don't be scared," she said under her breath. "He's fine once you get to know him."

"Why am I here, really?"

"Shh. You'll see."

"Ladies, if you can take your seats," he said.

Sarah made herself comfortable on the Chesterfield sofa facing the screen as he stood facing them. He referred to his watch. While they waited, she used the opportunity to update him on their meetings with the caseworker, and later with Fr. Brian.

"I've seen the psychiatrist's report," he said. "Frankly, I don't think it was of much use. And I'm not surprised at Fr. Brian's reaction to the suggestion of demonic activity. He follows the dictates of the Church, as he should."

"But if he's not in favor of an exorcism, how—"

"Let me worry about that."

His tone was dismissive, and it alarmed her. Since meeting with him the last time, she'd assumed she and her friend were equal partners and not merely employees like the housekeeper and the maid.

Carter patted her hand. "You're right, he's fine."

"Shut up."

He looked at his watch and pointed at Mary, who connected the laptop to the TV screen. Soon, a Skype window appeared.

"It's time," the attorney said.

He turned his gaze to the girl, and she gripped the arm of the sofa, unsure what to expect.

"Sarah already knows I sent someone to Guatemala to investigate Ana Robles. I invited you both here to meet him and hear his report. Feel free to ask any questions you like."

She didn't say anything and continued staring at herself in a small window in a corner of the screen.

"Okay," he said. "He'll be coming through any minute."

Soon, the session began, and an older gentleman with white hair and kind eyes smiled at them. From the looks of it, he was in a hotel room.

"Can you hear me okay?" he said.

"You're coming in loud and clear. I'd like to introduce you to my colleagues, Sarah Greene and Carter Wittgenstein. Ladies, Charlie Beeks."

"It's nice to meet you. I'm Sarah, by the way." Then, when the girl didn't say anything, "And this is Carter."

"Great meeting you as well. Shall we get started? Harlan, I'm not sure how good this connection is, so I hope I don't lose you."

"Fire away, Charlie."

"Sarah, since you are both new to the team, I'll provide some preliminary background."

The PI explained everything in great detail. While he recounted the interview with the senior pastor at Iglesia Evangélica de Palabra Viva, the internet connection became unstable, and eventually the session dropped. After several tense seconds, it was restored.

"Okay, looks like we're back," he said.

As he was about to continue, Sarah raised her hand. "Something's been bothering me. Rev. Sloane described Tomás as a kind, caring person. Yet he abused Ana to the point of breaking her arm."

"I was getting to that. We made a thorough examination of the place where Ana's husband had imprisoned her. And we discovered this."

He held up a black notebook.

"This book may hold some answers. It contains detailed notes on the sessions Tomás Morales conducted with his wife at the shack. Harlan, I'm FedExing it to you in the morning."

"Okay, thanks. I'd like the women to examine it."

"Fine. But I warn you, what he wrote is disturbing. Besides beating Ana, he had sex with her while she was restrained."

"Oh, my God," the girl said.

Sarah stood and inched closer to the screen. "Do you have any photographs you can send us?"

"Lots. I'm setting up a Dropbox folder so you can download them along with a copy of my report."

She was concerned that Carter hadn't asked any questions. It was as if her mind were somewhere else. She touched her friend's hand.

"Did you want to ask anything?"

"I'm good."

The attorney rubbed his hands together. "Okay, great work. Keep me posted on anything else you find out. I'll see you back here in about a week. Goodnight."

"So long, everyone."

Mary disconnected the session and switched off the screen. Sarah stood as Harlan opened the library door, and to her surprise, led his guests out. *So, we're not discussing the Guardian thing?* At the front door, he shook hands with the women.

"Thank you again for coming," he said. "I hope the information was helpful."

"Very," Sarah said, disappointed. "Goodnight."

Carter was about to follow her when he gently laid a hand on her arm. "I'd like you to stay."

"What? Why?"

"There's something important I need to discuss with you." Then to Sarah, "I'll see to it she gets home safely."

Caught off-guard, she gave the girl an awkward hug and said goodnight to them both.

Carter felt lost, and she had the urge to bolt. She told herself her friend would never intentionally put her in any kind of danger. Nevertheless, she felt overwhelmed, as if taking on a burden she hadn't asked for. She stared at her bracelet, wondering about the real reason Harlan had given it to her. Getting hold of her fear, she decided to accept whatever was coming.

"Let's talk in the library," he said. "Would you like coffee?"

On the ride home, Sarah felt as if Carter had betrayed her. But how was this her fault? And besides, she needed to know the truth about Harlan if she was going to help Sarah going forward. She'd been sure he would say something at dinner, but it seemed he had other plans. In any event, the situation was beyond her control, and she concentrated on Joe.

It was almost one a.m. in New York, and she toyed with the idea of calling him. Most likely, he'd be awake. They hadn't spoken today, and she worried her refusal to join him had done irreparable damage to their relationship. *You're being ridiculous.* They'd known each other for years and would get past this.

Her watch vibrated. Glancing down, she saw it was Joe and grabbed her phone, putting it on speaker.

"I was just thinking about you," she said, trying to contain her relief.

"I know it's late. But between going to the hospital and spending time with relatives, it's been nonstop. How are things?"

"Not so good. I miss you."

"Miss you too. Look, I realize I was out of line about you not coming."

"It's okay. And as long as we're all apologizing, I should've told you about the women's shelter. I meant to."

"Never mind, it's better this way. There's a lot of family stuff I need to deal with. No use you being in the middle of it. My mother sends her love."

"Thanks. Hey, when you come back and I'm done helping at the shelter, do you think we could get away for a few days?"

"Boy, that sounds good. Anywhere in particular?"

"I don't care. As long as I'm with you."

She felt weepy and had to clear her throat. "I love you."

"I love you too. And I'll come home as soon as I can. In the meantime, start thinking of places we can go."

"I will. Night, Joe."

As she made her way back to Dos Santos, she thought about everything they'd been through over these past years. And, like so many times before, she prayed that, married or not, they'd always be together.

Carter rang Nellie's bell, and soon she answered the door wearing glasses.

"Hey, what are you—"

"I swear I never do pop-ins. Are you busy?"

"Just reading a boring research paper on contextual fear conditioning in transgenic mice."

"Sounds hilarious."

Nellie was about to say something when the other girl took her face in her hands and kissed her. She melted.

"Those stupid mice can wait," she said, pulling her lover inside.

Later in bed, Carter lay in Nellie's arms, warm and content, putting her meeting with Harlan out of her mind. The blonde girl stroked her hair and kissed the top of her head. She used her index finger to outline the anime tattoo on Carter's bare arm.

"Is this a scarecrow?"

"Sort of. Did you see *Howl's Moving Castle*? He's a prince who's under a curse. And Sophie, who was turned into an old woman by a witch, saves him."

Nellie pointed at the colorful multi-character tattoo on her other arm. "And those?"

"They're from different anime movies. This one's a Totoro. And this is a kind of dragon, which is really a river spirit. What can I say—I love Studio Ghibli."

"You seem sad."

"Do I?" She gazed at her arms. "This is fantasy, you know? And they can do anything."

"I wish you'd tell me what's bothering you. Maybe I can help."

"I can't. So, how's your research going?"

"It's going." Nellie turned on her side. "Do you remember the night we met at the bar?"

"Renown? Sure."

"Something odd had happened that afternoon. I didn't want to talk about it then. It's just so weird. I was in my office doing my weekly status report, and I was really jumpy for some reason. When someone said my name, I almost freaked. I saw it was Heidi and laughed. She said I looked tired and should go home."

"Sounds like she was concerned about you."

"The thing is, I didn't feel tired. In fact, I was getting my second wind. Anyway, I promised to leave soon. She said goodnight and left, and I got to work. But then, I heard what sounded like... It was like someone exhaled. It reminded me of when my father was in the hospice."

"Aw, man."

"It's okay because he died peacefully. Then I distinctly heard Heidi say my name again, only this time the voice came from outside my office. When I turned, no one was there. So, I went out and looked around. Even though I knew I was alone, I called her name."

She took Carter's hand and interlaced their fingers. Carter squeezed gently and kissed her hand.

"When I went back to my desk, I stared at the monitor. The page I'd worked on was gone. And in the middle of the screen there was something I hadn't written."

"What did you do?"

"I shut down the computer and got the hell out of there."

"Do you remember the words?"

"Wait, I wrote them down."

Nellie got up and dug through a pile of papers on her desk. Grabbing a note, she handed it over and climbed into bed.

Carter squinted at the page. "Your handwriting's atrocious."

"Which is why I'm going to make an excellent doctor someday." She took it and read aloud. "*Doors. Must choose. Don't want to go. Choose. They said so. Don't want to. All right, I'm ready.*"

"I feel like it's a conversation."

Nellie stared at the note. "These were the words my father said before he passed—the exact words. He'd been in the hospice for only a week. My mom, brother, sister, and I took turns visiting him. I was the last one to see him alive. What do you think he meant?"

Carter studied the words. "I read a book on death and dying once. Yeah, I'm a sicko. There was something in there about the dying being between worlds—this one and the next."

The other girl sat up straight. "It's interesting you say that. Because I remember now, he was staring at the wall like, I don't know, someone was standing there."

"Sounds to me like he was being asked to make a choice, and he didn't want to."

"He was stubborn, my father. But it doesn't explain how those words appeared on my computer."

Carter shook her head, remembering what Fr. Brian had said about knowledge of hidden things. Unless Nellie had told someone her story, there's no way anyone could've come up with the words of a dying man. Of course, she might have unconsciously typed them, but she didn't believe it for a second.

"I think I know," she said. "But you're not gonna like it. Something demonic may have put those words there for you to see."

"Great. Well, how am I supposed to document that in my research?"

Carter put her hand on hers. "Can I stay here tonight?"

Nellie gazed at her. "You never have to ask. Ever. Okay?"

Embracing, they kissed, their passion igniting. Any fear or anxiety Carter had felt earlier melted like snowflakes in sunlight. And she opened her heart to feelings she'd managed to cut off for so many years—since she was thirteen and living in Sausalito.

That was the year her world had come apart.

FOURTEEN

The smell of coffee woke Nellie. Stretching, she looked over and saw she was alone. She threw on some clothes and wandered sleepily into the kitchen, where Carter was setting a perfect pancake on a tall stack of other perfect pancakes. She watched the other girl adjust the tower to make it uniform.

"I bet you're fantastic at Jenga," she said.

"Actually, I suck at it—and cooking in general. Pancakes are the only thing I know how to make."

Carter handed her a plate of crispy bacon, which she set on the table.

"Be right back," she said.

After placing the ginormous flapjack stack in the middle of the kitchen table, Carter poured out two cups of coffee and sat. In a moment, Nellie returned and sat, her face washed.

"Okay, this is way better than any breakfast I ever made," she said, picking up a fork. She hesitated. "It's such a nice tower, I hate to— Wait."

She grabbed her phone and composed an Instagram-worthy photo. Then she snagged two pancakes and plopped them on her plate.

"These are fantastic," she said.

"Okay, here's a secret I can share with you—orange zest."

Nellie laughed. "Thanks for the reminder. I keep buying oranges, but I never eat them."

After a few moments, Carter glanced at the pile of case files sitting on a chair in the corner.

The blonde girl saw where she was looking. "That chair's broken."

"No, I was wondering about the files. I hope you don't mind, but I sneaked a peek. You were reading about Ana."

Nellie put down her fork. "You know what you said before about being careful? I figured I could learn something about her while we conduct the tests."

"And?"

"Well, one thing's for sure. She has all the symptoms of PTSD. Pretty much what I expected. Dr. Curtis, the psychiatrist who interviewed her in LA, noted that she has bad dreams."

"Probably of her late husband?"

"No doubt. Also, she suffers from headaches. The doctor thought they might be migraines, but they don't present that way. There are also some photos in there from the MRIs they took."

"Anything weird?"

"You mean, like a lesion? No, her brain appears healthy."

She dug through the files until she found what she was looking for and laid a photo in front of Carter.

"See the brightly colored area? It's the amygdala. It's what controls our fear response. You know, fight or flight."

"Which is why you were reading about the mice."

"Correct. When we see something threatening, the amygdala triggers the release of stress hormones. Our brains become hyperalert. The pupils dilate, and we breathe faster. Also, our heart rate and blood pressure rise."

"And then we run," Carter said.

"Or fight. Apparently, Ana does neither. I was hoping to find something to explain her behavior when those other women had their accidents. And also, why her presence seems to have such a strange effect on them."

"Wait, you think she's...contagious?"

"It's a hypothesis. There is such a thing as mass psychogenic illness, also known as mass hysteria."

"Wait, that's really a thing?"

"Oh, yeah. There are recorded cases going back as far as the middle ages. I remember reading about one particular case—the dancing plague of 1518. For no reason, people in Strasbourg, Alsace, started dancing. Soon, everyone was doing it. And here's the thing—they couldn't stop. Some had heart attacks and died."

"How long did it go on?"

"About a month, as I recall."

Carter pushed aside her plate. "So, you're thinking Ana's arrival triggered something in the other women."

"Not sure yet. In Ana's case, the psychiatrist was able to induce a fear response by showing her a series of images."

Nellie removed a page from the file, and putting on her glasses, scanned it. "All the symptoms were there. Her heart rate increased to one-eighteen."

"She reacted normally, right—as expected?"

"Not exactly." the blonde girl took a breath. "She was laughing."

Carter examined the photo. "But that would mean..."

Nellie looked at her gravely. "Whatever it is terrifying Ana?"

"She likes it," Carter said.

Sarah savored her cup of Earl Grey tea as Roxanne made a note. She'd dreaded telling the therapist about her disastrous yoga session, feeling the news would disappoint her.

"And these children you saw…"

"Were as real as you and me."

"I see. Tell me what you've been doing to help yourself."

"Well, I've been running more."

"Excellent. Exercise is a wonderful way to reduce stress. Also, it sharpens your thinking and improves memory."

"So, you think I'll be okay if I stick to an exercise plan?"

"And I would watch your alcohol intake. Some patients have a tendency to self-medicate."

Sarah thought of her new bottle of Talisker going untouched. She and Joe had enjoyed so many wonderful evenings together, sipping the whiskey and listening to jazz. It was therapeutic. *Said the tipsy psychic.*

"I wanted to ask you something," she said. "I learned recently that my dad recommended you."

Roxanne didn't say anything, but Sarah thought she saw a flicker in her eyes, and she persisted.

"Can I ask how you know him? Did he come to see you after my mother died?"

"I'm afraid that information is confidential. Your time here is better spent focusing on you."

Sarah was taken aback by her sternness. When the

session was over, the therapist walked her to the front door as usual.

"I need to know," Sarah said.

Roxanne looked past her to the street, her expression troubled. Finally, she took her patient's hands.

"Why not speak to your father about it?" she said. "See you next week."

On her way to the office, Sarah continued thinking about Eddie. When her mother was ill, he must've gone through emotional hell and needed therapy. Or what if after her death, he was clinically depressed? She went over what this period of their lives had been like for the family. She was seventeen and about to start her freshman year at UCSB. Rachel was fifteen. There was no particular incident that stuck out in her mind. Then, like a flash grenade, a powerful memory came back to her.

It was the weekend after her mother's funeral. Sunday dinner had always been special, and Sarah recalled vividly how much her dad enjoyed cooking for his girls. Unfortunately, he was in no shape. When she saw the mess he was making in the kitchen, she suggested they go out to dinner.

She recalled the restaurant, dark and smelling of Mexican cooking and lady customers' perfume. She remembered they were sitting at a table near the front doors. Pigeons milled around the entryway, forever being shooed away by passing waiters. Her sister thought it was hilarious and laughed.

When the food came, Eddie was about to eat when she reminded him they needed to pray first. It had always been her mother who enforced the rule. Irritated, he set down his fork. Staring at his plate, he wept. Then Rachel cried. Not knowing what else to do, Sarah took his hand.

"It's okay, Dad," she said. "We can get this to go."

By the next day, everything had changed. Rachel was at a friend's house. When Sarah returned from a shopping trip, she found all of her mother's things boxed up, ready for Goodwill. Angry and confused, she confronted her father. From now on, he told her, she and her sister were to call him Eddie—not Dad. *This must've been it.* He'd been grieving and needed Roxanne's help.

Walking into the realty office, she decided to put the whole business to rest. What did it matter anyway? Still, there was the way the therapist had looked at her when she mentioned her father.

"She knows something," Sarah said.

At The Cracked Pot, Sarah did something she rarely did after taking a booth by the window—she studied the menu. She thought she knew it by heart and was surprised to find chilaquiles. She sipped her coffee when Carter appeared.

After leaving her behind at Harlan's house, Sarah had thought her friend would tear her a new one for setting her up. But she wore her professional server smile. And Sarah was relieved to see her wearing the leather bracelet.

"Ready to order?" Carter said.

"You guys do breakfast all day, right?"

"For you, yes."

Sarah quirked her eyebrows. "Chilaquiles," she said, handing over the menu.

"Good choice. We have fresh tomatillo salsa. I'll make sure you get extra."

It wasn't that the girl was acting rude. No, what was the word? Efficient? *Curt.* As she turned to go, Sarah gently took her wrist.

"We should catch up."

Biting her lip, Carter looked away. Then, "I get off at four."

"Can you come by the house?" Sarah put on her best puppy dog pout and whimpered.

Her friend laughed. "I guess I can be there by five-thirty."

"Perfect. I'll make us something special."

Sarah felt the muscles in her neck and shoulders relax. Had she imagined things being worse between them? When broaching the subject of Harlan Covington, she would be cautious. She had no idea what the attorney had told Carter, and she prayed it hadn't spooked her. Sarah needed her.

While she ate, she gazed out the window. An impossibly thin man with sunken eyes glowered at her from across the street. He was poorly dressed and, though it was hard to tell through the scraggly beard and the grime, he looked to be in his thirties. Passersby ignored him.

The reflections on the glass coming from the interior lights made it difficult to make out his features. But there was something unnerving about him. His expression was one of complete malevolence, and it was directed at her. There was something else—his eyes.

Carter returned with more coffee. Sarah tugged at her friend's sleeve and indicated the window. But when Carter looked, she saw nothing unusual.

"There was a man," Sarah said, her voice hitching. "And his eyes were completely black."

Sarah had finished preparing steak frites with thick-cut French fries and steamed broccolini, when the doorbell rang. Gary waited expectantly next to the counter. Setting aside the meat to finish cooking, she brushed back her hair, pointed a warning finger at the cat, and went to answer the door.

Wearing skinny jeans, a top Sarah recognized from Nordstrom, and her leather jacket, Carter proffered two bottles of wine.

"From your cellar?"

"I didn't know what we were having, so I brought red and white."

They entered the kitchen, where Sarah uncorked the Bordeaux to let it breathe.

"It smells so good in here," the girl said.

"Let's hope it tastes good too. Can you grab the salad bowl?"

Carter placed the salad on the dining room table. A glass bowl of white camelias stood in the center. The flowers reminded her of her parents' garden.

"I was going to tell you this before," she said, "but I was mad at you."

"Oh, boy."

"It's okay—I figured it out. Something happened to Nellie the other day at St. Rita's. And I think it supports our demon theory."

When she'd finished her story, she looked at her friend, whose eyes were glued to her.

"And she's sure those were her father's last words?" Sarah said.

"Absolutely."

"Maybe she was thinking about him and unconsciously wrote them herself."

"I considered it, but I don't think so."

"Well, I would mention it to Fr. Brian, but Harlan made it pretty clear he's in charge."

"Yeah, that kind of pissed me off too."

Sarah spooned a dollop of Roquefort butter on each steak and brought everything out. She returned with the wine and her aerator.

"What's that for?" the girl said.

"I noticed the sediment in the bottle. We should filter it out. Want me to teach you?"

Carter got to her feet and stood next to her friend, who handed her the device.

"This is an aerator. Set it on the glass and slowly pour the wine."

Careful not to spill a drop, the girl was meticulous.

"Now swirl it a little and breathe it in. Then take a sip."

"Aw, man—smooth."

"It'll probably get even better in ten to fifteen minutes." Sarah poured a glass for herself. "According to my therapist, I'm supposed to cut back. Wow!"

Things were quiet for a time as they ate. Gary trotted over, and meowing, rubbed against Carter's chair.

"Ignore him," Sarah said.

The girl looked down at the cat. "I was told to ignore you."

The cat stared at her with the forlorn eyes of the

damned. Relenting, she picked him up and placed him on her lap. Then she dangled her fork over the broccolini.

"I feel bad for acting so weird before," she said.

"It's fine. This business with Harlan was a lot to lay on you out of the blue. I didn't know he was going to do it that way. Do you want to talk about it?"

"I need to, and you're the only one I can tell, since we're both sworn to secrecy. By the way, is he okay?"

"He's being treated for cancer. Why?"

"We were in the middle of a conversation, and he almost passed out. I had to get Mary."

Sarah remembered the episode in the lawyer's garden. "He's working too hard."

"After he explained everything, I got scared. I mean, we're talking *The Exorcist*. I've always known there's this other... world, but. And the first thing I thought was, why me?"

Sarah refilled her wineglass. "What exactly did he tell you?"

"Everything. About him being a Guardian. And the evil infesting Dos Santos. He even told me about the demons."

"Wait a second, what?"

"Come on, you know. They've been after him for years."

"I didn't know." She remembered the restaurant. "The man I saw..."

"Do you think they're here now? In Dos Santos?"

Before Sarah could answer, a loud noise startled the women and sent the cat running.

"Shit, what was that?" Carter said, turning.

Sarah hurried to the foyer and peeked out her window. A car had slammed into a streetlight. The driver, apparently unharmed, stood next to the vehicle, holding his phone to his ear.

"Traffic accident," she said and returned to the dining room. "I don't think anyone was hurt."

"Scared the shit out of me."

Picking up her glass, Sarah swirled the wine and gulped it. She'd come to the question that was plaguing her—one she was afraid to hear the answer to.

"Are we still a team?" she said.

She always knew when the girl was stressed. She'd slump in her chair, look away, and twirl the hair over her left ear. And now, she was doing it again. Sarah worried she might lose not only a partner but a dear friend.

"Carter?"

When the girl looked up again, her eyes were filled with tears.

"There's something I need to tell you," she said.

Carter sat on the living room sofa next to her friend. Each had a glass of Talisker. To soften the mood, Sarah had put on one of her favorite Chet Baker albums, simply called *Chet*. As the sad ballad "Alone Together" played over the Bluetooth speaker, The girl steeled herself.

"I love the music," she said, looking down. "I never told you the real reason I left Sausalito. Something happened. And it, um... Well, it just about destroyed me."

"Are you sure you want to—"

"It's fine. My parents spent a fortune on psychiatrists. They thought it had to do with my, you know, psychic abilities. Finally, after seeing Dr. Kagan, things got better. I guess she was the only one who got me."

She wiped away tears with the back of her hand. "I told her the truth." Her eyes met her friend's. "I was raped."

"Oh, no! How old were you?"

"Thirteen. It wasn't until I was fifteen that my folks learned what happened. The whole time, Dr. Kagan encouraged me to tell them. But I never wanted to because... Because he was my best friend's dad."

"Seriously, you don't have to—"

"You don't understand. If I can talk about this, then I control it—not the other way around. It's what Dr. Kagan always said.

"He must've thought he'd gotten away with it because I'd never said anything. My parents had always wondered why I stopped going over to Franny's house. I made up a story about her being jealous over a boy who liked me."

"Was he ever arrested?"

"My father is a very influential man and didn't bother with the police. He went straight to the DA to make sure Franny's dad went to prison for a long, long time."

"And did he?"

"No. While he was out on bail, he..." Carter finished her drink. "He hanged himself. After the funeral, Franny's family moved away. I never saw her again. At school, the last thing she said was how much she hated me for what I'd done."

Sarah set her glass on the coffee table, and taking the girl's hands, pulled her close and held her as she cried.

"The thing is, none of it was my fault. And I lost my only friend—my best friend. She was a talented artist, and I miss her so much."

"Listen," Sarah said. "Harlan and I can handle the women's shelter."

Carter pulled away, her mascara running down her pale

cheeks. "That's exactly what I *don't* want. You almost died because of Peter Moody. I guess we're both a little broken."

"I know, but—"

"Do you remember when I told you that as a kid I used to go sleuthing around the neighborhood?"

"And you found a dead cat."

"I lied—it wasn't a cat. It was a baby."

"Dear Lord. How old were you?"

"Eight. Harlan said something that frightened me, but it also made perfect sense. He said I'm meant to protect you."

Sarah felt a chill and held herself. Outside, she heard voices and what sounded like a tow truck winch.

"Did you tell him about finding the dead child?"

"That's just it," Carter said, wiping away her tears. "Somehow, he already knew."

FIFTEEN

It was early when Sarah started her run. The air was crisp, and the low, gray clouds seemed to weep, drizzling a fine, steady mist over the muted landscape. Though the evening had been an emotional one, she was proud of herself for having cut back. She'd had only one glass of wine and barely a taste of the Talisker. *What would Joe think?*

Mile One. She made her way west instead of north. It had been more than two months since she'd run in the forest. Later, she would check on Greene Realty's latest renovation, which was nowhere near Casa Abrigo. Eventually, she knew she would have to return to Devil's Bluff. If only to look down at the huge pale rocks and remind herself that she'd survived.

Mile Two. Since seeing the demoniac—or whatever he was—outside the restaurant, she wondered if there were others like Peter Moody waiting in the shadows to attack her. Harlan had promised to perform rituals to keep her safe. And after what he'd shared with Carter, she suspected he had decided to do the same for her.

Carter. In the short time they'd known each other, she loved the girl, heart and soul. All the misfortune, and yet, she was still a kind and caring person. And her friend was right. Each of them in their own way was broken. Had they been destined to meet? If Carter was fated to protect her, then Sarah vowed to watch over her friend as well.

Mile Three. Traffic started to build, and she turned down a side street that would take her past Resurrection Cemetery. Though she dreaded the place, she'd gotten more confident now that she had confronted some of the things lying hidden there. The cemetery gates stood at the top of an incline. Breathing hard, she pushed all the way up the rise and stopped while running in place.

The redwoods and tanbark oaks, wet with morning rain, cast slow-moving shadows all across the grounds, giving the impression that the property was underwater. Something in the darkness flickered. When the birds stopped singing, she stopped moving and watched. Someone was there in the dead silence among the graves— she felt it. A dark green golf cart with a truck bed attached stood parked to one side, and she assumed what she'd seen was a cemetery worker.

She was about to take up her run again when she looked down. There on the ground, a sparrow lay on its back, its wings shuddering violently as it tried righting itself. Crouching, she picked up the delicate thing in her hands and held it. The rapid beating of its frightened heart pulsed against her fingertip.

The dying creature looked at her with one coal-black eye and screeched, the sound piercing her ears. When it burst into flames in her hands, she panicked and dropped the burning mass. Looking around frantically, she recognized the murderous black entity that had been pursuing her. *The Darkness.* Inexorably, it floated toward her. And when it did, it began to take on an almost human shape.

She looked at the ground again. There was no bird—only wet leaves. Her chest throbbing with anxiety, she ran faster than she ever had in her life.

Joe held his mother's hand and looked into her tired eyes. Neither of them had gotten much sleep the past few days. They sat in the kitchen, and vaguely, he heard the teakettle whistling.

"What you did was wrong," he said.

She squeezed his hand, then turned off the fire. Using a colorful potholder bursting with daisies, she poured the boiling water into two ceramic mugs.

"It was to protect you."

"I know, but—"

"And I would do it again."

Her hands trembled as she placed a teabag into each mug. He carried their drinks to the table. When they were seated again, he took a sip.

"You were only sixteen," she said. "Getting ready for college—your future. Do you remember what I said to you?"

"You told me I would make a great doctor."

"Because of your kindness. I couldn't let anything ruin that for you."

"But it was an accident—the police said so. Nothing would've happened to me."

"A file would exist somewhere. Things have a way of coming back."

He looked at his hands, reliving the awful day. It was sunny. First, there was the ball—a blue plastic ball, and it had bounced into the street. He'd been over it a million times. He should've stopped. But for some reason, he thought he could shoot past it. And that's when the girl appeared out of thin air. By then, it was too late. In an instant, she was in front of him, and he hit her as his mother screamed.

Even now, he could hear the sickening thud as the bumper struck her small, slight body. But it wasn't the sound that had haunted him all these years. It was the look in her eyes—those bright blue, beautiful eyes—as she stared at him with an expression of complete, utter surprise. As if he was the one who wasn't supposed to be there.

And then, the jouncing of the vehicle as it rolled over her body, crushing her little arms and legs. He had come to a stop immediately after and exited the car. There were no witnesses, other than the birds watching from the power lines. His mother must've called 911, because he thought he heard a faint siren.

He went to the girl to see if he could save her. The asphalt was red where she'd hit her head. Kneeling, he took her frail hand and felt for a pulse. But there was none—she was dead. As he stood, his mother looked at him sternly. Grabbing him by the upper arms, she pulled him to her.

"Listen to me, Joseph," she said. "The police will be here soon. This is what you're going to tell them."

When he looked up again, he saw his mother's care-worn face. None of the sternness of that long-ago day was there now—only a resigned sadness. And he realized, as if for the first time, how she'd sacrificed everything for him. It was all so that he could make his father and her proud.

But he'd failed them. He never went to medical school. Why? Because somewhere in him, he knew he didn't deserve it.

"I'm sorry," he said.

"For what?"

"Everything. You deserved better."

She stroked his cheek. "Your dad and I have never stopped being proud of you. You've made a life for yourself, and that's all we ever wanted. For you and your sister. Of course—"

"I already know what you're going to say. And I'm still not sure whether I'm cut out to be a father."

"Think about it, that's all I'm saying."

She rinsed their cups in the sink. As she dried her hands with a dish towel, he stood behind her, and towering over her, hugged her.

"Come on," she said, patting his arm. "It's time to go to the hospital."

Sarah was scheduled to meet a couple in Santa Barbara to show them a single-family home. Plenty of time to grab a to-go coffee from The Cracked Pot. The pre-lunch crowd was light, and she wished she had had time to eat.

What happened on her run had terrified her. In her mind, she saw The Darkness racing toward her. Though it was an amorphous, cloud-like thing, she felt it was looking at her. She touched her St. Michael medal as she approached the counter. To her surprise, Carter was at an espresso machines, expertly crafting a cappuccino.

"Carter?"

"Oh, hey. Marty didn't show up—again. So, I'm filling in."

"Well, can I get doppio to go?"

"Sure. Give me...one sec."

As Sarah waited, she gazed at the crowd. She always did that—seeing if she could spot out-of-towners looking to purchase a home in Dos Santos. When she saw Rachel sitting in a corner booth toward the back, she started over. Then she stopped when Lou Fiore walked out of the men's restroom and sat opposite her sister.

"What the—"

"They've been here awhile," Carter said.

When Sarah turned around, she saw the to-go cup and accepted it. "Really?"

"At first, I thought it was a little weird, but I dunno. They seem kind of—"

Sarah pointed a warning finger. "Don't say it. Thanks for the coffee."

After paying, she walked out of the restaurant so quickly, she almost ran into an elderly woman who was coming in.

"Oh, my gosh—my fault," she said and held the door open for her.

On her way to the office, Sarah wondered whether her sister had made up that story about her car. Just before entering the realty office, she stopped. *What's wrong with me? Lou's a nice guy. I should be happy. Why am I not happy?*

Recognizing the couple she was supposed to meet waiting inside, she took a calming breath and walked in.

Standing at the doorstep of her father's house, Sarah had second thoughts. Eddie had maintained the same school schedule for years, and she knew this was the day he worked from home grading papers. He probably hadn't heard her car. She could leave now, and he'd never be the wiser.

It was better she didn't know. His past was his past. On the other hand, he was the one who recommended Roxanne. But why her? Groaning, she used her key to unlock the front door. Standing in the foyer, she called out.

"Hello? Eddie?"

A moment later, her father emerged from the kitchen. He was unshaven and wore the sweater she'd given him last Christmas. They kissed each other's cheek.

"To what do I owe the honor?" he said. "Car acting up?"

"It's running fine. I wanted to talk to you before Rachel and Katy got home."

"Ooh, sounds serious. Want a beer?"

"No, thanks."

She followed him into the kitchen and sat at the table, where she found school papers spread out. Eddie grabbed a Modelo from the refrigerator. While he tidied up the mess, she picked up a paper and scanned the first paragraph. Awful.

"So, any budding Nancy Chodorows?"

"There's one girl. Pretty smart, like you. Graduated high school at sixteen."

"Impressive."

"So, what's on your mind, mija?"

She lay down the paper and looked at her father. Had he lost weight? His face was thinner, and his eyes were a bit sunken. *You can still back out, Sarah.*

"This is hard for me," she said. "But it's been bothering me a lot."

"You mean, about what happened to you?" He pointed at her wrist.

"Partly. I just— Can you tell me what your connection is to Roxanne Marsh? Because I know it was you who recommended her. Joe told me."

He took a swallow of beer and eyed his papers. "You really shouldn't worry about—"

"Is it because you were a patient?"

She tried touching his hand, but he got up and opened a cupboard. After rummaging through the packaged goods, he slammed the door shut.

"Man can't even have regular potato chips in his own house."

"Eddie?"

"Look, whatever connection I have to Roxanne is my business. You don't always have to go poking into other peoples' lives, you know. Worry about yourself."

Ignoring her, he went back to grading papers. "Was there something else?"

Why is he being so defensive? It frustrated her to know so little of her father's life. She couldn't recall ever seeing any photos of him as a kid. And he'd never shared stories about living with her grandmother, who she and Rachel had never met. All she really knew was that he was an only child and was ten years older than her mother when they married. She decided she wasn't leaving until she uncovered the truth.

"So, did you see her after Mom died?"

He glared at her. "What do you want from me?"

"I want to know why you recommended Roxanne Marsh."

"Is she helping you?"

She looked away and rubbed her wrist. "She is. But I know you have a connection to her, and I want to know what it is."

"Why?"

"Because I need answers!" She looked at him dead on, her eyes glistening. "I'm pretty sure I'm in danger."

"What?" He scooted his chair next to her. "What kind of danger?"

"I don't know, I— There was this man, only I don't think he was a man. It was his eyes, they were black."

Before she could stop herself, she told him the whole story, beginning with Peter Moody's warning. But she left out any reference to Harlan Covington. When she'd finished, he banged his hand on the table, startling her.

"This is why I never wanted you to get mixed up in this supernatural business!" he said. "We live, then we die. That's the end of it."

"It wasn't my choice. When Alyssa appeared to me the first time—before Mom passed—I knew. This is who I am."

He lowered his voice. "You don't have to be. Turn your back on it."

Turn my back on what? "Eddie, do you see things too?"

He stared at her as if she were crazy. "I'm a regular guy, no different than our mailman."

"Then why did you see Roxanne?"

He took another swallow of beer. "You're not letting this go, are you?"

"You know me."

"Okay—mierda. It was because of your grandmother."

"Did she hurt you?"

"Nothing like that. She was...like you."

"Abuela was psychic? How could you keep that from me?"

"She was always telling me about the things she saw. I grew up hearing stories that would make your skin crawl. After she died, I went to see Roxanne. I didn't want to think about ghosts and... I was in my early twenties. All I wanted was to live my life and raise a family."

"Did the things she told you scare you?"

"At first. Then I thought it was funny. But after a while, I convinced myself she was loca, and all those stories were made up. It was the only way I could survive."

"Did she ever use her abilities to help anyone?"

"Neighbors would stop by the house all the time seeking her advice. Soon, others from our parish started coming. She never took any money. Mainly, she offered them comfort. I used to resent all those people. I was doing poorly in school, and she seemed to be always busy with strangers. Why did you come here?"

"Because I'm scared. Knowing what you know, can't you help me?"

"But don't you see? I don't know anything about what you're going through. Seeing spirits or hearing voices or having nightmares. What can I do?"

"I don't know. Did Abuela ever give you any advice about how to deal with something like this?"

"It hurts me so much that these things are happening to you. I can't pretend to know what it's like, but I can give you one piece of advice she gave me. It was right before she died. She told me that evil is everywhere around us, but so is goodness. We must always seek out the good and turn our backs on the evil."

"Okay. Did she say how?"

"Prayer."

And there it was. It always came down to that. Prayer was what Fr. Brian had recommended. And it was also what Harlan had talked about. She hugged her father.

"See? You did help me," she said. "Oh, and don't mention this to anyone."

"What happens in the kitchen stays in the kitchen."

"Te amo."

"Igualmente. Take care of yourself."

As she started her car, her watch vibrated with a new message. She tapped the device and saw a text from Harlan.

> Book arrived. Expecting you and Carter tonight at eight.

"So much for a quiet evening at home," she said and put the Galaxie in gear.

SIXTEEN

Elsa had laid out the food buffet style, which meant this wasn't a leisurely dinner. Sarah wasn't very hungry and prepared herself a modest plate of broiled fish, vegetables, and salad. It had been a job coordinating with Carter, who was scheduled to end work at ten. Fortunately, one of her coworkers had agreed to cover her shift for the extra money.

When they took their seats, Harlan reached into his briefcase and removed a black journal. Sarah recognized it as the one Charlie and Sister Elizabeth had retrieved from the shack in the forest. He hadn't gotten any food, and she was struck by his sallow complexion. He laid the book on the table and took a sip of his sparkling water.

"This doesn't contain all the answers I'd hoped for," he said. "But what it does have are clues to what happened in the wretched place."

The girl had hardly touched her food. Sarah thought she seemed troubled. On the way over, they'd talked about the wisdom of continuing their investigation since what they were dealing with was dangerous—even life threatening—

and was taking a toll on them both. In the end, they'd agreed to see it through for the sake of the women.

"How do you want to do this?" Carter said.

The attorney seemed thoughtful, and her voice appeared to have startled him. "I want each of you to give me your honest impressions."

"Now?" Sarah said, glancing at her friend.

"Finish your meal."

She was trying to decide when to tell Harlan about the things she'd seen recently. Better to get it over with.

"I need to tell you something," she said. "I saw The Darkness again at the cemetery."

"You didn't—"

"I ran away. Also, I saw someone watching me. He was, I don't know, not—"

"Human?" the attorney said. "I've already discussed these things with Carter. They're demoniacs, and they've been after me for some time now."

"But are they human?"

"It depends."

"I don't understand," the girl said.

"Demons can take many forms. They can appear as you or me, for example. In this case, what you perceive is not human. They can also possess the living."

"So, what I saw may or may not have been a man," Sarah said.

"What were his eyes like?"

"Completely black."

"Most likely, he was a demoniac."

"Wait," Carter said. "Are these people taken over against their will?"

"Not always. In demonic possession, there is sometimes an implicit agreement between the victim and the possessor. These people have invited a demon or demons to take them."

Sarah leaned in. "Which means…"

"They have given themselves willingly to the Evil One, and they serve him."

"How many are there in Dos Santos, do you think?"

"Impossible to know. But their numbers have been growing since—"

"Since I discovered the damned mirror," she said.

He patted her hand. "This is not your doing—it was bound to happen. Whatever evil exists in Dos Santos has been festering for decades, long before you were born. And there are other sources, things we don't have time to discuss tonight."

"And Ana is a part of it?" the girl said.

"Most certainly. But I don't know how yet. Shall we?"

As the women followed him into the library, Carter took her friend's hand. "There was no way for you to know about the mirror."

"If only I'd stopped before…"

"It's like he said—it would've happened anyway."

When they entered the library, the large TV was there again. Mary sat at the desk, with the laptop in front of her. Harlan laid the journal on his desk and gestured to a tray where a pot of coffee stood. Grateful, his guests helped themselves.

"I hadn't planned on having another videoconference," the attorney said. "But he's turned up additional evidence I think you should hear."

"Evidence?" the girl said.

"Proof that Ana coming to Dos Santos was no accident."

"It's time," the housekeeper said and started the Skype session.

Soon, the PI's face filled the screen. He looked tired.

"Good to see you, Charlie," Harlan said.

"You too. Hello, ladies."

The women waved. The PI cleared his throat and opened his notebook.

"I finally tracked down Ana's uncle. He wasn't thrilled to see Sister Elizabeth and me. He's fond of money, though. Seems he enjoys hitting the casinos in Guatemala City. So, I paid him five hundred US dollars to talk to us."

"Smart thinking."

"He told us he never intended for his niece to leave the country. And then, he said something else. If you'll recall, Ana began getting debilitating headaches at fifteen. Turns out her father had been sexually abusing her for years, starting when she was eight."

"How awful."

"And though there's no proof, I'm pretty sure the uncle had something to do with his brother's disappearance. Somewhere along the line, he met a woman—an American—who seemed to know about Ana's history. She convinced him she could help his niece, and that it would be better for her if she lived in the US."

"Interesting. Do you have a name?"

"Grace Zielinski."

"What?" Sarah and Carter said at the same time.

"Do you know her?" Charlie said.

Sarah was on her feet now. "She's the caseworker we met with. The one who arranged for Ana to stay at St. Rita's."

The attorney took out his handkerchief and coughed. "Are you absolutely sure about this?"

"Positive. Lou attended the meeting—you can ask him."

He pointed at the screen. "I need you here as soon as

possible. We need to know her background, her connections, everything."

"I'll be on the next flight to LA."

"Is there anything else?"

"Sister Elizabeth. I drove her to Guatemala City rather than put her on a bus."

"There are no trains?"

"The train system here is pretty much nonexistent. I knew our investigation has had quite an effect on her. She assured me she was fine, but."

"Has it tested her faith?"

"I don't think so. But it frightened her on a profound level. Though she's never met Ana, Sister has developed a deep affection for her. I wanted to mention it in case there was anything—"

"I'll get in touch with her superiors," Harlan said. "Sounds like our beloved nun is long overdue for an all-expenses-paid vacation."

"Okay. I'll email you my notes."

"Thanks, Charlie. Safe travels."

"How is it possible that Grace already knew about Ana?" the girl said. "And if she thought the woman was dangerous, why would she wanna expose the other residents?"

"She told the uncle she was trying to help her," Sarah said. "Remember when we met her? She was passionate about protecting these women."

The attorney retrieved the journal. "Thank you, Mary."

Taking her cue, she left the room, closing the door after her.

"There's no use speculating about Grace Zielinski until we have all the facts," he said. "I think it's time we focused on this book."

Sarah felt a pain in her stomach. "I guess I'll start."

Instead of handing it to her, he walked over to Carter. "I'd like to see what you can make of it."

Though Sarah had been afraid to touch the journal, getting passed over offended her. After all, this was her case. Rather than sitting there seething, she got more coffee. When she returned, the girl was gripping the worn black book with both hands. She had a strange, distant look in her eyes Sarah had never seen before…

Carter was no longer in the library. Somehow, she'd been transported to the horrifying shack in the forest. Now, as she floated face down against the ceiling, she felt a moist draft on her back. Below, there was only darkness. And out of it, she heard singing.

Vamos a la mar, tum, tum.
A comer pescado, tum, tum.
Boca colorada, tum, tum.
Fritito y asado, tum, tum…

As she mouthed the words, a dim, vaporous light shone on the table. Ana lay on her back, naked and shackled, to the sound of someone chanting. It was a prayer they repeated over and over. Though it was in Spanish, she understood the words perfectly.

I acknowledge my sin unto thee,
and mine iniquity have I not hid.
I said, I will confess my transgressions
unto the Lord;
and thou forgavest the iniquity of my sin.
Selah.

Tomás Morales emerged from the shadows, clutching the journal. He was also naked. Dropping the book, he scrambled onto the table and mounted his eager wife as she beckoned him with febrile eyes. As soon as he entered her, she arched her back in the throes of dark animal pleasure.

Carter tried to leave, but something powerful held her there. As Tomás thrust violently, Ana laughed like a madwoman. Now, the girl saw herself lying on the table, shackled. She was thirteen again. And the one violating her was not Ana's husband, but her best friend's father.

She screamed...

When Carter came to her senses, Sarah was holding her close and stroking her hair. The journal lay open on the oriental rug.

"Shh. It's okay."

She could barely get the words out through her choking sobs. "It was so horrible!"

When she looked up, Harlan was standing there, proffering a glass.

"What is it?"

"Cognac."

She accepted it and drank. Though it burned her throat, it warmed her.

"He was chanting something. It began, *I acknowledge my sin unto thee, and mine iniquity have I not hid.*"

"Psalm 32," he said.

Sarah stared at the book, reluctant to touch it. When she turned to him, he nodded. Closing her eyes, she made the Sign of the Cross and prayed. Reaching down, she picked up the cursed thing.

Sarah stood in the middle of the shack, which was

empty. The smell of rotting vegetation, sweat, and blood made her want to vomit. Outside, she heard rushing water. Tomás stood in the shadows, holding the stick he used to beat his wife. He had on the clothes he'd worn on his wedding day. Only now they were bloodstained.

As he moved toward her, he took her hand and led her outside. Instead of the forest, she stood next to a violently rushing river. It was night, and the only sound was the water and the faint cries of feral, nocturnal creatures.

He let go of her hand and walked to the river's edge. She tried calling to him, but no sound came out. He gazed at the turbulent water. Then he glanced at her, and dropping the stick, flung himself in. Instantly, the powerful current carried him away.

Across the river, something shone. It looked like a pillar sickening yellow wavy light. She knew there was something inside the light—something evil. When she turned to go, she came face-to-face with Tomás.

His body was dripping and bloated, the skin a puckered bluish white. His eyes were scaled over and sightless. As he tried to speak, a torrent of foul, brackish water gushed forth. He opened his mouth wide and square, the skin at either side tearing bloodlessly.

His shriek was a cry from Hell.

The call came early. Unable to shake the effects of her vision, Carter had spent the night at Sarah's. But she'd slept poorly, and her head pounded. Those feelings had been so intense, and they reminded her of the nightmares she'd had for years after the rape. It was Dr. Kagan who had shown her how to cope. In her head, she repeated the words the psychiatrist had asked her to memorize—words she'd relied on ever since to keep her from going insane.

What happened was not my fault.
Out of the darkness, the light within me shines.
I am a good person, and I am loved.

She reached for her phone. One missed call. Soon, a voicemail came through. After playing it, she scrambled out of bed and bolted into Sarah's bedroom.

"Sarah!"

Her friend was asleep on her side. Purring and kneading his paws on her back, Gary looked up with squishy eyes.

"What? What's wrong?"

The girl was out of focus, standing in the doorway wearing a pair of Sarah's gray lounge pants and a white undershirt.

"Something's happened. We have to go to the shelter."

Sarah sat up. "What do you mean?"

"It's Nellie!"

"I don't..."

Tears sprang from Carter's eyes, her arms open as if pleading. "We need to go now!"

When Sarah arrived with Carter, Myrtle Street was jammed with police cars, a ladder truck, and an ambulance. Seeing the crowd and the barricade tape, her chest tightened. She found a space on the street and parked.

She left the Galaxie and pushed her way through the

crowd with her friend close behind. Lou, Tim, and Heidi stood on the other side of the tape, looking up. Behind them, the ladder truck was in position, and a firefighter was already climbing it. Carter pointed at the roof.

Wearing a fringed gray peasant top and jeans, Nellie stood on the ledge watching the crowd below. Her eyes were vacant. Spotting the women, the police chief said something to Tim. He lifted the tape and escorted them through.

"Thank God you're here," Lou said to the girl. "She keeps asking for you."

"I don't understand what's going on!"

He grabbed her hand. "No time, come on."

Sarah started to follow when he stopped her. "She'll only speak to Carter."

As they raced up the steps to the entrance, Sarah kept her eyes on the blonde girl. There was a strong wind, and she prayed Nellie wouldn't lose her balance.

"How long has she been up there?" Carter said as they rode the elevator to the top floor.

"Maybe an hour. An orderly saw her go up. She told him she needed some air."

When the elevator doors open, they entered the bright hallway and headed for the stairs to the roof. The police chief banged open the door and held it for Carter. Inside, she found steps leading to another door labeled Roof Access. She climbed up.

Though she was terrified, she pushed open the door. A frigid blast of air hit her. Sensing Lou behind her, she continued toward the girl, who looked down, her arms dangling lifelessly at her sides.

"Nellie?"

Slowly, she turned around. There were dark circles under her eyes, and she grinned in a way that chilled Carter. As if she knew a terrible secret she couldn't wait to share. When the cop tried moving closer, she pointed at him.

"Stay back!"

Raising his hands, he inched away and remained meekly in front of the door. Carter looked at him desperately, then focused all her attention on the blonde girl. Blinded by tears, she made her way slowly to the edge of the roof.

"Talk to me."

"It's beautiful, isn't it? He said it would be. I never told you, but I once tried to kill myself in my car. Everything was so mixed up back then."

"Nellie, don't do this."

"He let me see my future." She stroked Carter's face. "And you're not in it. It's fine." Then she lifted her arms to the heavens. "Thank you for showing me my place!"

She pulled Carter close and pressed her head against her shoulder. Then she crooned in her lover's ear.

Vamos a la mar, tum, tum.
A comer pescado, tum, tum.
Boca colorada, tum, tum.
Fritito y asado, tum, tum...

Carter was afraid to move—even an inch—for fear of losing her forever. There had to be a way to get her away from the ledge. Soon, the ladder with the firefighter swung toward them.

The lonely graduate student with the fine blonde hair moved away, her expression dark and erratic. When she spoke, the voice was no longer hers but instead a demonic chorus.

"Ella aparenta ser una mansa paloma, pero no lo es."

Her face brightened. Taking Carter's face in her hands, she kissed her with a deep and lasting passion, which spoke of a lifetime together that would never be.

The firefighter was about to reach the edge of the building. Ignoring him, she backed up as Lou sprinted toward them. Closing her eyes, she raised her arms to the sky and fell into pure air as the firefighter tried and failed to grab her.

Horrified, Sarah watched as Nellie hurtled to her death. When her head struck the edge of the sidewalk, the sound it made—a wet crunch—sickened her. The suicide lay motionless, one vacant eye staring at her. Gasping, the crowd pressed in luridly against the barricade tape as the police ordered them to move back. Sarah hadn't realized Heidi had taken her hand.

Carter stood at the edge of the roof, looking down, feeling cold and empty and alone. She turned to the police chief, and in a burst of fury, pummeled his chest with her small fists.

"She wouldn't have done it if you'd stayed back!" She was sobbing now. "I could've saved her. She didn't deserve to…"

Gently, he took her hands. Vulnerable, she held him, her tears staining his shirt.

"Why did she have to die?" she said. "Why in God's name did she have to die?"

Sarah adjusted the duvet over Carter, who was fully clothed. Shards of late morning light leaked in between the slats of the white wooden shutters, making the room glow like a world within a world. She left the guest bedroom, closing the door behind her.

When she saw Gary looking at her and meowing, she picked him up. Kissing his head, she carried him into the living room. Setting down the cat, she grabbed her phone lying on the coffee table. As she sat on the sofa, she noticed Gary staring at the front window, his eyes alert.

"What is it?"

His ears flattening, the cat let out a low, persistent yowl. Concerned, she went to the window and peeked out. No one was there. She felt cold and returned to the sofa. Then, she made a call.

"Joe?"

As soon as she heard his voice, the tears came. He tried to say something, but she cut him off.

"Can you please come home?" she said.

SEVENTEEN

Outside the women's shelter, the street was deserted except for Lou's SUV and another police cruiser. Though the sky was bright, a chilly wind blew, making the barricade tape twist. The ambulance carrying Nellie's broken body had already left for the morgue in Santa Barbara. Next to the building, a maintenance worker hosed down the sidewalk, doing his best to wash away the blood, bone, and hair after the forensics team had collected their evidence.

The police chief met with Heidi and Harlan in the conference room. He rubbed his eyes with the heels of his hands. He'd forgotten to ask someone for coffee and was in the throes of a monumental caffeine withdrawal. Not that he was addicted or anything. The director, whose eyes were red-rimmed, gathered her strength for what was to come.

"But where will they go?" she said, her eyes pleading with the attorney.

"I promise we'll find them accommodations, but they can't stay here. It's too dangerous."

"I agree," Lou said. "Though there's no evidence of a

crime, I think it best we move the residents someplace safe."

Resigned, she folded her hand. "What about Nellie's research? Technically, it belongs to the university." Again, she looked to Harlan for answers.

"I'd prefer it remain here for the time being."

The way he studied him made the police chief uncomfortable. "You think there might be something in there?" he said.

"We must remain open to the possibility."

Classic lawyer-speak. "Heidi," Lou said. "Everything in Nellie's office—including her computer—is to be considered police evidence." Then to Harlan, "Good enough?"

"Thank you, Chief."

"I'll let the staff know," she said. "Excuse me."

After she'd left the room, Lou wrote something in his notebook. He hoped the attorney had some place to be. But he sat there patiently. Then, predictably, he went over the game plan according to Harlan Covington.

"Chief Fiore," the attorney said, "I'm going to contact the archdiocese to arrange temporary housing for these women. I am aware of several shelters in LA and Camarillo."

Lou nodded. "And Ana is going with the others?"

"No. She is to remain here."

"But how will you manage without putting the staff in danger?"

"I take full responsibility. And I promise to give you a full report once I've made all the arrangements." He left before the police chief could object.

"Great," Lou said. "Now, I'm working for him."

Sarah opened the door as Lou walked up.

"Thanks for seeing me," he said.

She waved him in. "Try to keep your voice down. Carter's asleep."

"How is she?"

"Pretty shaken up."

"Were she and Nellie, um…"

"I don't know. Maybe?"

As she led him toward the kitchen, he admired the décor. He wished he could afford a place like this, but what with the alimony and child support payments, he had to settle for a one-bedroom condo on Church Street. When they walked in, Gary stared at the stranger. He approached the cat, his hand extended. Hissing, the animal scurried away.

"Huh," she said. "He's usually pretty friendly."

"Most pets don't like cops. It's okay, I'm used to it."

"I made us some coffee."

She poured two cups and took a seat on a barstool next to him. "Hey, can I ask you something?"

"Sure, anything."

"Are you seeing my sister?"

He choked mid-swallow and coughed into his hand. "Too hot. Uh, you see, we just. Well, I gave her a ride that one time and…"

She reached over and laid her hand on his. "It's okay. I'm very protective of Rachel."

"Uh-huh."

"And if you break her heart, I'll make you suffer. Are we clear?"

"I would never—"

She squeezed his hand hard. "Are we clear?"

"Yes."

He took back his hand and massaged it, watching her warily as she adjusted herself on the stool and drank her coffee.

"So, how's the investigation going?" she said.

Her voice was pleasant, and she acted as if they hadn't just done a scene from *The Bold and the Beautiful*. Getting his wits about him, he filled her in on his earlier meeting.

"What about Ana?" she said.

"Hold on to your hat."

As he was about to continue, the girl drifted into the kitchen, looking haggard. Her face was splotchy, her eyes red rimmed.

"What're you doing up, honey?" Sarah said. "Come on, take a seat at the table. Want some coffee?"

"Okay."

She jerked her head at the police chief, which he took to mean they were moving the show to the butcher block table. Touching Carter's hand, she brushed the hair from her swollen eyes.

"Lou was about to give me a report. Do you feel up to it?"

She cleared her throat, her mouth set. "I wanna know everything."

As Sarah poured a cup for her friend, he repeated the story. "And here comes the fun part." He looked at Carter. "Harlan wants you to move into the women's shelter—with Ana."

"Like hell!" Sarah said, taking her hand.

"You'll be safe, I promise. I've assigned Tim to stay with you."

The girl scoffed. "Like that's gonna help."

He poured himself more coffee. "Anyone else?"

"He can't be serious," Sarah said. "And by the way? Why are you telling us this and not him?"

"He said he had to take care of something and didn't want to wait to let Carter know."

The girl ran her fingers through her hair. "I need a cigarette."

"And what am I supposed to do while everyone else is at the sleepover?" Sarah said.

"You'll be with Covington and the PI. What's his name, Meeks?"

"Beeks," Carter said, looking miserable.

Sarah held her friend by the shoulders. "You don't have to do this."

The police chief rolled his eyes. "Harlan warned me not to let you talk her out of it."

"Okay, I've had just about enough of him and the Guatemalan Freddy Krueger!"

Both she and Lou were on their feet now, glaring at each other across the table as Carter sat perfectly still, her head in her hands.

"Why are you yelling at me?" he said. "I'm the messenger."

"Funny, I thought you were the police chief. Why didn't you tell him to take a big, fat hike?"

"Guys," the girl said.

The cop ignored her. "Oh, like that's so easy. Maybe I should've drop-kicked him too. Wait a second. Is this about me and your sister?"

"What? That's nonsense!"

"Hello?" Carter said.

Sarah shook her head. "This whole thing has gone off

the rails. And to top it off, Barney Fife is supposed to keep her safe?"

"Hey, Tim's an excellent officer. Why would you—"

A piercing whistle stopped them in mid-fight. the BattleBots turned to see the girl glaring at them. When she was sure she had their attention, she spoke in a calm, determined voice.

"I'll do it," Carter said.

There was so much to do. Harlan and his assistant had spent the day on the phone making calls from his offices in Santa Barbara. Working with his connections in the archdiocese, he arranged housing for everyone. Heidi insisted on remaining at the shelter with Ana. They also retained a cook, two orderlies each working twelve-hour shifts, and a security guard. And the attorney had paid everyone else's salary through the end of the month.

He'd made a point of letting Grace Zielinski's superior know what was happening, but he didn't refer specifically to the caseworker. He didn't want to tip her off—not yet. If she were guilty of something, she might be tempted to make a move. And he wasn't ready.

The pain in his prostate and joints was intense, and he foresaw another trip to the doctor. He decided to take a walk. Later, he planned to meet with Charlie, who'd arrived on a mid-morning flight at LAX and was en route to Santa Barbara.

It was chillier than he'd expected. As he walked north on State Street, he was aware a man and woman were following him, obviously pushing through the crowd to get closer. Lately, he'd seen more and more of them and wasn't surprised.

At the corner, he crossed the street on the light with a group of college students, hoping the couple would give up. But they didn't. As he made his way toward a small gourmet shop, which sold organic smoothies, his pursuers quickened their pace. He entered the shop and waited near the front window to observe them.

They looked to be in their late twenties and sloppily dressed. Each had a head of greasy hair, and he imagined they smelled bad. No one on the street reacted to their coal-black eyes but him.

He realized the sketchy couple didn't plan to enter the store, so he walked up to the juice bar and ordered a berry smoothie. In a few minutes, he was sipping his drink through a paper straw. When he'd finished, he looked out the window. They were nowhere in sight. He disposed of the cup and walked out.

As soon as he reached the corner, they closed in. The Don't Walk sign flashed, but he crossed anyway. By the time he'd reached the other side, the demoniacs were in the middle of the crosswalk. Concentrating, he raised his right hand as if to make them halt. They grabbed their heads and wailed like wild dogs as the light turned red.

A truck driver blasted his horn, but it was too late. The enormous vehicle struck them head on, knocking them flat on the street. It crushed their limbs under its wheels, leaving a red swath in its wake. Bystanders screamed. The driver hit his brakes and stopped dead in the middle of traf-fic, the tires smoking and his trailer shimmying danger-ously. Ignoring the chaotic scene, Harlan made his way briskly toward his building.

When Joe arrived, he set down his bag in the foyer and went to the kitchen, where his ex-wife was busy cooking something that smelled wonderful. Jazz played through the Bluetooth speaker sitting on the counter. She had her back to him as she stood over a pan of sizzling olive oil. Eager to hold her, he moved closer. Something dark lay on the floor. It was the cat's headless body.

"Sarah?" he said, barely able to get the word out.

She didn't turn around. "Dinner will be ready soon, hon."

His legs were like water. With naked hands, she grabbed the hot pan to show him what she'd done. He was powerless to look away. It was the cat's furless head, dripping in oil, the teeth exposed and the eyes deflated.

"I know how much you enjoy my cooking," she said. "So I made you something special."

The squeal of the plane's enormous wheels hitting the runway startled Joe. He looked around the first-class cabin. A flight attendant read off gate information over the PA. He rubbed his eyes and stretched.

He still had a long Uber ride to Santa Barbara. As soon as he was off the plane, he'd call Sarah. But he wouldn't tell her about the disturbing dream. Instead, he'd bury it along with the other bad dream about the blue bouncy ball.

"What did you do?"

Sarah gazed up from her computer monitor. Rachel

stood in the doorway, her posture stiff, wearing a look of anger mixed with incredulity.

"Excuse me?"

Her sister marched in and closed the door, but she didn't sit. This was not a good sign.

"What did you say to Lou?" she said.

"Oh, that. Nothing. I was curious. And by the way, thanks for telling me you were seeing him."

"Don't you dare change the subject." Her shoulders slumped, and she sank into the guest chair. "I didn't say anything because we haven't even been on a date yet. It's been coffee and one or two phone calls."

The look on her sister's face sent a pang of guilt through Sarah. Why did she have to meddle? Rachel was a grown woman. A lovely single mother with a preteen daughter and a heart as big as the moon. *Sure, and someone any man could easily take advantage of.*

"I thought I was being protective," she said.

"Yeah, well, now you've got him terrified. I think he was going to ask me to dinner. I guess that's not going to happen. Never mind."

Sarah came around her desk and took her sister's hand. "Do you really think being involved with a cop is a good idea? Besides, he's divorced."

"So are you."

"Not relevant."

"Oh, really? I'm thinking if some new guy comes into your life, I'm going to warn him."

"Look, I know you're angry. But I think I know what's best for you."

"What's best for me is for you to stay the hell out of my personal life!"

When Sarah looked into her eyes, she saw the same determination she recognized in herself. "Rachel, I—"

"I mean it, Sarah," she said. "Stay out of my business."

When Joe reached the front door, Sarah was already waiting for him. Having put her run-in with her sister behind her, she'd showered and changed into skinny jeans and the tight-fitting white cashmere sweater she knew he loved.

"Welcome home, weary traveler," she said.

She was barely able to keep from flinging herself at him as the Uber driver backed out of the driveway and peeled out. Without words, he grabbed his bag and walked in.

"Where's Gary?" he said.

She grabbed his arm and made him face her. "Want to try again?"

Setting down the bag, he kissed her. Then he moved to her neck and continued showering her with passion as she snaked her arms in the air, her knees going weak.

"That's more like it," she said, flushed and breathless.

The cat trotted over, and Joe acted as if he were a long-lost friend. He picked up the animal and scratched behind his ear, making him purr and knead his paws in the air.

"Want a glass of wine?" she said.

"Absolutely."

He followed her into the kitchen. She'd set two places at the dining room table. A vase of fresh flowers stood in the center, and she'd brought out her expensive crystal wine-glasses.

"Boy, looks like you went all out."

"I did."

"I really need a shower."

"Okay, dinner should be ready in ten."

He grabbed his bag. As she removed the pan of stuffed pork chops from the oven and set it on top of the range, the shower came on. The cat watched her, and feeling generous, she pulled off a tiny piece of meat and laid it in his bowl.

"Looks like you got lucky tonight, buddy," she said. *Hope that makes two of us.*

EIGHTEEN

Carter was on the roof again. It was morning, and there was no sound. Everything seemed to move in slow motion. Screaming, she reached out helplessly as Nellie tumbled off the edge, her slender arms windmilling in frigid, empty air. The firefighter on the ladder tried catching her, but he was miles away.

Then everything stopped.

With a hammering heart, Carter grabbed her by the wrist. She tried pulling her to safety, but the girl was immobile—made of glass. Then, like a movie reel out of control, everything speeded up. Nellie's hand snapped off bloodlessly. Carter watched dumbstruck as she fell to her death. As she looked down, she gasped.

She was still holding Nellie's hand.

Carter sat bolt upright in bed, holding her chest as her heart continued its rapid thumping. Morning light filtered through her bedroom's pale miniblinds. She stared at her empty hands and caressed her bracelet. Then she cried all over again.

Sarah savored the Mexican organic brew The Cracked Pot offered, trying to mask the awkwardness she felt as she sat across from the police chief. Though she'd promised herself she wouldn't meddle any further in what might be the beginnings of a healthy romantic relationship, something made her think she'd been right all along.

Rachel had suffered untold pain after Paul died. He was a soldier. Lou was a cop and also at risk of being killed in the line of duty. Sarah shuddered at the thought of her sister losing a loved one again. The police chief being divorced had nothing to do with it—she realized that now. It was the unknown—the danger.

"Lou," she said.

"No need to say anything. It's forgotten."

"But—"

"You weren't out of line. All I ask is that you give me a chance."

What if he were meant for Rachel? She'd prayed countless times for her sister to meet someone and fall in love again. Had God answered her prayer in the form of the Dos Santos police chief? *How about a little faith, Sarah?*

"Okay," she said.

"Really?" He'd already drained his triple espresso, and appearing relieved, started in on a stack of bacon.

She raised a finger. "Heart attack, table for one."

"Ever heard of the keto diet? So, Joe's home?"

"You didn't ask me to breakfast to talk about my ex-husband." Leaning in, she quirked an eyebrow. "Or did you?"

He pushed aside his plate. "Listen, I realize you get queasy around morgues…"

She'd raised a forkful of blueberry pancake to her mouth when she stopped mid-bite. "Oh, no. You want me to touch Nellie's body to see if—."

"Well…"

She scoffed. "It was suicide. Everyone saw her jump."

"I know, but…"

"But you think something made her do it."

"She wasn't what you'd call suicidal. I know—I was there. Look, I realize it's a lot to ask. I'm prepared to donate a kidney, should the need arise."

"Tempting offer. Can I collect now?"

As they ate, Carter appeared with fresh coffee. Sarah's friend had been crying again, and she was surprised the girl had shown up for work.

"You should be at home resting."

"I'm fine. So, what's doin'?"

"You don't want to know. Apparently, I'm needed down at the morgue."

"Okay, what time?"

"You want to come?"

"Of course."

The manager walked over and pulled Carter aside. "These orders aren't going to serve themselves."

She nodded contritely. Then to her friend, "I get off at two."

"Make sure not to eat anything," Sarah said, a little too loudly as the girl hurried off.

When she turned around again, Lou was grinning at her.

"Thank you."

"Look, the only reason I'm doing this is because of Carter. Otherwise, I would've told you to—"

"Yeah, yeah. I get it. I'll let Frank know we'll be there around three, okay?"

"I guess. Now, let me eat my pancakes in peace."

"Want some bacon?" he said. "I have plenty."

Carter had changed into gray Lululemon straight-leg pants and her black leather jacket. As they made their way south toward Santa Barbara, she stared at her phone.

"Last chance. Are you sure you want to do this?" Sarah said.

"I feel like I owe it to Nellie."

"Yeah, me too. I hope you didn't eat lunch."

"Only a protein bar and coffee."

"I guess we'll see if your stomach is any stronger than mine."

Sarah got off at the exit and made her way through traffic until they arrived at the coroner's office. Walking in, she was determined not to have a repeat of her last visit, when she puked violently, almost nailing the ME's shoes.

Inside, it was pleasant. There were potted palms in the lobby, and bright afternoon sun was streaming through the windows.

"This isn't so bad," the girl said.

"We've only just begun, my friend."

An assistant came through a security door and greeted them. She'd also witnessed Sarah's barf fest.

"Hey, Sarah."

"Okay, I'm embarrassed. I don't remember your name."

"Annie."

"This is my friend Carter Wittgenstein. Lou asked us to join him."

"Come on, I'll take you back."

She used her ID badge to unlock the door and led them down a hallway that was familiar to Sarah. As they approached the autopsy room, her knees buckled. *This is not happening again.*

When they reached the door, the assistant went in first. Sarah gave the girl a pained look as they followed. Inside, Dr. Franklin Chestnut, the Santa Barbara Sheriff-Coroner, stood next to the last stainless steel table. Wearing a medical lab coat, he chatted amiably with the police chief. She swallowed hard and walked toward them.

"Thanks for coming," Lou said.

The ME extended his hand. "Nice to see you again, Sarah."

"Likewise."

"This is Carter Wittgenstein," the police chief said.

"Ah, the other half of the dynamic duo. Loved your article."

"Thanks." Blushing, she glanced around, fascinated by everything in the room.

"If I were you, Frank," Sarah said, "I'd step back about three feet. Considering what happened the last time."

"You'll be fine. It takes a few minutes to get used to the smell. Once you do, you shouldn't have a problem."

"You ladies ready?" Lou said.

Sarah shrugged. "Bring it on."

The ME pulled back the sheet to reveal the corpse's head and shoulders. There was no Y-incision, which meant he hadn't yet performed an autopsy.

It was hard to tell whether this was Nellie Watson.

One side of the skull—the side that had hit the side-walk—was bashed in. As a result, the face looked contorted, with wildly asymmetrical eyes. Whereas she'd been pretty, the monstrosity Sarah stared at resembled something you'd see in a funhouse mirror. She was about to say something when her friend hurled.

Annie had returned and immediately went to get a bucket and mop. The men looked at the body matter-of-factly.

"I'm pretty confident," Frank said, "the autopsy will confirm the cause of death as consistent with head trauma and internal blood loss as a result of a fall. Manner of death is suicide."

The cop cleared his throat. "I agree with you. However..." Then to Sarah, "If you wouldn't mind."

"Right."

She was relieved she hadn't thrown up. As she moved closer, Carter touched her hand.

"No, let me," she said.

"Are you absolutely sure? You don't know what you'll see."

"I have to do this."

Closing her eyes, she cleared her mind. For no reason at all, she pictured herself at eight, exploring an abandoned house with Franny, her best friend. She dismissed it. When she'd gotten herself into a complete state of calmness, she reached for the corpse's shoulder. Her hand trembling, she touched the body.

Carter hurtled down a hole made of swirling dark smoke. Voices wailed as hundreds of hands attempted to grab her as she fell. Down, down. Her arms and legs were splayed, and there was nothing to hold onto except the grasping, skeletal fingers she refused to touch.

Eventually, she reached the bottom, and the wailing stopped. Someone wept softly. In the void, her breathing echoed. Dimly, she could just make out someone hunched over and wringing her hands, her shoulders quivering. As she approached the phantasm, she realized who it was.

"Nellie?" she said.

The ghost turned to her. Here in this place, she wasn't disfigured. She wore the clothes Carter had seen her in that damnable day. Nellie tried speaking, but her mouth didn't seem to work properly, and what came out was a kind of moaning from someone with no tongue.

"Why did you take your life?" Carter fought back the tears. "You didn't even give us a chance."

Her words were clearer now. "I told you—he showed me my future. You weren't in it."

Carter touched her. "Who showed you?"

"No, go away! I can't let him find me!"

"Who?"

"*Him*. And you mustn't let him find you either. If he does, you'll end up here, like me." She wailed pitifully. "I don't know where I am!"

Carter's heart was breaking. A powerful feeling came over her, and she knew what she had to do. Grabbing Nellie's hand, she placed it on her leather bracelet. As soon as she did, a powerful white light illuminated the ghost. As she watched in wonder, Nellie became luminescent. But before the light could absorb her, she said something.

"Carter, run!"

Then she was gone, and with her, the light. Carter stood in the void alone. Suddenly, a noise. It was like the keening of a dying animal mixed with hellish grunting and lowing.

The sound terrified her. As the cursed thing moved in, she felt herself being pulled up through the tunnel of smoke into a weak light that gradually brightened.

Now, she was once again in the autopsy room, with everyone staring at her.

"So, it didn't work," Lou said, disappointed.

"What?"

"You touched the body for only a second."

But Carter's friend understood. "No, she saw something."

The others gaped at her. She went to the girl, who was shaking, and held her.

"She saw everything," Sarah said.

It was early when the women arrived. Sarah had never heard of the bar and knew immediately it wasn't her kind of place—too hipster. But she'd agreed to accompany Carter. Luckily, they'd found a booth.

"So, Renown?" Sarah said.

"It's stupid, I know. But I feel like I'm honoring her by coming here."

"Then we should drink a toast." She raised her wineglass. "To Nellie."

The girl did likewise with her glass of Guinness, and they clinked glasses. Though they sat in a corner, they kept their voices low so no one would overhear the conversation.

"Do you want to talk about it?" Sarah said.

"She was in this really dark place. Not hell, I don't think, but. It was like..."

"A void?"

"Yes. And she was so scared."

"Did she say why she..."

Carter looked away. "She said it was because she saw her future. And I think she saw her own death too."

"Could Ana have shown her something?"

"She kept referring to someone—maybe the thing we saw at the shelter. But how can anyone predict the future?"

"They can't. And if they say they can, they're selling something. What about depression? Maybe he said something he knew would make her despair."

"Before she— She told me she'd tried killing herself before."

"It's possible this demon is preying on those hidden, vulnerable places in these women and exploiting them."

"But what about the other residents? They're just as vulnerable."

"It's possible they're stronger. It was the same in Guatemala, remember? Charlie said only three women in the Christian church mutilated themselves, but no one else. And then, there was the apartment manager's wife. She was close to Ana, yet nothing happened to her."

The girl shook her head. "But Nellie wasn't acting depressed. Just the opposite—she seemed happy."

"Whatever this thing is, it can play tricks on the mind."

"A trickster demon?"

"I don't know."

"I think I saved her." Carter held up the bracelet. "With this."

"St. Benedict?"

"When she touched it, she was surrounded by this beautiful light. It was so bright, but it didn't hurt my eyes."

"It might mean her soul is free, and she's not trapped anymore."

She looked at Sarah with fear in her eyes. "There's something else. And I think it's related to Ana."

"The demon?"

"I think it knew I was there, and it was coming for me. Sarah, I'm so scared."

"It'll be all right. Remember, you're not alone in this."

"I know." She touched the medal on her bracelet.

"You have St. Benedict," Sarah said. "But you also have me."

Lou read through the report one more time, ignoring the autopsy photos and concentrating on the manner of death.

Suicide. Though he'd witnessed Nellie Watson hurtling off the building, there was something that bothered him. She hadn't acted like a suicide. The former homicide detective had never actually witnessed someone killing themselves, but he'd read plenty of reports. And what he believed were the reasons always made sense. He recalled an article on the six reasons people killed themselves. Mentally, he ticked off the list.

Depression. Was she depressed? From what Carter had told him, she was happy. When he spoke to her professor at the university, he said she loved her work and was looking forward to completing her doctoral thesis. Besides, depression was not what he'd observed on the roof.

Psychosis. She wasn't psychotic, as far as he knew. The report showed there were no drugs in her system. And there was nothing in her background to indicate she'd been diagnosed.

Impulsivity. Again, it would be the result of a drug problem. She wasn't wild and crazy, from what he'd observed. She seemed like a sensible girl—quiet and focused.

A cry for help. She didn't want help. In fact, it was the opposite. She seemed to be saying goodbye. Was this why she insisted on Carter being there?

A desire to die. No, that was typical of people with a terminal illness. And from what he knew, they didn't jump off buildings—they took pills.

Guilt over some mistake. What could this poor girl have done to make her want to end her life? And again, she hadn't acted like someone who was remorseful.

He closed the folder and rubbed his eyes. When he glanced at his watch, he saw it was after seven. The circumstances surrounding Nellie's death continued to nag at him. He thought about the others—the women who had harmed themselves at the shelter. They all had something in common.

Straightening up in his chair, he pawed at his desk, looking for his notebook. Seeing it under a pile of papers, he flipped it open and scanned the pages until he found what he was looking for. It was the interviews he'd conducted with the residents who were with Marcy Lund when she mutilated her hand in the garbage disposal and showed it to them. *She was giggling,* one of them had said.

He flipped to a new page. Interview with an orderly. Another resident, Julie Talbot, had tried to swallow a knitting needle. The orderly discovered her and took it away. *She was laughing,* he said. And a final interview with a volunteer, Rupinder Anand. She'd been the one to find

Roberta Stanton, who'd smashed her hand with a brick. *She looked happy.* And Nellie? She too was happy.

Wearily, he grabbed his jacket and headed for the door when he ran into Tim.

"Working late?" the officer said.

"I can't seem to get a handle on what's happening at St. Rita's. Has Harlan gone over everything with you?"

"Yes. The other residents are leaving soon, and I'm about to take my stuff over there."

He'd always thought the kid was a solid cop, if a little green. But he liked him and even felt a little protective.

"Just watch yourself, okay?"

"I will."

"And stay away from Ana Robles."

"What do you mean?"

"She might be dangerous," Lou said and walked out.

NINETEEN

Grace fidgeted in the uncomfortable chair with the dodgy wheel while the program manager, Irene MacAllister, sat at her desk reading the report. She was around fifty—ten years younger than the caseworker. A humorless woman, Grace felt, who wore too much makeup. And her perfume!

Behind the program manager on a bookshelf stood a maple wood statue of St. Rita of Cascia, patroness of abused wives. She wore a nun's habit, a rosary dangling from her belt, and she cradled a large crucifix. Irene had purchased the statue on a trip to Italy, and the caseworker was aware how much she cherished it.

Laying down the report, the program manager removed her tortoiseshell reading glasses and looked at Grace without expression. There was a black mole above her lip. The caseworker wondered how much it would bleed when you stuck a pin in it.

"I'm afraid I agree with Heidi Lewis," Irene said.

"But—"

"Until we can understand what's happening at the women's shelter, it is to remain closed."

Furious, Grace had to remind herself who was in charge. "What about Ana Robles?"

The program manager looked at her pointedly. "What about her?"

"How in the world can you permit her to remain there by herself?"

"I'm sure Heidi has the situation under control."

The caseworker stared at the floor. "It's all the lawyer's doing."

"What?"

Grace felt the beginnings of a migraine. It always started behind the eyes. "Ana is a special case. She—"

"Look. We all know about your special cases."

Irene had become exasperated and instantly regretted what she'd said. She took a breath as the caseworker seethed.

"Tell me again how you found Ana," she said. "It was while you were traveling in Guatemala, was it not?"

"What? I... I told you. It was during my vacation. I visited a church there, where I happened to meet her uncle. We struck up a conversation, and he told me about his niece, who was being abused by her husband. He asked for my help."

"He asked you."

"That's what I said."

"I see." The program manager flicked the corner of the manila folder. "You've done quite a bit of traveling, it seems."

"What of it? I have a lot of vacation saved up. I don't see what any of this has to do with—"

"And you always seem to find women who are in trouble. Tell me, do you carry a divining rod?"

Irene was doing it again, but she didn't care. Grace Zielinski was her least favorite employee. And despite her impeccable references, she regretted having hired her.

"I beg your pardon?" the caseworker said. "Are you suggesting I—"

"I'm not suggesting anything. Look, no one is doubting your commitment to these unfortunate women. But once you place them, they're no longer your responsibility."

"You don't think I know that? I've been in this business longer than you."

The program manager's face darkened. "Don't go there, Grace." She glanced at her watch. She couldn't afford to be late to the Archbishop's meeting.

"I suppose you think Ana is responsible for what's happened?"

"I can't say. But what I do know is that somehow her presence upsets the other residents. And now, a young woman is dead."

"The girl was unstable."

"And how exactly would you know?"

"It stands to reason. People don't just fling themselves off buildings."

For a second, Irene pictured the unpleasant woman doing a swan dive off the top of the Los Angeles Cathedral. She'd have to confess that on Saturday. As if reading her thoughts, Grace gaped at her.

"I'm hoping we can reopen St. Rita's as soon as possible." The program manager grabbed her purse and stood. "You'll have to excuse me—I have another meeting."

Though Irene had left the room, the caseworker didn't get up. She tried thinking of a pretext to visit the women's shelter. She'd never met Harlan Covington, but she'd heard of him. And she knew he was on the board, which meant had influence with the archdiocese.

And what had possessed her superior to ask about Guatemala? Had the lawyer insinuated something? The last thing she wanted was an investigation into her travels. Something had to be done.

Glancing over her shoulder, she didn't see anyone in the hallway. She picked up the report and scanned the pages, flicking one to the next. The director had recommended keeping Ana under observation. Dr. Roxanne Marsh would conduct daily therapy sessions.

As she continued reading, she noticed the report mentioned Sarah Greene and Carter Wittgenstein. Where had she heard those names? *The psychics she'd met.* What kind of game was Harlan Covington playing?

The pain was unbearable, and she wanted to vomit. Holding her head in her hands, she moaned. Vaguely, she felt herself leave her chair and return the report to its place on the desk. A familiar dark wailing emanated from a point precisely in the middle of her brain, and she saw flashes of light.

Steadying herself, Grace made her way to the door and looked out over the endless rows of cubicles. People worked at their desks. Others hurried up and down the aisles. Two coworkers laughed over a shared joke. Insects, all of them.

Everything looked wavy and blurred, as if viewed through the intense heat of the desert. The ceiling lights were blindingly bright. She'd find a way to deal with the elderly attorney and those two meddling bitches. But now, she had to find a dark room. Shielding her eyes, she went in search of a utility closet.

Smelling smoke, an administrative assistant hurried

into Irene's office. Though there was no fire, the smell was intense. Confused, she approached the desk and saw the program manager's beloved statue of St. Rita on the bookshelf. The area surrounding it was black and charred. A circle of white ash circumscribed the base.

But the statue itself was unharmed.

Carter pulled her MINI Cooper into a free space at the end of the building and turned off the engine. Absently caressing the silver medal on her bracelet, she considered what she'd say to the priest. She felt drawn to the old Irishman. When she called, the assistant had been pleasant but all business. The girl didn't blame her. A non-Catholic taking up his valuable time was not high on her agenda.

What did she expect to get from the meeting? Comfort? No, clarity. Though she hadn't known Nellie well, the woman's gruesome death devastated her. And more than anything, she wanted to understand why she had to die. Why—the eternal philosophical question. What was it Nietzsche had said? *He who has a why to live can bear almost any how.* Had Nellie lost her reason for living? She'd seemed happy in her work and happy with her newfound relationship with Carter. *So, why?*

Brushing the fresh tears welling in her eyes, she entered the parish office. Mrs. Ivy wasn't there.

"Hello?" she said. "Fr. Brian?"

"In here."

The room looked different, but she couldn't say how. Dismissing the thought, she recalled what her friend had told her when they visited the first time. The books, the smell of British Sterling. These were wonderfully old-fash-ioned things, which brought a sense of comfort. Though the books were there, she could detect no odor other than something that smelled faintly of smoke. It was acrid and irritated her throat.

The priest looked at her, immobile, his eyes intense. Somehow, they weren't the kind eyes she'd remembered from her last meeting.

"Have a seat," he said.

Coughing into her hand, she slid into a chair. The last time, he'd offered his hand. Now, he just looked at her. His expression was strange, as if he were distracted.

"Is this a good time?" she said, unsure now of why she'd come.

"Of course. What's this about, Carter Wittgenstein?"

"I... It's about what happened at St. Rita's. My friend Nellie... I feel like I need to talk to someone."

"A real tragedy." He was dismissive as he glanced at some papers on the desk. "Suicide is a lamentable choice. But sometimes, it's the only way. Wouldn't you agree?"

"What?"

This wasn't at all what she'd expected. Though she wasn't religious, she was certain the Catholic Church did not condone the taking of one's own life. Was he testing her?

"It was so unexpected," she said.

"Are you Catholic?"

"I..."

He'd already asked her when they met the last time, and she had answered. He was old—maybe his mind was slipping.

"No," she said.

"I'm not surprised. You must be Jewish then. A great

people, the Jews. So much suffering, though. You know, history is filled with human suffering. The things I've seen... Do you think perhaps you might deserve it? Philosophically speaking?"

She felt feverish. "I don't know what you want me to say."

He leaned forward and looked at her darkly, his expression absent of all compassion. "I want you to tell me what you believe in. Isn't that the real reason you're here?"

"I... I'm not religious."

"Hmm."

He leaned back and gazed around the room, as if seeing it for the first time. Something wasn't right, and she didn't want to be here.

"I don't blame you. Religion isn't what it used to be. You start with six hundred thirteen commandments. Then, some so-called prophet from a backwater town barely on the map boils them all down to two. Very convenient. But a rather slippery slope, don't you think?"

Dizzy, she got to her feet, and trembling, made her way to the door. "Thanks for your time, Father."

"Glad I could be of help. Be sure to say hello to Sarah Greene."

Outside, she exhaled, and keeping her eyes to the ground, started toward her car. Maybe it was all a dream. Her heart pounded as she tried to understand what had just happened. Unaware, she nearly collided with someone.

"Hey, watch out!" a familiar voice said.

Looking up, she stifled a scream. It was Fr. Brian.

"Carter, what's wrong?" he said.

Sitting in the priest's office, Carter sipped her Irish Breakfast tea. Her hands were still shaking, and she had to be careful not to spill the hot liquid on herself. The room that was so foreign moments earlier was once again warm and familiar. And this time, she smelled his cologne, which comforted her.

"Again, my sincerest apologies," Fr. Brian said. "I was asked to handle a situation in a fifth-grade classroom. When I got there, the teacher insisted she hadn't called me."

"He looked exactly like you." She was on the verge of tears again. "I don't know what's happening to me."

"Have you spoken to Harlan Covington?"

"What?"

"It's all right. I know you and Sarah are assisting him." His expression turned serious. "I'm afraid there may be demonic forces at work here after all."

She laughed bitterly. "Ya think?" Then, "That was rude."

"I'm sure he's explained it to you. Demons can appear as anyone they wish—even a humble Irish priest. Unfortunately, my hands are tied since your experience doesn't relate directly to Ana Robles."

"But—"

"You have a strong sense of what is good and what isn't. Many people don't—they live in a fog. But you knew immediately something was wrong. Never doubt yourself."

She wiped away her tears. "He tried telling me that sometimes suicide was the only way."

"Satan's greatest weapon is despair. Because once we fall into such a state, he can deliver our souls to hell. I know the girl's death was a great shock to you. But whatever you do, don't despair."

"Is that what you think happened to her?"

"I don't know. Look, I realize you're not—you don't practice a religion. I said this the first time we met, and it bears repeating. Prayer is a powerful arrow in your quiver."

"But since I'm not Catholic..."

"Have you considered exploring Judaism?"

Taken aback, she looked at him sharply. "Wait, you're not gonna try and convert me?"

He laughed. "Of course not. Our job is to spread the Good News. It's up to the listener whether they follow. Matthew said it best in the Parable of the Sower."

"I'll think about it."

"If you like, I can put you in touch with a friend of mine—a rabbi. He's a wonderful human being. I'm sure you two would hit it off. By the way, his wife makes the best latkes."

Relieved, she placed her cup on the desk and got up. "Thanks for everything, Father."

He came around the desk. Then he took her gently by the shoulders and looked deep into her eyes. His were clear and sparkling—not at all like the other creature.

"In the meantime," he said, "I will pray for you—for your peace of mind and for your safety."

"Thank you so much."

Before she could stop herself, Carter hugged him. Then, her soul at peace, she left without looking back.

TWENTY

"Aunt Sarah?"

The familiar voice seemed to come from a distant place, like a sweet memory buried under soft piles of colorful yarn. Sarah held her wineglass, seeing yet not seeing what was inside. She'd thought after Joe returned, things would return to normal—whatever that was. Though he had been affectionate when they made love, she sensed something was different. Almost as if he were another person. Ridiculous. This wasn't *Invasion of the Body Snatchers*. He was the same person, only he was hiding something. He'd never kept anything from her as far as she knew. Why now?

Turning, she beheld the face of her beautiful niece. Had she grown since the last time they were all together? Her face seemed radiant, her hair like the sun as she sat perched on the chair, wearing her Notre Dame School uniform. The girl reminded her so much of Rachel at that age.

"What?"

"Earth to Sarah," her sister said.

"I must've checked out."

"I'll say. Eddie asked you a question hours ago."

"Oh, boy. What was it?"

Her father looked at her with those discerning eyes, which could cut through any bullshit she dished up. She prayed he wouldn't bring up their previous conversation. Sure, he'd promised not to. But Rachel and Katy were family. And often, families shared secrets. She took a large swig of her wine and pretended to be interested in the food.

"I was asking about Joe's dad," he said.

"He's better, thank God. They moved him to a private room. Joe's hoping he'll be able to go home soon."

"Who's going to look after him?" her sister said.

"I think Evelyn is arranging for a private nurse."

Eddie's eyes widened. "Sounds expensive."

She squeezed her niece's hand. "I need me some chisme. Tell me what's going on at school."

"Oh, you know, the usual. Got a C on my math test." She noted her mother's sidelong glance. "What? Math isn't my thing. Alexis got food poisoning—again. And..."

"And?"

"Oh, there's this boy in band—Richard. I don't know. He's always hanging around."

The sisters exchanged a look of concern.

"*And?*" Rachel said.

"And nothing. I just wish he'd stop bothering me."

"What exactly is he doing?" her grandfather said.

She groaned. "I don't want to talk about this anymore."

"Too late," The women said at the same time.

"Fine. He brings me stuff. Last week, it was a pack of Twizzlers, which I love, by the way."

"I know," her aunt said, overly serious.

"And because he knows I like to draw, he gave me this cool Japanese gel pen with some anime character on it. I think it's No-Face from *Spirited Away*. And yesterday, he left a book for me in the office."

"What kind of book?" her mother said, narrowing her eyes.

"Poetry."

"Hmm."

"Okay, so the boy likes her," Eddie said.

Katy's mouth fell open. "What? Ew!"

Sarah touched her sister's arm. "If he's bringing her poetry, I'm pretty sure you have nothing to worry about, Mom."

"Let's hope not."

"And if he gets out of line, tell me." She waggled her fingers at the girl. "I'll turn him into a ghost."

Laughing, Katy got up from the table. "I need to practice."

"I'm out too," her grandfather said. "Papers to grade. I'll clean up the kitchen later."

Rachel shooed him away. "Don't worry about it. Sarah and I can handle it."

"Gracias, mija."

"De nada."

Sarah cleared the table while her sister rinsed off the dishes and placed them into the dishwasher. Before long, the dulcet sounds of an alto saxophone wafted through the house as she warmed up with a series of accomplished scales.

"Kid's got talent," Sarah said. "Hey, I've been meaning to ask. Are we okay?"

Her sister stopped what she was doing. "I appreciate

you wanting to protect me. But I'm not a kid. I don't know what's going to happen between Lou and me—if anything. But it's nice being with someone, you know? I mean, you have Joe. Speaking of which, do you want to tell me what's going on?"

"Nothing. Everything. He's been acting strange ever since he got back."

"Give the guy a break. He's concerned about his father. And he can't be thrilled about you being back in action so soon."

"You're right. And then, there's Carter. I'm worried about her, Rache."

"How's she doing?"

"Not well."

"The other girl's death was tragic, but I didn't think they knew each other very well."

"Me neither. But they seemed to be, I don't know, crazy for each other."

"Any clue why she'd take her own life?"

"None."

"Is Carter staying at St. Rita's?"

"As far as I know. She and I are supposed to meet Harlan tomorrow to discuss next steps."

"I don't know if I trust him. From what you've said before—"

"He's fine. Turns out I misjudged him."

When they'd finished, Rachel refilled their wineglasses and headed for the living room. "And you? Are you fine?"

Sarah followed her. "I'm better now that Joe's back. Which reminds me." She lowered her voice. "You never mentioned anything about him and me to Katy, did you?"

"No way am I putting sophisticated ideas in her head.

As far as she knows, you're good friends who work together."

They didn't notice that the girl had stopped playing and was in the kitchen. When she walked out holding a bottle of water, she'd overheard the conversation.

"I knew it," she said and returned to her room to practice the first alto saxophone part to "Let It Go."

Rachel raised a finger. "I still say—"

"I know, I know. Why aren't we married? The eternal question. We'll probably end up buried next to each other. Maybe on our headstones, they can write *Why weren't they married?*"

Her sister giggled. "How about this? On his, *What do you want to do?* And on yours, *I don't know, what do you want to do?*" No reaction. "Oh, come on, not even a smile?"

"Don't quit your day job," Sarah said.

"How was dinner?" Joe said.

Sarah was in the bathroom, brushing her teeth. She had on the oversize Knicks jersey he'd given her. She rinsed and wiped her mouth with a hand towel.

"Fine. I think my niece has a boyfriend. Well, not an actual boyfriend, but..."

"What is she, nine?"

"Eleven. This is how it starts, my friend. First, it's poetry, then breaking up via text message with emojis."

"A little bitter for you."

"Bitter or realistic?"

She got into bed and found him shirtless, looking at his

phone. She had to admit, having him in her bed waiting for her was the best thing ever.

"Joe?" she said as she slid in under the covers.

"I refuse to recite any poetry."

She touched his bare arm. "Are you okay?" No answer. "I know the thing with your dad has been tough, but you seem a little distracted."

He set his phone on the nightstand and took her hands. Now she was getting worried.

"You're right," he said. "Seeing him in the hospital, lying there and barely conscious—it was hard. And the way it's affecting my mom... It did something to me."

"I can't even imagine."

"But the whole time, I was thinking about us."

Her heart stirred. "Really?"

"I don't know what's going to happen. But I want us to be together always."

She melted in his arms and kissed him. Somewhere, Gary meowed. He probably wanted more food. They ignored the cat, and as she fell onto her back, Joe's touch and his kisses electrified her.

"I want..." she said between kisses. "Oh, I want..."

Sarah sat next to the window at The Cracked Pot, watching the morning street traffic, as she waited for her friend. The last time she was here, the terrifying demoniac, filled with all the hate in the world, had glowered at her. And she worried he might make another appearance. *Better not—too beautiful a morning.*

She felt phenomenal despite her lack of actual sleep.

Her lover had been strong and untiring, bringing her to ecstasy twice, then again in the early morning as they showered together. All thoughts of Joe being distant had evaporated. She had him back, and she was happy.

Carter slid into the booth opposite her and groaned. The poor girl must have been exhausted. Her face looked drawn, and her pale skin was almost deathly.

"Hey," she said.

"Excuse me for saying this, but you look awful. Maybe you should see a doctor."

"I haven't been sleeping."

Instead of making small talk, Carter told her about her encounter with Fr. Brian's evil twin. When she was finished, Sarah's heart was pounding.

"I've read about things like that," she said. "And he was identical to the priest?"

"Sarah, it was him."

"What do you think it means?"

"I keep thinking he wanted to keep me from finding out the truth. Also—don't laugh—it seemed like it was pumping me for information."

"Or he's afraid of you?"

"Me? I doubt it."

"So, are you working later?"

"I asked for the day off." A server brought her a coffee. "Thanks, Mark."

"No prob. Hey, you don't—"

Sarah cleared her throat in his direction, and he scurried away as her friend warmed her hands around her mug.

"So, game plan?" Carter said.

"Okay, I'm just going to say it. I don't like the idea of you staying at the shelter with Carrie."

The girl showed her the bracelet. "Protected, remember?"

"I know, but."

"And besides, we need to solve this. After what happened at the parish office, I believe it more than ever. And with Harlan's help, I know we can."

"When did you become so gung ho about paranormal investigation?"

"I don't know. It's partly because of what happened to Nellie. But also, I remember how it felt when I was a kid."

"How what felt?"

"You know. Unraveling mysteries? Discovering the truth. It's been three months since the Peter Moody case. And well, I guess I miss it. Don't you?"

"Maybe a little."

"Come on, admit it. When Rupinder told you her story, you could've given her a lot of sympathy and done nothing. But you were in from the get-go."

"Yeah, I was. I suppose I can't help it. But that's me. I'm not the one who lost..."

"It's okay. Sure, losing Nellie was hard. I can't imagine what I'd be like if we'd been a couple. But you lost someone too—your friend Alyssa. And your mom. And yet, you're still at it."

"Only because Alyssa won't leave me alone."

"That's a cheap excuse, and you know it. You were made for this, and so am I."

"Fine, you win. So, what are we doing about Harlan?"

"I'm going to do whatever he says."

Sarah took the girl's hand. "You know what? I love ya, kid."

Carter blushed. "That goes for me double. Let's do this."

Sarah pulled into Harlan's driveway. An unfamiliar car, which looked like a rental, was parked on the street. Mary greeted the women at the front door, and when they walked in, she directed them to the dining room. Charlie Beeks chatted with the lawyer over the remnants of breakfast.

As she and Carter found places at the table, the men rose, making Sarah feel as if she'd fallen into an old black-and-white movie.

"Hello, boys," she said, using her favorite line from the television series *Supernatural*.

"It's great to finally meet you two in person." The PI extended his hand warmly.

After getting coffee, the women took their seats.

"Charlie was just telling me..." Harlan shook his head. "Counsel is testifying." Then to the PI, "Proceed."

Charlie consulted his notebook. "I've been looking into our friend Grace Zielinski. At first, I discovered nothing out of the ordinary."

He reached into his messenger bag and pulled out a manila folder.

"This is a copy of the background report the program manager, Irene MacAllister, ordered as part of the hiring process. It describes a woman who'd lived in Seattle for many years, working for Mary's Gift, a Catholic social services agency. So, I did some more digging.

"She owned a home, had no credit card debt, and never learned to drive. Also, she was in the hospital briefly when she had a procedure to remove endometrial polyps. And she has no other family."

"Wait," the girl said. "She doesn't drive?"

"She didn't when they ran the report, which was around seven years ago. Here's where it gets interesting."

He grabbed another folder and removed what looked like lab test results and showed them to the women.

"According to the hospital where Grace had her surgery, her blood type is O Positive. Also, she suffers from adult onset diabetes."

As the men exchanged a glance, Sarah rolled her eyes. "Well, are you going to tell us?"

He cleared his throat. "About a month ago, she went to the doctor complaining of headaches. They ran a series of tests and determined that she suffers from high blood pressure."

"Maybe from the stress of the job," Carter said.

"They did a full work-up." He pointed at the results. "This time, no diabetes was detected. And there's something else. According to the tests, her blood type is AB negative."

Sarah felt her stomach drop. "So, what you're saying is the woman we met at the parish office..."

Her friend cut in. "The one who drove herself there..."

The lawyer folded his hands, and glancing at the PI, said, "Short of a miraculous cure and a change in blood type, the woman calling herself Grace Zielinski is an imposter."

The girl scoffed. "Perfect. So, now what?"

Harlan stood and got himself a bottle of water. "I'm sending Charlie to Seattle to investigate further. It's possible there was a mix-up, but I need to be sure."

Now Sarah was confused. Hadn't Lou said she'd be working with these guys while Carter was occupied at St. Rita's?

"I want to go too," she said.

Chuckling, the PI made a show of pulling out his wallet and handing his employer a crisp one-dollar bill.

She glared at Harlan. "What's going on?"

"I bet Charlie you'd volunteer, but he insisted otherwise. I can't tell you how delighted I am. You two are invaluable to me and our cause."

Laughing, she shook her head. "I need to work on not being so predictable. What will Carter do while we're away?"

He looked at Sarah's friend. "I'd like you to study Nellie's notes and video recordings of the sessions she conducted. They might hold clues to Ana's illness."

"But I don't know anything about psychology," she said.

"You'll do fine—you're smart." Then to Sarah, "I've already purchased the plane tickets, and I made reservations at the W in Seattle. You leave tonight."

She exhaled through pursed lips. "It shouldn't be a problem."

As she and Carter walked outside, Sarah realized there was a problem.

How do I tell Joe?

Sarah finished arranging the takeout she'd purchased at El 600. The white tapas plates looked elegant and inviting. She was about to pour the wine when she heard Joe's truck outside. A moment later, he walked in through the front door. When he saw her travel bag, he made a face. Ignoring his reaction, she kissed him. Then she took his hand and led him into the dining room.

"I didn't have time to make dinner," she said. "Why don't you wash your hands so we can eat?"

He took a sip of wine and went into the guest bathroom. A moment later, he returned and sat. She said a silent blessing and tried a dish.

"This is so familiar," he said. "Only this time, it's you who's leaving."

He grabbed a plate and ate without enjoyment. Though he rarely got headaches, he felt an intense throbbing at his temples.

"Harlan needs me to go to Seattle with Charlie." She didn't make eye contact.

"The PI? When did you find out?"

"Today."

He sat there for several seconds without moving. Why would she go away? Hadn't she practically begged him to come home? Now that he was home, he'd decided to tell her about Leah Talman. In fact, he'd planned to tell her tonight.

"What's in Seattle?" he said, his voice tuneless.

"We think a woman may have been murdered."

He brought down his fist, nearly knocking over his wineglass. "Dammit, Sarah! Is this how it's going to be from now on? You running off on these little adventures? Putting yourself at risk?"

"Harlan needs my help."

"And what if something happens?"

"It won't. We're interviewing respectable people."

"Is Carter going with you?"

"She'll be at St. Rita's. Look, if this is about me being safe, Charlie's an ex-cop. I need to do this."

"Why though?"

"Because..." Looking away, she sighed. "Because it's who I am."

"Have a safe trip."

Grabbing his jacket, he marched out the front door. A moment later, he backed his truck out of the driveway, tires squealing. Gary trotted in and rubbed his back on the leg of her chair. She looked at him, her eyes glistening.

"I did nothing wrong here," she said.

TWENTY-ONE

As Sarah settled into her first-class seat next to Charlie, she replayed the earlier scene with her ex-husband. She'd never seen him so angry and wondered about their future together. Clearly, he was worried about her. But he'd known about her abilities for years. Why was he so upset about it now? *Because you almost died, stupid.* They'd had rough patches before. She'd call him when they landed.

And as if her personal troubles weren't enough, she'd left Carter behind to face whatever it was lurking in the women's shelter. She reminded herself that her friend was strong. She seemed to have abilities the dark forces they were battling feared—gifts going far beyond the bracelet. Before parting, the women had promised to keep each other informed. If either was in any real danger, the other would go to them immediately.

She glanced at her traveling companion, who read a small black bible. "I'll bet it comes in handy in your line of work."

"It does." He laid down the book. "I won't bore you with

the things I've uncovered over the years. Let's just say I've seen the depth and breadth of humanity."

"Does it get any easier?"

"I find I'm always surprised, which may be one reason Harlan picked me for this assignment. I try to keep an open mind. Sister Elizabeth told me something when we left that godforsaken shack in the forest. She said, *Something evil happened here.* Simply put, and I agree."

"So, have you known Harlan long?"

"This is the first time we've worked together."

"Interesting. Do you think he Googled PIs and found your name?"

He laughed. "Hardly. I don't advertise. My business is based strictly on referrals."

"I wonder who told him about you."

"He wouldn't say, but I suspect it was an old friend of mine—a priest assigned to the Vatican. What about you? How do you know Harlan?"

Now it was her turn to laugh. "Our first meeting wasn't exactly pleasant. I was helping the police chief with a cold case, and we met with Harlan since he'd been the family's attorney."

She gave him the highlights of the Peter Moody case, including the part where she almost died.

"I have to say, in all my years... Ravens, you say?"

"Ravens. When I agreed to help St. Rita's, our paths crossed again. And now, here I am."

"I can tell he respects you. And Carter."

The flight attendant set down their meals. Sarah made the Sign of the Cross and said a blessing. It was nice seeing her companion do the same.

"Any idea what we'll find in Seattle?" she said.

"The truth, I hope. I'm not clear on why Grace Zielinski

—or whoever she is—would seek out a mentally unstable woman from Guatemala and bring her all the way back here."

"To control her?"

"Okay, but to what end?"

She recalled the apparition she and her friend had seen at the women's shelter. For some reason, it was drawn to Ana. She thought again about demonic possession. Fr. Brian had explained the criteria the Church uses, and so far, the only thing they'd observed directly relating to the woman was her aversion to Carter's bracelet. Not exactly a slam dunk.

They spent the rest of the meal talking about other things—travel, relationships. He told her about his late wife. They'd been married forty-three years when she had her stroke. She never woke up and died in a coma. Sarah thought of Joe's father and wondered if he was headed for the same fate. The PI shared with her his plan to retire in San Diego.

"It's going to be a lot of books, golf, and all the television shows I've missed over the years," he said.

"Sounds like a great life."

"You sound worried."

"I was thinking about the hellhole you and Sister Elizabeth found in the forest. And I remember how it felt."

"Really? How?"

"It happened when I touched the journal you sent us. It was like being there."

"Pretty handy talent. Could've used you in New Hampshire when I was a homicide detective."

"Wait, you're from New Hampshire?"

"Born and raised in Plainfield."

"Shouldn't you have a New England accent?"

"Worked hard to get rid of it. Seems people take me more seriously when I don't say things like, 'Open the doh-wah so we can go down cellah and see the body.'"

She laughed. "So, what happened in New Hampshire?"

"Oh, boy. Now, there's a story. We'd arrested a woman—a novelist—who wrote books about serial killers. Somewhere along the line, she went batshit crazy and began committing the murders she described in her books. Not very original. When we arrested her, she said she couldn't remember anything."

"Sounds to me like she was a nutcase."

"I thought so too. Until I watched her levitate two feet above her chair in the interrogation room."

"Seriously?"

"There's more. After her little trick, she stared as if seeing right through me. And I remember her voice. Gives me chills thinking about it. It wasn't like a woman's at all—it was deep and guttural-sounding. And she was laughing. Then she turned serious and said, *Danny sends his regards.*"

"Who's Danny?"

"My late nephew. He died of leukemia when he was seventeen. There's no way she could've known."

"Wow. So, what did you do?"

"Do? I prayed. Later, I quit the force and moved to California with my wife. We ended up in Orange County."

"I can't imagine what you must think of this case."

"If I hadn't witnessed the event in New Hampshire, I would've dismissed everything to do with Ana Robles as a product of silly superstition. But I know better now."

"So, you're a believer?"

"Yes." He held up his bible. "Which makes this even more important."

After the meal service, the cabin lights dimmed. Sarah closed her eyes. As soon as she did, she was out.

The ride from Sea-Tac to Seattle was uneventful. As they traveled north on WA-509 in the rented Escalade, all Sarah saw through the rain was blackness. She'd tried reaching Joe, but her calls kept going to voicemail. Maybe he was still angry. *He needs some time, that's all.*

When they reached the city, they had to pass through decaying neighborhoods populated by the homeless huddled in clusters, trying to stay warm. Charlie slowed to a stop at the intersection. The light turned green, and he accelerated. Out of nowhere, a delivery truck shot past, barely missing them. Her chest tight, she turned to see where the vehicle had gone, but it was nowhere in sight. They drove the rest of the way in silence.

She missed Joe so much and decided to try him again when she got to her room. As they approached the elevators in the parking garage, she thought she saw something moving in the shadows. She didn't like this city and would be relieved when they were on a plane headed for LAX.

She peered into the darkness as they stood in the elevator waiting for the doors to close. Someone was there —she was sure of it. There was an outline of a man. He wasn't moving, but instead waited. She exhaled as the elevator doors closed.

When she entered her room and switched on more lights, she noticed a gift basket sitting on the desk. Excited, she tossed her bag and purse on the bed and hurried over. As she tore open the red cellophane, she discovered a box of

Godiva chocolates, a selection of fresh fruit, and a bottle of Talisker with two crystal whiskey glasses.

"Joe," she said, wiping her eyes.

She kicked off her shoes and made two drinks. Then, she called him. "So unexpected. I poured two glasses. Care to join me?"

"I wish. About before—obviously, I'm an idiot."

"You're not, babe."

"You haven't called me that since we were married."

"Maybe it's time I got in the habit again."

Silence. Then, "Everything okay?"

"So far."

She didn't want to mention their near-accident or the dark stranger in the parking structure. Another silence fell, and she sensed there was something between them that wasn't right.

"Did you feed Gary?" she said.

"Of course. I miss you."

"Me too."

"Sarah, listen." *Here it comes.* "There's something we need to talk about when you get back."

She felt cold suddenly. "Is it bad?"

"We can discuss it then. I have to go."

Reluctantly, she said goodnight. Feeling unsettled, she took a sip of the Talisker. Was he planning to leave? *I'm being ridiculous.* They'd been friends too many years. It had to be something else. She eyed the chocolate. *Oh hell.*

Six pieces of candy later, she tossed aside the box. She wanted to hit the gym early before the business travelers took it over. After brushing her teeth and washing her face, she slipped under the covers. She thought again about the stranger in the shadows. Reaching for her purse, she removed her rosary and said a decade for the man she loved before drifting off as the wind and the rain pummeled the land outside.

Carter had gotten a late start in the morning and didn't have time for breakfast. She was starving. When she arrived at the women's shelter, the first thing she saw was a rental truck parked in front. Two men in T-shirts already soaked with sweat carried boxes of clothes and other belongings to the vehicle. Heidi and Tim stood off to the side, observing the constant procession. They acknowledged the girl as she approached them carrying her bag.

"Thanks for coming so early," the director said.

"No worries. Hey, Tim."

He reached for her bag. "Want me to take that in for you?"

"Sure, thanks."

After the cop had gone inside, Heidi took Carter's hand. "I don't know what Harlan thought we'd accomplish here, but I'm so glad you came. Will Sarah be here later?"

"She's out of town on an investigation."

"I must say, you gals take your work seriously."

"Should we go inside?"

They headed up the steps, barely avoiding a mover whose arms were loaded with boxes.

"All the residents moved out last night," the director said. "All except Ana."

"How's she doing?"

"Hard to say. She never made any friends, and I'm worried she'll withdraw even more once it sinks in how everyone else has left. Roxanne is coming by later to conduct a therapy session. I'm hopeful she can get through to her patient."

As they stood outside Heidi's office, the girl gazed off down the hall. "I'd like to get started on Nellie's research," she said. "Would you mind if I went in there now?"

"Of course not. I take it you know—"

"It's this way, right?"

"Shout if you need anything. Lunch begins at 11:30."

"Okay, thanks."

Nellie's scent filled her office, and Carter's heart ached. She hadn't considered the emotions being in here would stir and focused on what she had to do. A computer keyboard and monitor sat on the desk. The computer itself stood on the floor under the desk. As in Nellie's apartment, there were messy piles of research everywhere. Picturing her beautiful, disorganized lover, she wiped away the tears.

Her hunger had gotten the better of her, and she thought there might at least be some coffee in the kitchen. The room seemed cold and vacant, though there was plenty of light streaming in through the tall windows. Shuddering, she dismissed the memory of Marcy holding up her mangled hand. A Latina, who looked to be in her fifties, was busy prepping for lunch.

The girl continued toward the kitchen and spotted Ana standing against the wall. She seemed so small, like a lost child. Though Carter recalled the awful images of the woman's husband on top of her in the shack, now she seemed. innocent. A feeling of compassion overcame her, and she crossed to Ana, not at all sure what she would say.

"Excuse me. Are you okay?"

The diminutive Mayan woman looked up at her. Her teeth were extraordinarily white, and she didn't blink. The girl's heart raced.

"You are going to die in here," Ana said and marched off.

Climbing out of the Escalade, Sarah walked up to the house in Beacon Hill with Charlie. Though it was modest, the architecture was pleasing. It was a two-story traditional, faded green with white trim. Barren trees and empty flower beds surrounded the building. All appeared gray and lifeless. When they'd reached the door, he rang the bell. An Asian girl answered, her shiny black hair held in place with pretty barrettes.

Sarah crouched. "Are your parents at home?"

She nodded and ran off. A moment later, a well-dressed woman, who looked to be in her early forties, waited for an explanation.

"Hello," he said. "I'm Charlie Beeks, a private investigator. And this is my associate, Sarah Greene. Are you Mrs. Park?"

Warily, she looked them over. "Yes."

"We'd like to have a few words, if you don't mind. It's about Grace Zielinski."

They showed her their IDs, and she invited them in. He was about to enter when Sarah nudged him, pointing at the shoes outside the door. Then she removed hers, and he did the same.

She gazed at the interior as they followed. Though not extravagant, the living room was comfortable. She especially liked the alpaca sofa cushions, one of which featured a Korean mud horse. A beautiful antique mantel clock ticked softly, giving the place a sense of peace.

"Would you like tea?" the homeowner said.

The PI was about to respond when Sarah nodded. "That would be lovely."

Mrs. Park gestured for them to sit and left the room.

"Why do I get the feeling you know something I don't?" he said.

She leaned over. "A Korean family used to live next to us when I was growing up. I learned a ton about good manners."

It wasn't long before the woman returned with a tray with four steaming mugs on it. Her daughter had followed and helped her mother arrange the tray on the coffee table.

"Please," Mrs. Park said.

Thanking her, they accepted the tea. The girl handed her mother a mug and kept the last one for herself. He removed a photo of Grace from his bag and handed it to Mrs. Park.

"Do you recognize this woman?" he said.

She squinted at the photograph. "No."

"Well, you bought the house from her, right?"

"No."

"Are you positive?" Sarah said.

"I am sure. The lady who owned this place was nice. This one is..." She said something to her daughter in Korean.

"My mother says she looks mean."

He cleared his throat. "Did Ms. Zielinski happen to mention why she was selling her house? Or what her plans were?"

"Mm. She said she don't like the cold winters anymore and wanted to live in Arizona. A retirement community, I think."

"Do you recall which one?"

"I am sorry."

"When was the last time you saw her?"

"Emma was very small. Eum, seven years ago? After we move in. Ah! Because it was my daughter's birthday, and we were going out for the day."

"Do you remember the date?"

"January eleven. Emma was two."

"Did Ms. Zielinski say why she stopped by?" Sarah said.

"Was going to have dinner with a friend from work, and she wanted to see us. Make sure we were fine. She was so nice. Good Christian woman."

"And that was the last time you saw her?" he said.

"Yes, like I told you. Is she all right?"

"We won't trouble you anymore."

As they got to their feet, Sarah walked over to the fireplace and examined the mantel clock. Then she turned to Mrs. Park. "Is this yours?"

"Belong to Ms. Zielinski. She gave us many things."

Feeling herself drawn to the antique, Sarah touched it.

She was in the middle of a forest surrounded by conifer and deciduous trees. The air was biting. Moonlight shone through branches that quivered in a sharp wind. Strangely, her surroundings were tranquil. But there was something else. Directly ahead, there was a tree trunk, its top bent completely over and back into the earth. It formed a huge upside-down U.

As she moved toward it, a voice whispered something inside her head, the words indistinct. Turning, she saw rays of yellow light falling on what looked like an opening in the foliage. She moved closer and crawled through. Inside, it was still. Then something grabbed her ankle.

Startling, she looked down and discovered a hand

jutting out of the frozen earth. It was covered in dead leaves and insects. Wisps of skin clung to the white bones like gossamer, and spiky fingertips dug into her flesh. It resembled a woman's hand. Releasing Sarah, the fingers slowly splayed to the sound of brittle, grinding bones.

And then, the index finger pointed at something.

Sarah and Charlie sat at a corner table at Starbucks. Outside, cars and pedestrians made their way through the rain matter-of-factly. She wasn't hungry and picked at her salad.

"The tree," she said. "I can't get it out of my mind."

He slid his pen and notebook over to her. "Do you think you could draw it?"

"I can try. My niece is the real artist in the family."

"Take your time."

Lightly, she made black strokes and carefully drew the outline of the tree trunk. She tried capturing the surrounding area—the isolation of the place—but she wasn't successful. Finally, she handed him the notebook.

"You'd think someone who studied art history would be better at this."

"What about the hollow?"

"No way, pal. But I'm sure there's someone buried there."

"Are there any other details about this place?"

"I don't think so."

He wrote in the notebook. "What was the ground like?"

"Almost frozen. I keep thinking it might've been a trail.

There were sharp rocks. And a dusting of snow on the ground."

"What about the sky?"

"It was night."

He gazed out the window at the oppressing gray of the cloud-swollen sky. "Chilly?"

"Freezing."

He got out his laptop and opened Google Maps.

"What are you looking for?"

"Photos to help you." He slid the laptop around so she could see.

"Mt. Rainier National Park?"

"It's a long shot, but a lot of what you described can be found there along the various trails."

"There are a million other forests." She scanned the images on a tourist website. "Not ringing any bells."

"I'll make some calls to see if we can get a lead on the tree. There can't be too many like it. Meantime, I'd like you to work on remembering more of what you saw or heard. For now, we should focus our efforts on our mystery woman."

She thought again of the images from her vision. It was the hand—the bleached, bony thing. And the pointing finger.

What does it want me to see?

TWENTY-TWO

Sarah stepped out of the Toyota Prius that had brought her to the house in Beacon Hill. It was late afternoon, and the rain had stopped. Though Charlie had advised her not to trouble the family further, she insisted she needed to dig deeper into the mystery of Grace Zielinski's presumed disappearance. Eventually, he relented. While he met with the director of Mary's Gift, she planned to learn as much as possible as long as Mrs. Park was willing to cooperate.

As she walked up the steps, she wished Carter were with her. She'd come to rely on her friend for strength, and also for her keen insight. After adjusting her clothes and hair, she rang the doorbell and waited. This time, the little girl's mother answered. Sarah extended her hand.

"I don't mean to bother you, Mrs. Park. May I come in?"

The other woman said nothing as Sarah removed her shoes and went inside.

In the living room, she gazed at her surroundings again, hoping to spot something to help her visualize the location of Grace's body. Mrs. Park stood nearby, her hands clasped behind her.

"I knew you would return," she said.

"Oh?"

"When the man—"

"Charlie."

"When he did not answer my question."

"Which question?"

"I ask him if Grace was all right."

From the petite Korean woman's tearful expression, Sarah knew how deeply she cared about the former owner. "I didn't want to be the one to tell you. We think Grace may be dead."

Mrs. Park covered her mouth. As Emma drifted into the room, she noticed the distressed look on her mother's face and went to her. Mrs. Park sat her down and hugged her. Then, looking at her guest, she pointed at the mantel.

"You saw something when you touched the clock."

"Yes."

Nodding thoughtfully, she patted her daughter's knee and rose. "You come with me now."

She said something to Emma in Korean. As the girl eagerly obeyed, her mother led their guest upstairs to the landing. There in the middle of the ceiling was an attic door. Emma reappeared carrying a long metal pole with a hook at the end.

"Umma," she said.

Mrs. Park took it from her and used it to open the door. When the metal stairs appeared, she reached for a ring and pulled them down. Laying the hook on the floor, she climbed up nimbly.

Sarah scrutinized the opening and turned to the girl, who twisted from side to side. "You first."

Emma shook her head. "I'm not allowed."

"Fine." Taking a breath, Sarah climbed. "Good thing I'm not afraid of heights."

She beheld the attic, which was filled with lamps, artwork, and stacks of storage boxes.

"All this stuff belong to Grace," the Korean woman said. "She was supposed to send for it after she moved. Maybe you can find something in here to help?"

As Sarah perused the boxes, she came across one labeled PHOTOS.

Charlie sat in the social services office waiting room, texting Harlan a quick status update. Parents—mostly women—with their noisy children surrounded him. When he looked up, he saw a little Latina with huge brown eyes and braids observing him.

"I like your bow," he said.

She raced back to her mother. A woman wearing a pantsuit approached him.

"Mr. Beeks? I'm Carla Wainwright. We can talk in my office."

After shaking hands, she led him through a secure door to a large open area where people in cubicles were on the phone or typing on computer keyboards. Continuing on, she directed him to her office.

"I appreciate you taking the time to see me," he said.

"To be perfectly frank, I was surprised you wanted to talk about Grace Zielinski. She hasn't worked here for many years."

"I am aware." He opened his notebook. "Was Grace well liked here?"

"Strange question. Yes, absolutely. She was one of the kindest people I know. Gave a thousand percent to her clients—especially the children. She was always handing out candy and little toys she used to pick up at the 99 Cent Store."

"Did she get along well with her coworkers?"

"Grace was friendly to everyone. There was another woman who came to work here. I'd say she and Grace were trying to become friends."

"Interesting way of putting it."

"If you'd met her, you would understand."

"Does she still work here?"

"She left around the same time Grace retired to Arizona."

"Would you mind telling me her name?"

"I would need to see some ID first."

"Of course." She examined the card. "Her name was Laurel Diamanté."

"*Diamanté.* Like the brooch?"

"I suppose."

He wrote down the name and flipped to the inside cover of his notebook, revealing a photograph of Grace. He handed it to the director.

"Is this Ms. Diamanté?"

"Why, yes. And she was no Grace."

"What do you mean?"

"It's hard to explain. She was odd—volatile even. Not at first, though. When she interviewed for the job, she seemed pleasant and knew her stuff. But after a while... Sorry, it makes me uncomfortable talking about a person's behavior when they're not here to defend themselves."

"I understand perfectly, but this is important."

"Okay. Sometimes she would get agitated over nothing at all. For example, every year, we have a May crowning ceremony. The children love it. As they were singing 'Immaculate Mary,' Laurel lost her temper. She said their voices were too loud. Then she left the building, complaining of a migraine."

"Unusual for someone who works with children."

"Now that I think about it, the incident may have been why Grace took an interest in her. I think she was trying to help Laurel become a better caseworker. Hmm..."

"What is it? Did you remember something?"

"I seem to recall the two of them were going to have dinner together on Grace's last day. I assumed Laurel was trying to pay her back for her kindness."

"And do you know if they ever did?"

"Afraid not. I never saw Grace again after her last day."

"Did she have any hobbies or interests?"

"Oh, yes. She loved the outdoors. And she couldn't wait for summer to go hiking."

"Any particular spots she liked?"

"Well, I know she loved the Longmire area of Mt. Rainier National Park." She laughed. "She was always showing us photos of her latest adventure."

He turned to the drawing Sarah had made in his notebook and handed it to her. "Does that tree look familiar to you?"

She squinted at it. "It's possible I've seen it, but I can't be sure."

He put away everything and got up. "This has been extremely helpful."

"Mr. Beeks, did something happen to Grace?"

"As you can imagine, my work is confidential. But I can tell you we are looking into her current whereabouts."

"She's not in Arizona?"

"We're uncertain."

Turning to leave, he glanced at a set of photos on the wall and walked over. One was a portrait of the staff and included Grace. Laurel Diamanté stood next to her. She was shorter and wore a stern expression.

"Would it be all right if I borrowed this? I promise to send it back."

"Sure, if you think it'll help."

"Thank you again for your time," he said, shaking her hand.

Charlie stepped onto the street and considered the dark clouds. A stiff wind sent leaves and debris hurtling as he made his way to the parking structure. He planned to pick up Sarah from Beacon Hill and hoped the rain would hold off long enough for them to return to the hotel.

As he approached his vehicle, he spotted a heavyset man of undetermined age standing across from him. Despite the cold, he wore a light jacket, jeans, and workman's boots. He stared at the PI, the belligerence on his features startlingly specific.

Though Charlie almost never thought about the weapon he carried, his hand reached for it. As he did, someone grabbed him and spun him around. Before he could shout for help, he was on the ground, staring up at the man with the angry face. Another man stood next to him. He resembled a weasel, his teeth small and sharp.

"What do you want?"

"Delivering a message," the larger one said. "The lawyer will understand."

In the weak light of the parking structure, Charlie

thought he saw their eyes darken until they were solid black. The weasel-like man kicked him in the ribs, making his victim cry out. Rolling onto his side, he endured more blows, and to his horror, realized they meant to kill him.

Steeling himself against their repeated assaults, he managed to slip his hand into his jacket. Relieved, he felt the leather holster. Taking hold of his gun, he fell onto his back and fired a round at each of his assailants. Howling in pain, they limped off, leaving twin blood trails.

"What in God's name were those things?" Charlie said.

Sarah stood near the front window, looking at the empty street under a brooding sky. She was glad she'd found what she was looking for and was eager to share the details with Charlie. Mrs. Park had been so patient, and Sarah decided she would send Emma a present when she returned home. It rained as the black Escalade pulled into the driveway.

"Okay, I'm leaving!" Sarah said.

The mother and daughter stepped out of the kitchen and came toward her.

"Thanks for everything."

"Are you sure you don't want the other photos?"

"I have what I need."

Crouching, Sarah put her hand on Emma's face and brushed the hair from her eyes. Then she stood and hugged the kind woman.

"Good luck, Sarah," Mrs. Park said.

She ran to the car. The passenger door was already open. As she fastened her seatbelt, she saw his scuffed shoes and torn pant leg. The PI backed out and headed toward the main road.

"What happened to you?" she said.

"I slipped and fell." He peered through the beating windshield wipers. "Any luck back there?"

"As a matter of fact. I have a photo that might help. You?"

"I got some good intelligence." As he turned the wheel, he cried out.

"Okay, what is going on?"

He side-eyed her and saw she was serious. "I ran into some trouble in the parking structure. Two me attacked me."

"Oh, shit. Do you need a doctor?"

"I'm fine. Just need a hot shower and some food."

"Men," she said as they made their way through the downpour.

Facing the mirror in his hotel bathroom, the PI gingerly touched his damaged ribs and winced. The hot shower had helped, but he was in a lot of pain. Slowly, he put on his clothes and sat on the bed. How in the world would he get his shoes on? His phone vibrated, and he looked over. It was a Seattle area code. He took the call.

"This is Charlie."

"Mr. Beeks? It's Carla Wainwright. I hope I'm not calling too late."

"Not at all. What can I do for you?"

"This is going to sound silly, but I kept thinking about

that tree of yours. I did a little digging on my own and, well, I think I may have located it."

Straightening up, he reached for his notebook on the bed. "Go on."

"It's on the Trail of the Shadows in Longmire. I can text you a photo."

"Fantastic—thank you so much. Speak soon."

A moment later, he received a text message. When he opened it, he saw the photograph. The tree was nearly identical to the drawing. A sudden muscle spasm caused him to drop his phone. Reaching to pick it up, he cried out in pain.

"I've had worse," he said without conviction.

Sarah abhorred the interior of the hotel's restaurant—its trendy black-and-white furniture, rainbow lighting, and the most unattractive light fixtures she'd ever seen. The total effect looked like the mad ravings of a Danish interior designer on Ecstasy. But she and Charlie settled on this place because he was in too much pain to go out.

He'd forwarded her the photo of the tree, and she was looking at it when their food arrived. She had ordered the ribeye. He'd gotten a steak salad.

"It's the same tree—I'm positive," she said.

"So far, so good."

As he opened his notebook, she recognized the photo she'd taken from the house in Beacon Hill. It showed Grace —the real Grace—on a hike. When she touched the photograph in the attic, she was transported there with the gentle woman, feeling the warmth of the day and smelling pine. She sensed this was Grace's favorite place in the world.

He returned the photo to his notebook. When he looked up again, his dinner companion was watching him.

"What is it?" he said.

"I can't stop thinking about those men who attacked you. And you say they mentioned Harlan?"

"One said they were delivering a message."

"How strange. Do you think they know about our investigation?"

"I'm sure of it." He shuddered. "And those eyes."

"Black? I've seen them too in Dos Santos."

"What are they?"

"Demoniacs. Hey, are you sure you're okay? From what you said, they worked you over pretty good."

"Might have a couple cracked ribs. Guess I should see a doctor when we get back. Look, I don't pretend to understand the paranormal or occult or whatever you want to call it. But who would send these things?"

"I don't know. But I'm beginning to think it has to do with Dos Santos. Harlan told me once the evil there is spreading like a cancer."

He became thoughtful. "If that's true, then Laurel Diamanté might be connected to it."

"Which means Ana is a part of it."

"I did some checking on our friend Laurel and came up with nothing. No Social Security Number, no driver's license, and no passport."

"So, is it safe to say we think she murdered Grace?"

"So far, I've been working on a theory purely based on my years in law enforcement. I'd love to run it by your friend Lou to get his thoughts."

"Okay, so let's hear it."

"We know Grace was set to meet a friend for dinner. Mrs. Park said so, and Carla Wainwright confirmed the friend was Laurel Diamanté."

"But Laurel was not her friend and planned to kill her."

He picked at his salad. "Right. She needed to assume Grace's identity."

"Why?"

"Not sure. But we know she moved to Los Angeles, got a job as a caseworker, and later traveled to Guatemala. So my idea is this—she and the real Grace met as planned. And Laurel murdered her."

"But wouldn't there be witnesses?"

"Not if the killer was smart. She could've drugged her victim first. Pretty easy to do. Slip something into Grace's food. The murderer wouldn't want to waste time. So, she takes Grace somewhere local yet out of the way."

"Like a national park," she said. "But this is all conjecture."

"Unfortunately. Unless we can find witnesses, the only way to know for sure is to get Laurel to confess."

"I've met the woman, and I'm pretty sure anything she's guilty of she'll take to the grave."

"The important thing now is to retrieve the body."

"Well, now we know the general area, but won't it take forever to dig all around there?"

"I've been in touch with a company, which claims it can locate a body using GPR."

"Which is?"

"Ground Penetrating Radar. Of course, we need to go to law enforcement, but it shouldn't be a problem. I have a friend in the Seattle PD who I think can help us. And if Harlan covers all the costs, we should be fine."

She took a swallow of her pinot noir. "When do you think we can do it?"

"It'll take days, weeks to arrange."

Such a disappointment. She had an overwhelming urge to find Grace and put her soul to rest.

"I'm pretty sure I can locate the body," she said.

He gaped at her. "You're not serious?"

"Why don't we head out there tomorrow?"

"It'll be slow going, what with all the rain and the mud. We'd need the right clothes and shoes. And I don't think I'm in any shape to hike."

"Then I need Carter. After dinner, let's call Harlan and give him the news." She saw his expression. "You seem doubtful."

"Do I?" He tried laughing and groaned from the pain.

"Okay, this is ridiculous. You, my friend, are seeing a doctor. Now."

He didn't argue. She came around the table and helped him up. When they'd reached the hotel's front entrance, she headed toward the first car in line at the taxi stand and helped Charlie into the backseat.

"The nearest emergency room," Sarah said to the driver.

TWENTY-THREE

Lou ignored his complaining stomach as he approached the front door. Sarah's warning played in his head. *And if you break her heart, I'll make you suffer.* What did that even mean? Though she'd since softened her stance, he worried he might make a mistake and suffer the unknown consequences. He carried a box of long-stem yellow roses under his arm. The florist had encouraged him to go with red, but he was afraid the symbolism would send the wrong message.

He struggled to remember the last time he'd dated. When the faded memories finally dislodged themselves from some disused corner of his caffeine-addled brain, they brightened into full color, which made his palms sweat.

Becky Driscoll.

She was a cop at the Santa Barbara PD who worked dispatch. They'd flirted on and off for months after she transferred from LA. She was an attractive woman with a sharp sense of humor. And though she was ten years his junior, he'd had no problem imagining a long-term relationship with her. Unfortunately, it wasn't meant to be.

Clearing his throat, he rang the doorbell. This was it. The door opened, and a cute middle school-age girl answered. Rachel's daughter, he recalled.

"Hi, Katy. Nice to—"

"Mom! Your date or whatever is here!" Then to him, "Come in, I guess."

He remembered he was holding flowers and thrust them at the girl, anxious to be rid of them.

"Don't you want to give those to my mother?"

"Oh, yeah."

Why was he being awkward? He was a cop, for crying out loud—the Dos Santos Chief of Police. To his relief, Rachel Zamora walked down the stairs. She had on designer jeans, a light beige silk shirt, and black suede high-heel booties, which made her appear incredibly tall. And she carried a black leather jacket. He thought she looked stunning.

"Honey, you remember Chief Fiore," she said, putting an arm around her daughter.

"You're wearing Aunt Sarah's jacket."

"I am."

Eyeing the flowers, she waited for him to hand them over. Then, "They're beautiful. Let's go into the kitchen a minute so I can put these in water."

"This should be good," Katy said to herself as they followed her mother.

When they walked in, he saw a familiar face—a man in his mid-sixties with graying hair and a mustache. He sat at the table, drinking beer and playing solitaire.

"Eddie, I'd like you to meet Lou Fiore."

Balefully, he looked up at the cop. "We already met while searching for Sarah at Devil's Buff."

"Oh, right. I forgot."

The girl stood in the doorway, covering a mischievous grin with her hand. Her grandfather rose and extended his hand.

"Thank you again for what you did for my daughter," he said.

"No problem. Sarah's a dear friend."

"Want a beer?"

Finished with the roses, Rachel slipped in between them and pulled her date toward the door. "Actually, we're late. We have a dinner reservation."

"Have fun," her dad said.

Eddie and Katy watched the two leave the house as if they were double-parked in front of a fire station. She tugged at his sleeve.

"So, do you think they'll get married?"

"God, I hope not. It's good she's getting out, though."

"Yeah. I feel like Mom can use the distraction," she said.

The sky was clear as Lou drove along State Street. He felt the worst was over. Time to relax and concentrate on getting to know Rachel. The few times they were together had been promising, and he wondered again why he hadn't paid attention to her before. She'd always seemed to be in the background, whereas Sarah... He had been attracted to her older sister for the longest time. Now, though, he saw this lovely woman in a new light.

"That went better than I thought," he said.

"My father has enormous respect for you. Ever since..."

"Teacher, right?"

"He's at the community college."

"I like him too. Look, I appreciate you doing this. I know Sarah isn't really too hot on us—"

"Let me worry about my sister," she said.

When they reached Victoria Street, he turned and found parking a short distance from Bouchon Santa Barbara. Before he could make it around the vehicle to open Rachel's door, she'd already gotten out and stood on the sidewalk, admiring the tree-covered entrance to the restaurant. Offering his arm, he walked her to the front door.

Inside, it was bright and a little noisy. There were decorative mirrors mounted along one wall, and the tables were set with white linen.

"So fancy," she said.

"I've always wanted to try this place, but..."

"No date?"

"Exactly."

It wasn't long before someone showed them to their table. After getting settled, he ordered drinks. They said little until their wine arrived. Holding up his glass, he made an impromptu toast.

"Here's to..."

"Good friends." When his mouth fell open, she laughed and clinked glasses with him. "You should see your face."

"I'm not trying to rush anything here. I thought—"

"Lou, there's something you need to know if we're going to continue seeing each other. I'm not like Sarah. With the jokes, I mean. I'm the opposite. I operate in stealth mode."

"Uh-huh..."

"You probably won't see it coming."

When she saw the confused look on his face, she reached over and touched his hand. He felt a thrill.

"I like you, okay? If I didn't, I wouldn't have agreed to

this. It's been a long time." She took a swallow of wine. "Boy, has it ever been a long time."

"Me too. When I was in homicide."

"Are we talking *Laura* or *Someone to Watch Over Me?*"

He laughed. "Okay, I've actually seen both those movies, and neither. She was a police officer."

"Don't tell me. She was into macrame."

"There's your stealth humor again."

He regretted having brought it up and wondered how to change the subject without offending her. Primly, she waited for the rest.

"So, are you going to tell me or what?"

"Her ex threatened to kill me."

"Wow. Did you call the cops on him?"

"He is a cop. LA County Sheriff's Department."

As the story sank in, the server appeared.

"Thank God," she said. "I want to hear all the specials."

He was a wiseguy and smirked. "Date going badly?"

As she laughed out loud, Lou rubbed his eyes.

"Not you too," he said.

It was after ten, and Carter's eyes burned with fatigue. She'd spent the day and most of the evening reading Nellie's research notes and watching videos. The only breaks she'd taken were for meals and to speak to Sarah on the phone. After the call, she texted a server at The Cracked Pot, asking if he would cover her shift tomorrow. Fortunately, he said yes.

She'd poured hours into going through what the researcher had produced. Nothing seemed to shed light

onto Ana or how she had influenced the accident victims—
and the girl. And the scientific lingo didn't help. Though
Carter had read her share of research papers in school, she
was lost in a labyrinth of PTSD and IPV, resilient behaviors
and interactional models. And the footnotes! Nellie Watson
was a true scientist with a sharp mind, which made her
death all the more heartbreaking.

Before retiring for the night, she decided to take one
more stab at the videos to see if she'd missed anything. As
she browsed the folders on the computer, she came across a
new one named "Personal Observations." She double-
clicked it and discovered another set of files.

"Why did you hide these?"

Thank goodness she'd numbered the files because the
names were not helpful. She clicked the first one. Instead of
the testing room, Nellie's face appeared in closeup in her
office, sending a pang of sadness through Carter's heart.
Looking down, the girl cleared her throat and faced the
camera.

"Okay, so this is not part of my official research. I
needed to capture what I was thinking as I tested Ana
Robles. It's strange, but when I'm in the room with her, it's
like there's someone else there too. And there doesn't seem
to be a rational explanation."

She stopped and looked off-camera, as if she'd caught
someone eavesdropping. When she tapped the keyboard,
the video ended abruptly.

Carter played the next video, dated the day after. As
before, Nellie spoke directly into the camera.

"I haven't been sleeping well. It started after I began
these tests."

She described the vivid dreams she'd been having and
her confusion over what they might mean. Most were

centered around being trapped. Though Carter heard nothing concrete in the girl's ramblings, she felt strongly the researcher had been scared out of her mind.

After the video ended, she proceeded to the next, dated the next day. This and most of the remaining videos said little about what might be going on. But one thing was clear—gradually, Nellie was losing her grip on reality.

When Carter got to the last video, she hesitated. It had been recorded early in the morning on the day of her death. When she played it, she saw a person who was ill and frightened.

"Carter, I don't know if you'll ever see this, but I'm making it for you." She whispered as if someone might overhear. "I know what's happening, and it's not Ana. There's someone else here and— You need to—"

As she explained, the file skipped. Bands of rainbow-like distortion chunked across the screen, overlaying her face and corrupting her voice. Carter was unable to make out anything. Frustrated, she paused the video and tried playing the section over. But it was no use—the same thing happened. She let the recording continue, hoping the problem would clear itself up.

The video seemed to skip frames as it moved forward jerkily. Finally, her face reappeared. Her eyes seemed distant, as if she were in a trance.

"It's too late," Nellie said. "He's here."

Suddenly, the power went out, leaving Carter alone in the dark except for the computer, which was connected to a UPS device. Someone shrieked. When the emergency lights came on outside in the hallway, the temperature in the room plummeted. A presence lurked behind her. She sat there frozen, her heart thudding.

Though the thing made no sound, an overwhelming

wave of malevolence washed over her, and she had the keen sense it wanted to destroy her. Shutting her eyes, she waited to see what it would do. It remained there, silent and murderous.

Then she remembered something—the prayer Sarah had advised her to recite if she was ever in danger. Her ears ringing, she couldn't recall the words. Slowly, so as not to arouse the creature's anger, she slid her fingers onto the keyboard and brought up Google. Then she typed *prayer to st michael*.

Stinking of sulfur, the creature bore down on her, its breath hot and dry like a scorching desert wind. Inside her head, she heard a crackling noise, similar to the sound kindling made when you lit it. Her voice breaking, she recited the words.

"*St. Michael the Archangel, defend us in battle. Be our protection against the wickedness and snares of the devil.*"

The monster hissed at her menacingly, warning her to stop. Undeterred, she went on.

"*May God rebuke him, we humbly pray—*"

Now, it howled in pain, its voice like a chorus of rabid dogs being torn apart slowly.

"*And do thou, O Prince of the heavenly host, by the power of God...*"

A hideous claw thrust itself forward and tried grabbing her right hand, but when it brushed the St. Benedict bracelet, it withdrew instantly, wailing in almost human voices, which seemed to plead from a place far, far below the earth.

"*Cast into hell Satan and all the evil spirits who prowl about the world seeking the ruin of souls. Amen.*"

She waited, the blood in her head turning her vision

red. She felt a rush of wind, like something expelled from the room.

Then, it was gone.

Slowly, she rolled her chair around and saw vicious claw marks dug deep into the area surrounding the doorframe. And words scrawled across the wall in what looked like blood.

Quid mihi et tibi est.

TWENTY-FOUR

Wearing a sweater, jacket, and boots, Carter hurried through baggage claim at Sea-Tac and saw Sarah waiting for her. She was dressed similarly. The women embraced as harried passengers brushed past them.

"Thanks so much for coming," Sarah said. "Need any help?"

"I'm fine."

"Really? Because you don't look fine."

"Tell you about it on the way. This is not what we're wearing out there, right?"

"Don't worry, I packed heavy."

Soon, they were leaving the parking structure in a rented Subaru Outback and heading south on the 167 toward Longmire. The sky was overcast, but at least it wasn't raining for a change.

"Does Joe know you're doing this?" the girl said.

"Why would you ask that?"

"Because I stopped by The Cracked Pot to grab a coffee,

and I saw him sitting with Lou. From what I overheard, he was trying to get information."

"Did you say anything to them?"

"No."

"Joe and I are fine. So, tell me what happened to you."

Carter hesitated. "I saw the demon again. Well, I didn't actually see him—I was too scared to turn around. But I felt him."

"Oh my God, did he hurt you?"

"No, but he wanted to. I said the St. Michael prayer. Thank you, by the way. I think it may have harmed him because he vanished."

She glanced out the window and looked at her friend, her eyes intense. "There's more. There were claw marks on the wall. And writing in Latin."

"Do you remember what it said?"

"Wait, I took a picture." The girl grabbed her phone from her back pocket and read aloud. "*Quid mihi et tibi est.* I looked up the translation. It's a question—*What have you to do with me?*"

Sarah nodded. "The Gerasene demoniac. It's from Luke's gospel. Jesus confronts a man possessed by a legion of demons. When they recognize him, the man falls to his knees and says those words.

"Actually, what he says is, *Quid mihi et tibi est, Jesu Fili Dei Altissimi? obsecro te, ne me torqueas.* Which means *What have you to do with me, Jesus, son of the Most High God? I beg you, do not torment me.*"

"Okay, so how do you even know that?"

"I had to memorize it for my Confirmation class in high school. It stuck with me for some reason."

"But why would the demon say it to me? Was he being ironic?"

"Possibly. Or because at that moment, you were close to God. You're wearing the bracelet, and you said the prayer."

"So, wait. Jesus was close to me? I'm Jewish."

Sarah smiled at her. "So is He."

It was early afternoon when they reached the national park. The sun wasn't out, and it was hard to tell how much daylight was left. Despite his protests, Charlie had returned to Montecito to stay with Harlan. The doctors confirmed he had several fractured ribs but no internal bleeding. Sarah had told Carter everything. Then, when she called the attorney, he agreed they should try to locate Grace's body. But he made her promise to call the police the minute they found anything.

Sarah parked near a public restroom. Though she was hesitant to go inside, they needed to change clothes before venturing into the forest. As she exited the vehicle, she shivered from the cold. The women got out insulated hiking boots, hard shell pants, and insulated jackets with hoods from the rear of the Subaru.

"Here, take these," Sarah said. "I also brought socks and gloves."

"Good thing. It's freezing out here."

After changing clothes, Sarah got out two backpacks, which she'd stocked with flashlights, first aid kits, bottled water, and energy bars. She handed one to her friend.

"No marshmallows?" Carter said.

"Funny." Sarah looked at the darkening sky. "Let's hope we don't get stuck out here."

They'd zipped up their jackets all the way and wore

their hoods. She checked the weather on her phone. "Thirty degrees."

"Lovely," the girl said. "Tell me again why we're out here in butt-freezing weather?"

"Because it's the right thing to do."

Sarah locked up the Outback, and they headed into the forest toward the Trail of the Shadows.

"Glad you know where you're going," Carter said, already breathing hard as she hurried to keep up.

They'd only been hiking for twenty minutes. Threatening clouds skated across the darkening sky. Sarah prayed it wouldn't snow. If it did, they might not be able to go further. As she continued on, she realized she was alone and turned around. The girl sat hunched over on a log, trying to catch her breath.

"I really need to quit smoking," she said.

"It's okay. Let's take a break."

Sarah set down her backpack and got out a bottle of water and an energy bar. As she ate and drank, she tried to appreciate the beauty around her. Snow dusted the dark green trees. A few birds sang, along with the rustle of small unseen animals as they made their way stealthily through the low foliage. Somewhere through the trees, she spotted a deer.

Carter took a bite of an energy bar and gulped some water. She wasn't cut out for this. A memory of her old high school PE coach, Mr. Zabel, flashed through her mind. He was screaming at the top of his lungs as she and the others did laps around the track. Ignoring his taunts, she'd decided to make the best of a bad situation. Which was what she needed to do now. Slapping her knees, she got to her feet.

"I'm gonna be so sore tomorrow," she said. "Did I ever tell you how much I hate exercise?"

"And look what happened."

The girl narrowed her eyes at her friend powering ahead along the trail. Then mockingly, *"And look what happened."*

Eventually, they came to a clearing. The sounds of birds and the wind had stopped. Everything was still. As Carter caught up, Sarah held up her hand.

"I think we're close," she said.

"Why are we whispering?"

"I thought I heard something."

"Oh, great. I hope you brought a gun."

Sarah unzipped a jacket pocket and removed the photo of Grace. Using her teeth, she peeled off her right glove and placed her hand on the front of the color print.

Suddenly, she was swirling, as if in the center of a merry-go-round. Images flashed past her. First bright sunlight, then wildflowers, and finally a small, dark hollow. As she came to a stop, she beheld the smooth, curved tree trunk from her vision.

She put away the photo and walked toward the tree, with the girl following. When she looked behind her, she noticed the hollow. In front of it lay a scattering of moss-covered rocks and pine needles. A small animal stared at her from inside the entrance. It had reddish fur, round ears, and shiny eyes.

"What is that thing?" Carter said.

"I think it's a marmot."

As Sarah approached, the creature scurried off. Crouching, she peered into the opening. With the light rapidly fading, it was hard to see the clearing in the center. After her eyes adjusted, she saw a nearly perfect circle that reminded her of a hidden grotto in a fairy tale.

"We're actually going in there?" the girl said.

"It's all right."

Amazed, Carter watched her friend crawl through. Rolling her eyes, she followed. The ground was wet, and she felt the coldness through her gloves and the knees of her pants. Still, it was beautiful inside. Sarah removed a black folding shovel. Standing, the girl observed as she turned in a circle, picked a spot, and dug at the ground.

"What if she's buried, like, really deep?" Carter said.

"Let's hope it's a shallow grave."

It wasn't long before Sarah discovered something—the hand from her vision when she'd touched the mantel clock. The bones were wet and dirt colored. Closing her eyes, she recalled an image. The index finger had pointed at something. She turned to look and saw only the enclosing foliage, which surrounded the hollow like a garden wall. When she touched the hand, scenes from a gruesome attack flooded her mind, making her dizzy.

"Are you okay?" the girl said as her friend stood.

Sarah shuddered. "That was intense. I just saw how she died."

"What about the killer's face?"

"I didn't see it. But whoever it was beat her with a shovel until she was dead."

"Oh, the poor thing."

Sarah got out her phone and took pictures. Then she held it up high, and squinting at the screen, shook her head.

"No service?" Carter said.

"Good thing I have this." Sarah reached into her backpack and brought out another device, which resembled a walkie talkie. "Iridium satellite phone. Charlie's idea."

"Then I guess we won't die out here."

Sarah switched on the phone and extended the antenna, making sure to point it toward the sky. She dialed a number and waited. The temperature had dropped further, sending a chill through her. The girl was nearby, stamping her feet to keep warm.

"Hello, Det. Martens? This is Sarah Greene, Charlie's friend? Listen, I think we found her. I've got the GPS coordinates. Hang on."

She tried remembering the instructions Charlie had dictated to her. Then, scrolling through the menu items, she stopped and read off the coordinates.

"Got it?" she said. "Listen, we need to head back. It's getting colder by the second, and I don't want to get snowed in. Sure, I'll let Charlie know. Talk to you later."

She disconnected and looked at Carter. "They're sending a team. I need to tell Charlie about my vision. Come on, we should get back." Then, reacting to her friend's expression, "What?"

"I'm amazed. Seriously, I've never seen this side of you before."

"I'll let you in on a little secret. If you hadn't come with me, I would've been a mess." She hugged Carter. "What do you say to a steak dinner with plenty of wine?"

"And dessert. Let's get out of here."

As they grabbed their backpacks, Sarah thought of Joe. And the more she lingered on the memory of their last conversation, the more worried she became. Something was plaguing him. But whatever it was, she vowed it wouldn't come between them.

Outside the hollow, Sarah looked down as she unzipped a pocket and put away her phone. She hadn't seen her friend frozen in place, staring at something.

"Um, Sarah?" Carter said.

Holding hands, they gazed into the yellow eyes of a large gray wolf. The fur on its legs and underside was smooth and white. Mist rose off its back, making it appear other-worldly. Its mouth was open—its breath visible—and it growled way in the back of its throat.

"What is it doing?" Carter said.

"I'm sure I don't know."

Slowly and with great care, Sarah removed her back-pack and set it on the ground, trying to make as little noise as possible. Without looking away, she felt around inside and removed the shovel. Her eyes fixed on the beast, she spoke in a low voice.

"We have to make a run for it."

"What? I can't outrun that thing."

"Right. Take off your backpack and set it on the ground —slowly." She waited as the girl obeyed. "Now, when I give you the signal, run as fast as you can."

"Which way?" She watched as Sarah pointed off some-where. "What about you?"

"I'll catch up."

"This is a horrible plan."

"Carter, do as I say."

"I'm not leaving you."

When Sarah saw the determination in her friend's eyes, she relented. "Fine."

"What are you gonna do?"

"I'm going to brain it. With this." Sarah held up the shovel.

"Wait, what about your wrist?"

"Oh shit, I forgot."

Carter reached for the shovel. "Let me. Then we'll both run."

So far, the animal hadn't moved. Instead of growling, it barked—but not like a dog. It made a whuffing noise, which sounded to her as if it were trying to speak.

"What do you think it wants?" the girl said.

"I don't speak wolf."

Carter looked up at the sky. "It's getting late."

On cue, it started snowing. Squeezing her eyes shut, she took one step forward and raised the shovel over her head. Then she let out a loud, comical roar and swung it in an awkward arc. When she opened her eyes, Sarah was grinning at her.

"Is it gone?" the girl said.

"It ran off when you went all Simba." She put away the shovel and grabbed her backpack.

Carter adjusted the strap on her backpack. "Do you think it was scared of us?"

"I think it ran back to tell its friends about the crazy lady in the forest."

With the heavy cloud cover, they were in almost total darkness. A steady snow fell as they reached the trail and stopped to grab their flashlights.

"That was close," the girl said.

They'd been walking only a few minutes when they spotted a figure up ahead. Sarah thought it might be someone from the police department.

"Hey!" she said, waving a hand in the air.

As they got closer, she realized it was a boy of around thirteen with long, dark hair and intense blue eyes. But what surprised her was how he was dressed—dirty, torn blue jeans and a dingy white undershirt stained with blood. And he was barefoot. Despite the freezing temperature, he didn't shiver. And there was something else—the snow seemed to fall *through* him as his eyes remained fixed on the women.

"Ghost," Carter said.

"And an angry one. I feel like he may have been killed out here."

"You mean, like Grace?"

Sarah knew in her soul something awful had happened to him, and his spirit had been left to wander the forest for who knew how long. Calming herself, she walked toward him.

"What are you doing?" Carter said.

"I can't just leave him here like this."

As she got closer, the specter turned the color of ash, its eyes flaming coals. She stopped, her heart pounding. Then, undaunted, she extended her hand. A blinding bolt of electricity shot through her arm, sending her on her backside. Gasping, she scrambled backward to rejoin her friend.

"I don't think we can help him," Carter said.

"You might be right."

Steeling herself, she took the girl's hand. Staring straight ahead, they marched past the wraith.

"Don't look back," Sarah said.

They'd gone perhaps fifty yards when Carter pulled on her friend's sleeve, forcing her to stop. As Sarah looked up, she saw them—all of them. They'd gathered on the trail directly ahead.

"No, no, no," she said.

A pack of girls—all under fourteen—and a preteen boy glared at them with lifeless eyes. Each was dressed similarly to the other boy, with hardly any clothes and immune to the intense cold.

"What now?" Carter said. "They might be like the other one."

Sarah took out her satellite phone. When she checked the screen, she discovered she had no signal.

"Charlie warned me this might happen. The satellites aren't in range."

Frantic, she tried adjusting the antenna. Nothing. Meanwhile, the specters continued watching them. She got out her mobile phone. No service. She thought of Joe again. How could she have been so stupid? Eddie was right—she should've turned her back on all of this. Lived a normal life.

"Try your phone," Sarah said.

Her friend took out the device and checked. "Nothing."

Sarah studied her surroundings, trying to think what to do. If they turned and ran, they might end up deeper in the forest. And worse—lost. But if they kept going straight ahead, these things might attack them.

"Show them the bracelet," she said.

Carter fumbled as she struggled to remove her glove. When her bare hand was exposed, she pulled up the sleeve of her jacket, and shivering, held up her arm in a power salute, facing the medal toward the deathly specters.

Something was wrong.

Instead of fearing it, they were attracted to the bracelet. In an instant, they were in front of the women, each the color of ash. Avoiding their burning red eyes, Carter felt the intense cold coming off them.

"What do we—"

"Run!"

Sarah sprinted down the trail back toward the hollow

and continued blindly into the forest. Trees, rocks, and foliage zipped past. She kept glancing at the ground, hoping she wouldn't trip. Without looking back, she called out to the girl.

"Be careful of rocks and fallen—"

She heard a thump and an *Oof!* When she stopped, Carter lay sprawled on the ground, her backpack askew. She ran to her fallen friend and reached out her hand.

"This is why I hate exercise," Carter said, getting up. "Are they gone?"

Sarah looked past her and didn't see anything. "I think so. You okay?"

"More or less."

As they started forward, the girl groaned. "Wait. I think I might've twisted my ankle."

"Could this be any more of a horror movie trope?"

"Shut up. I'm serious—it really hurts."

Kneeling, Sarah examined Carter's ankle. Fortunately, there was little swelling. "I don't think it's too bad."

"Easy for you to say. I need something for the pain. What's in the first aid kit?"

Sarah got out the small plastic box and dug past bandages and antiseptic wipes. At the bottom, she found ibuprofen. She pulled out two foil packets and tore them open. Then she uncapped a water bottle and handed everything to the girl.

"I'm supposed to take all four?"

"Joe once told me four of these equals one prescription Motrin."

"He's the doctor."

As Carter washed down the pills, her friend gazed at their surroundings and realized the trail had long since ended.

"Okay," she said. "So, the good news is, we're not being chased anymore."

The girl returned everything to the backpack. "And the bad news?"

Sighing, Sarah looked at her. "I think we're lost."

As Sarah brought up the Compass app on her mobile phone, Carter hobbled in a circle, muttering to herself.

"We're going to be fine," she said.

"But we're lost."

"Technically. But I'm pretty sure if we head north, we can find our vehicle."

"Meanwhile, it's snowing. The right thing to do. Ha! *Blessed are the weak who think they are good because they have no claws.*"

"What?"

"Spinoza. When I'm upset, I like to quote famous philosophers. Calms me down. Aw, shit."

"What now?"

"Looks like our buddy is back."

When Sarah turned to see where the girl was pointing, the gray wolf was standing like a statue in the falling snow, observing them, its head cocked to one side. Its fur was sleek, and not at all like the photos she'd seen in books.

"Shoo!" she said, waving her hands uselessly.

"Wait." Carter was next to her friend now. "This is gonna sound crazy, but I think it's trying to tell us something."

"What? That we're dinner?"

The animal turned its head and whimpered.

"I feel like it wants us to follow it," the girl said.

Sarah checked her phone. "Nope, wrong direction."

When she looked up again, Carter was already limping off as the wolf made its way even deeper into the forest.

"Shit," she said and ran to catch up.

The ground was completely white with snow as the women continued after the canine. If they weren't careful, they'd freeze, with no way to call for help. Silently, she prayed.

The animal moved at a steady pace, never looking back. Finally, as they reached a clearing, it stopped and did something curious. It whined again and sat, as if waiting for the women to move closer.

Sarah crept cautiously toward it, and when it didn't move, she crouched in front of it, feeling all her fear draining away. She removed her glove and gently reached out to touch the wolf's head. When it growled, she scooted away.

"Okay, fine," she said. "So, no *Planet Earth* moment for me."

The girl laughed. "I cannot believe you tried that."

The animal trotted to the center of the clearing and pawed at the ground. At first, it whimpered. Then it barked sharply.

Sarah took off her backpack and grabbed the shovel. The wolf moved back as she scraped away the fresh snow and dug into the cold, hard ground. A short time later, she stopped because her wrist was aching.

"Here, let me," Carter said.

She dug for another half hour when she put down the shovel and peered into the hole. What she saw made her shudder. Lying there was a part of a human jawbone.

"There's a body down here!"

The girl was about to touch the remains when the far-off sound of engines got her attention. Sarah brought out the satellite phone to check for a signal. This time, she had one and redialed the last number.

"Det. Martens? Me again. And we found another body. I'll read you our new coordinates."

In a few minutes, two bright red ATVs came into view as Sarah and Carter waved. The drivers, who were dressed warmly, stopped their vehicles in front of the women. One removed his helmet and ski mask.

"I'm Officer Stanislav. Det. Martens is at the first site. And you say there's another body?"

The girl pointed. "Over there. But you might wanna be careful, because of the—" When she turned, the wolf was gone. "Never mind."

"Okay," he said. "We'll alert the PI. First, let's get you two out of here. Good job, by the way. I won't even ask how you did it."

"Trust me, you don't want to know," Sarah said.

She and Carter each climbed onto an ATV and held on tight as the drivers made their way through the trees to the trail. All the way back, Sarah kept thinking about the second body. Was this the real reason they were supposed to come all the way out here?

The vision from the mantel clock came into sharp focus, disorienting her. Once gain, she saw the skeletal hand in the ground and the finger pointing at the place where the wolf had led them. All along, Grace Zielinski—the real Grace—had been trying to tell her where to find the other body.

"Dear Lord," she said through the biting wind, which had practically frozen her face into a grim mask.

The women would have a lot to tell Harlan when they

returned. Now, all she wanted was to take a hot bath and enjoy a magnificent dinner.

"With dessert," she said.

TWENTY-FIVE

Joe lay on Sarah's sofa, dozing fitfully. He'd felt unwell all afternoon and had left Manny and his sons to continue their latest renovation without him. Voices swirled in his head—conversations with his mother, then his sister, and finally Dr. Shapiro. But what was worse was he'd dreamt about Leah again. In the dream, everything moved so slowly—the view in front of him as he drove, the blue plastic ball bouncing into the street from his right. And then, the girl.

Killed in a bloody instant.

When he opened his eyes, he noticed it was dark outside. He glanced at his phone—after five. Sarah had mentioned something about Charlie being injured and Carter having to join her in Seattle. She'd refused to say any more and told him again how much she loved him. Would she feel the same way when she learned the truth about Leah? He sat up. Gary looked at him oddly.

"What? You hungry?"

The cat meowed and bounded toward the kitchen.

As he followed the animal, he heard a noise in the kitchen. It sounded like—no, it wasn't possible. It sounded like an airy plastic ball.

A bouncing ball.

His chest tightening, he peeked inside the dark room. Nothing. Hesitating, he switched on the light. The room was quiet except for the sound of the cat lapping up water from his bowl. When his phone vibrated in his hand, he almost dropped it. Seeing it was his ex-wife, he answered immediately.

"Hey," he said. "Are you guys okay?"

"We're fine. I'll tell you all about it when we get back. Harlan has us on a seven a.m. flight to LA. Carter and I are going to grab some dinner. But I wanted to check in first."

"I appreciate it."

"Are you okay?"

"A little under the weather. Can't wait to see you tomorrow."

"Me too. I'll probably go right to bed after dinner. I'm exhausted."

"No problem. Talk to you tomorrow. I love you."

"Say it again."

"I love you."

"Love you too," she said.

Putting away her phone, Sarah stood outside the W Hotel with Carter. The rain came down steadily, and traffic had slowed to a crawl. She turned to her friend, who looked at her expectantly.

"Well?" Carter said.

"He says he loves me."

"You don't sound happy about it."

"There's something he's not telling me. Never mind, I'm imagining things. Come on, let's eat."

She was about to walk over to the taxi stand when the girl stopped her.

"Why don't we walk? The Capital Grille's only a couple of blocks."

"Are you sure? What about your ankle?"

"The meds did the trick. Doesn't hurt anymore."

They headed north on 4th Avenue. After half a block, Carter turned to her friend.

"So, are you guys getting back together?"

"What? I don't know. I thought we were in a good place."

"Only what?"

"Last night, Joe said he needed to talk to me about something."

The girl waggled her eyebrows. "Maybe he's gonna propose."

"I don't think so. It sounded really...serious."

"I thought marriage was serious, though."

"Serious isn't the right word. Important? Ominous? Never mind. Guess I'll know soon enough. Look, there's the restaurant."

The concierge at the W had made their reservation, and when the women arrived, they were seated immediately. Which was good because Sarah was exhausted and wanted nothing more than to eat and go to bed. And she was sure Carter felt the same. After the server had poured a pricey pinot noir, the women clinked glasses.

"I wanna thank you for today," the girl said.

"Thank me? We almost ended up freezing out there. Not to mention the ghosts."

"And don't forget the wolf. No, it's just— I learned an important lesson. About myself, I mean. This is probably gonna sound stupid, but I'm stronger than I thought I was."

"I've always felt you were strong."

"But it's not how I saw myself. Ever since...the thing happened to me, I was a victim. But I realized that, although something bad did happen, it didn't change who I am. And it took you to show me. So, it's why I'm thanking you."

Sarah brushed the tears from her eyes and hugged her friend. Kissing her on the forehead, she raised her glass again.

"You'll always be in my heart," she said.

"Likewise. Let's change the subject before we start bawling like little girls. Do you think there's any connection between the body in the hollow and the other one?"

Sarah took a bite of her salad and considered the question. "I've thought a lot about it, and I get the sense they're not related."

"How long before they can ID the remains?"

"That's a Charlie question."

Sarah's watch vibrated. Raising it, she recognized the number of the incoming call and decided to use her phone to answer.

"Hello? Oh, hi. Yeah, we're fine. Just grabbing some dinner. No, it's okay, not inconvenient at all. What?" She noticed the other diners side-eyeing her. "Hold on a sec."

She slid out of the booth and maneuvered past a large group of businesspeople until she was outside the restaurant. Making sure she was alone, she put the phone to her ear.

"Okay, Detective. Go ahead."

"First of all, thank you for what you did today. Normally, we get the results from DNA testing in around six to eight weeks."

"Wow, that long?"

"Hang on. We discovered something interesting in the first grave. The clothing was fairly intact. And we found a patch sewn into the victim's jacket."

"What kind of patch?"

"Some people use them to alert others to their medical conditions in case they're unconscious. This one read *Diabetic Type 2*."

"And we know Grace Zielinski was diabetic."

"Right. We're tracking down her dental records, which might mean we'll get a positive ID much sooner."

"Wonderful—thanks for telling me."

"Now. About the other body."

By the time Sarah returned to their table, the entrees had arrived. She slid into the booth and took a huge swallow of wine.

"You were gone a long time," Carter said.

"That was Det. Martens. I think we might get a positive ID on Grace very soon."

The girl attempted to high-five her friend, who ignored her. "You're about to tell me there's bad news."

"Bad is relative. You know the body the wolf led us to? It wasn't the only one."

Carter blanched. "Oh, no. The ghosts we saw."

"Yeah, them."

"How many?"

"Twenty," Sarah said. "They were all kids."

Still wearing his uniform, Tim helped himself to more popcorn as he binge-watched episodes of *The Office* on Netflix. Though he was alone in the women's shelter dayroom, he wasn't uncomfortable. An only child who didn't easily make friends, he'd spent his early years alone, preferring books over people.

At his father's insistence, he'd joined the Boy Scouts, which awakened in him a new purpose—helping others. Which was why Harlan Covington had thought him the ideal choice to assist him in his work. The lawyer had told him he recognized in the young police officer a single-minded determination to do the right thing, something Tim felt his superiors didn't always appreciate.

Mr. Covington had intrigued him from the moment they met. The elderly attorney reminded him of his late grandfather, a formal man who wore banker suits and never drank or smoked, and who never swore. He loved his grandfather and missed him terribly. He pictured the old man's face, stern but with a light in his eyes, which assured his grandson he loved him too, though he'd never put it into words.

The first time Mr. Covington had asked him to assist was when Sarah Greene found the mirror at Casa Abrigo. Though he'd had no idea of the significance, he followed the attorney's instructions, making sure not to let anyone know of his activities—not even the police chief. And here he was again, helping in some mysterious new investigation whose nature he wasn't permitted to know. As instructed, he'd sent the attorney pictures of the claw marks and writing on the wall Carter had reported. What hellish thing could've caused that?

The popcorn had made him thirsty. As he opened one of the glass doors on the commercial stainless steel refrigerator, he thought someone had moaned. Since moving in to keep an eye on Ana Robles, he hadn't experienced anything remotely paranormal. Was this how it started? He guessed it was why Mr. Covington—and the police chief—had warned him to be careful.

He returned to the dayroom and put on the duty belt lying on the sofa. After switching off the TV, he listened. Nothing but silence and the faint sound of an icemaker. He glanced at his watch. Ten-thirty. Heidi was most likely asleep. And the security guard wasn't due to arrive until midnight. He would go on his rounds now instead of at eleven, and he'd wake the director only if it was urgent.

The elevator moved slowly to the top floor, and he had to admit, he was nervous. At one point, the car made a loud chunking noise, then continued up. When the doors opened, he stepped into the dark hallway and shone a flashlight beam in both directions. Going to his left, he walked all the way to the window overlooking the street and looked down. Someone had recently placed flowers near the spot where Nellie Watson had met her end. Probably a resident.

None of the rooms on this floor were occupied. Methodically, he checked each one by swinging open the door, playing the light from one side to the other, and closing the door again. He managed to cover the entire floor in only a few minutes.

Ana's room was on the fourth floor. Instead of the elevator, he took the emergency stairs. As he emerged, a sulfur-like odor made his stomach lurch. He went to his right and checked every room, leaving the Guatemalan woman's for last. When he reached the window, he stood before her closed door, hesitant to open it for fear of startling her.

Gently, he turned the doorknob and pushed open the door just enough to get his hand through. The flashlight beam shone on the floor, where he saw two pairs of shoes arranged near the bed. Clothes lay neatly folded on a chair. On the desk lay a hairbrush, comb, and hand lotion, as well as other toiletries. He raised the beam until it fell on the bed.

It was empty, with the covers pulled back.

Behind him, another moan—not one of pain but of carnal pleasure. The sound unnerved him. Pivoting, he shone the flashlight back and forth in the hallway. Something dark clung to the ceiling. His hand shaking, he shone a light on it.

It was Ana.

Impossibly, she was on her hands and knees, her head completely twisted around so that her face was right-side up. Naked, she watched him coolly. Stifling a scream, he backed away as a black, snake-like tongue, which was much too long, probed its way out of her mouth and flicked at the air.

"Take me now, cop," she said—only it wasn't her voice.

Dropping the flashlight, he ran to the elevator and repeatedly punched the Down button until the doors opened. Struggling for air, he slipped in and pressed 2 and waited for the doors to close. On the second floor, he jumped out, trying to recall which was Heidi's room. *On the right.* Light streamed from the bottom of the closed door. Calming himself, he knocked firmly.

The door opened, and the director, wearing pajamas, stared at him. One hand absently tugged her collar closed.

"What's happened?" she said.

Tim waited in the kitchen, rolling the flashlight back and forth in one hand as Heidi poured him tea. His head was swimming, and he couldn't get the disturbing image out of his mind. Though she was small, Ana had terrified him.

"I know what I saw," he said.

She handed him a cup. "And I believe you. But we both saw her in her bed asleep just now."

He blew on the tea and took a sip. "It's impossible, right? Hanging from the ceiling?"

"Well, it's not something you see every day."

He laughed weakly. "I'm not so sure I should put this in my report."

She patted his hand. "It might be better if you didn't. However, we must tell Harlan."

"Of course. I'll contact him first thing in the morning."

She gazed around the kitchen as if expecting an unwelcome visitor. "I'd better get to bed, or I won't be any use to anyone tomorrow."

"I didn't mean to alarm you, Ms. Watkins."

"You did the right thing. And for heaven's sake, call me Heidi. Will you be able to sleep?"

"Think I'm going to watch some television for a while."

"Okay, goodnight."

"Yeah. Night."

He took his cup with him to the dayroom and switched on the TV, wondering what he'd gotten himself into.

Shaking his head, he tried imagining the conversation with the police chief as he asked to be reassigned. No, he had to see this through. He'd promised Mr. Covington. The silence was oppressive, and for the first time, he realized he wasn't at all comfortable being alone.

And the realization made him cry.

TWENTY-SIX

Harlan was in his usual place at the dining room table, drinking coffee and reading the report Charlie had prepared for him on the plane. In considerable pain, the PI walked in, and wincing, took a seat. At the emergency room, the doctor had prescribed a prescription painkiller, but he preferred to rely on over-the-counter drugs. Better to maintain a clear head.

"Morning," he said.

The lawyer didn't respond. Elsa entered from the kitchen and placed a vegetable omelet in front of Charlie.

"Coffee?" she said.

"Thanks, Elsa."

After she'd left, he took a bite of the omelet and savored the mildly pungent taste of garden-fresh tomatoes, zucchini, and onion.

"I understand your inside man was here this morning," he said.

Harlan put down his pen. "He was. You must excuse me. I was thinking about what you wrote. How are the ribs?"

"Never touch them m'self."

"At least you haven't lost your sense of humor."

"So, what did our friend Officer Whatley have to report?"

"He was frightened."

After the lawyer finished telling Charlie about Tim's encounter, he handed the PI a photo of the claw marks and the writing in Nellie Watson's old office. Charlie let out a low whistle.

"Carter reported seeing it after experiencing something she insisted was beyond evil."

"I'll admit it. Sometimes, I wish I'd never taken your call."

Harlan chuckled appreciatively. "And sometimes, I wish you and I had met twenty years ago. I'm sure we would've been great friends."

"I don't have many left, which reminds me. How did your last treatment go?"

The lawyer refilled his cup as he considered the question and looked at the PI evenly. "Not as I had hoped."

"But I thought the cancer was in remission."

"It was. And now, it's back. Yesterday, I learned it's spread to my bones."

"How long…"

"Unclear. No matter. I've been preparing a long time. Ever since I was first diagnosed."

The PI felt cold, as if someone had let in a draft. "Have you shared this with—"

"Mary knows. And of course, Brian Donnelly. I advise you not to tell anyone—especially Sarah and Carter."

"You have my word. There's something I've been meaning to ask. You've kept things pretty close to the vest —even from me—which I can appreciate. But if I'm going to continue working with you, I need to know what's at stake."

"You're right." Harlan took a swallow of coffee and set down the cup. "This case is about more than a young Guatemalan woman and a murder."

Charlie waved the photo. "I know. There's something supernatural going on, which is why you've enlisted a couple of psychics."

"And it's centered in Dos Santos."

"But what has it got to do with you? You're a lawyer."

"Like you, I'm also Catholic. And I plan to spend whatever time I have left combatting evil in all its forms."

"I see. And when you say *evil*, how bad are we talking?"

"What's infesting Dos Santos has tentacles that extend far and wide. Those men who attacked you in Seattle, for example. They seemed to know what you were up to."

"I wonder if there are others."

"There are. I've been dealing with them for a long time."

"How?"

"The less you know, the better. What puzzles me is everything that's happened over the past two months— longer even—seems to have been orchestrated."

"By who?"

Harlan shook his head. "I keep coming back to John Dos Santos. Very little exists about him in the history books. It's almost as if the town intentionally tried erasing his memory."

"Was he some kind of Satanist?"

"Some said he was the devil. But he hadn't always been so. John had been a good Catholic. He was an altar boy, and he used to enjoy helping the less fortunate, especially at Christmas. But something changed after he returned from the war."

"Changed how?"

"He used to care about people. Of all the men from Dos Santos who went over to fight the Germans, he was the only one who came back. Then, all he wanted was money and power. And he got them. Convinced Santa Barbara County to take an unincorporated area and create a new town named after him."

A sharp pain in the lawyer's hips prevented him from continuing. He waited for it to pass and went on.

"There were rumors. Political corruption, murder. Stories circulated about what went on at his mansion. Underage girls, sometimes boys."

The PI refilled his cup. "What about the police?"

"They worked for him. What he said, went. Everyone was terrified of him. After he died, he was laid to rest in a mausoleum in Resurrection Cemetery without fanfare. They didn't even say a Mass for him. And no one other than his household staff attended the interment."

"Talk about a persona non grata. What else?"

Harlan saw his reflection in his coffee cup. "That's all I know. As I said, there's very little written about him."

"How did you find out what you did?"

"There was a diary written by a childhood friend who later became his housekeeper. Like everyone else, she was terrified of him. But she needed the work. Her husband had died in a factory accident, and she had children to support. She claimed he'd never mistreated her."

"Where's the book now?"

"In my library. You're welcome to read it. You look like you have something on your mind."

"Hmm? I was thinking about those other bodies the women discovered. Do you think they're connected to the case?"

"I don't know." The lawyer looked wistfully at the flower arrangement on the table. "Children are abducted all over the world. It's possible that when the remains have been identified, we can piece together the truth."

Mary walked in, holding Harlan's phone. "It's Heidi." She handed it to him and waited, her hands folded in front of her.

"Morning," the lawyer said. "No, of course not—I've been up for hours. Are things a little more settled after last night's incident? Good. How's Ana? Okay. Charlie and I plan to come over around nine. Right. See you soon."

He disconnected and handed the phone to his housekeeper. The PI's eyes followed her as she left the room.

"She's more than a housekeeper, isn't she?" he said. "Really looks out for you. She would've made someone a good wife."

"She almost became a nun and devotes herself to the Lord."

"Well, that's a shame."

"Missing your wife again, Mr. Beeks?"

"Always," he said and finished his coffee.

It was after nine when Sarah and Carter got off the plane at LAX. Harlan had arranged for a driver to take them to Dos Santos. When they reached baggage claim, they saw a nice-looking young man wearing a smart black suit, holding up a sign with the words GREENE-WITTGENSTEIN.

"Sounds like a law firm," Sarah said as they approached him.

"And a damn good one."

Once they were on the road, the women fell asleep. Sarah was surprised when the town car pulled into her driveway. She hadn't even awoken when the driver dropped off the girl at her apartment. She glanced at her watch—it was almost ten forty-five.

The driver helped with her bag, and when she entered her house, Gary was sitting in the foyer, looking at her with his head tilted.

"Hey, buddy."

She set down her bag, and picking up the purring animal, scratched behind his ears. Joe had texted her that all was well. He'd made an early start and had already taken care of the cat's food, water, and litter box. She and Carter were scheduled to meet Harlan and Charlie at St. Rita's in the early evening after her friend got off work. By now, the PI would've contacted Det. Martens, so she didn't need to report in.

Anxious to leave Seattle, she hadn't processed what had happened to Carter and her in the forest. She went into the kitchen and sat at the counter, working a ball of green exercise putty to strengthen her wrist. Though Rupinder had cautioned her to perform the ritual daily, she'd been lax.

It wasn't long before images of the ghosts of the sad young boy and all the others invaded her thoughts. How long had they haunted the forest, waiting until someone discovered their remains? Years? Decades? She felt certain they'd died violently—possibly after having been tortured. Ever since discovering the evil behind Casa Abrigo, she was beginning to see dark, disparate threads slowly being woven together before her eyes into...what? An abominable tapestry pointing to some universal evil eating the town alive?

Her watch vibrated, and when she looked down, she saw a text message from Rachel.

r u back?

She got out her phone and dialed her sister's number.

"Hey, you. Yeah, just got home. Sure, lunch sounds good. I'll be in the office shortly."

She carried her bag to her bedroom and left it on the floor. Grabbing a water from the fridge, she found her keys and went out through the garage. There was a woman on the corner, observing her as she backed into the street. She was bedraggled, her hair clumsily tied in a loose bun. Though she wasn't dirty, she seemed altogether shabby.

After backing out, Sarah put the Galaxie in first, then second, and accelerated past the odd-looking woman. As she did, the stranger turned her face toward her, not bothering to move her body. It was as if her head were on a swivel. Her blank expression became a scowl that spoke of pure malevolence. Looking away, Sarah drove on.

By the time she walked into Greene Realty, Sarah had driven the memory of the strange, frightening woman out of her mind. Rachel was busy helping Blanca with something on the computer.

"Hey, stranger," she said. The sisters embraced. "There's a café mocha on your desk."

"Did I ever tell you how much I love you?"

"Mm. Can I have a raise?" Silence, and Rachel sighed dramatically. "I figured you'd need the caffeine. Are we still on for lunch?"

"I need to check my email. Hi, Blanca. How's the family?"

The assistant looked up with mild irritation. "Everyone's fine." Then to herself, "Ni modo."

Rachel followed her sister into her office. As Sarah got settled behind her desk, she said, "What's with Blanca?"

"Manny might need back surgery."

"Oh, no."

"And there's a good chance Pollito's girlfriend is pregnant."

"The urgent care nurse?"

"Yep. Everything go okay in Seattle?"

"We'll talk at lunch."

"Roger dodger."

As Sarah sipped her coffee, she gazed at the photo of Grace Zielinski. Images of the skeletal hand reaching up through the snowy ground paraded through her mind. Now that the police had discovered the patch in her clothing, it was all but certain the body was hers.

Despite her efforts to concentrate, she continued to think about the murder victim, especially her last moments. Had Grace been conscious after the first blow to the head?

"You didn't deserve this," she said and laid the photo on her desk.

Sarah and Rachel decided to try an Argentine restaurant, which had opened recently. There weren't many customers. Not a good sign. Rachel shifted uncomfortably in her seat. Sarah knew her behavior well. When they were little, her sister would squirm whenever she had a secret she was trying mightily to keep.

"Okay, spill," she said, picking up her menu.

"I, um... Oh. Lou and I went on a date the other night." She rolled her eyes. "Look, I know you don't like this situation..."

Sarah laid down the menu. "Rache, you're an adult. It's not my business who you're seeing."

"We're not really seeing each other. It was just one date."

"It was nice, though, right?" No response. "What's wrong?"

"I don't know. I guess I'm having second thoughts. Not about him—he's a great guy and all. But I've got Katy to think about. Besides, I don't know if I'm ready to get back out there, you know?"

"What does your daughter think?"

"She seems all right. But with her, it's hard to tell. She keeps a lot of things to herself."

"Want me to talk to her?"

"I don't know."

"So, where did you guys go?"

"Bouchon."

"Wow, fancy."

"The food was great."

"And the company?"

Rachel laughed. "Poor Lou. He was so nervous. And I was like— I was different. Edgy."

"You edgy?"

"I don't know what came over me."

"Well, this way you can keep him on his toes. Let's talk about you getting your real estate license."

"Stop. Tell me about Seattle."

"I will. But you have to promise me you won't be upset. Because Carter and I are fine. I repeat, FI-UN."

"Uh-oh."

"Here's the good news—I got to see a gray wolf up close."

"You're killing me," Rachel said, blanching. "You know that, right?"

Lou stared at the medical examiner's report. Harlan's housekeeper had emailed it to him as soon as the lawyer received it from the Seattle PD. After checking dental records, the ME had confirmed the body Sarah and Carter found was indeed Grace Zielinski, age fifty-five.

The autopsy concluded the cause of death was cranio-cerebral trauma. Manner of death was homicide. The ME had surmised the victim had most likely been hit on the head more than once with a large curved object, such as a shovel.

Charlie had told the police chief who he believed was the prime suspect. It chilled Lou to know he may have met the victim's killer only a few days earlier. And he wondered how they would go about proving the woman calling herself Grace—Laurel Diamanté—murdered the social services caseworker from Seattle.

He glanced at his phone—a little after noon. Rachel had let him know she was having lunch with Sarah. He wondered if she would tell her sister about their date. Of course she would. Sisters didn't keep things from each other. He rubbed the back of his neck, imagining Sarah's lightning-quick, negative reaction. Ever the protective sibling, she'd probably tried to convince Rachel she could do better than a small-town cop with an ex-wife, alimony payments, and a kid.

"What am I saying?"

When no one answered, he looked around his office. The muted walls ignored him. Hadn't she stood down when they spoke about it the last time? He was out of practice, that's all. And if he was being honest, he was self-conscious. He needed to take things slowly. If a relationship with Rachel Zamora was meant to be, then nothing—not even a woman as formidable as Sarah Greene—could stop it.

Tim appeared at the door, about to knock when Lou looked up. "I'm heading over to the women's shelter."

"Come in a sec. And close the door."

The officer took a seat, looking at his hands.

"Heidi told me what happened."

"She wasn't supposed to..."

"This is no reflection on you. You're a good cop. If you say you saw something you can't explain, that's good enough for me. And I don't expect you to put the incident in your report."

"I appreciate it. But it's just so...odd."

"Trust me, kid, I know. Ever since getting mixed up with Sarah Greene, I'm starting to question my own sanity. There are some strange things going on around this town. All I wanted to say was thank you for doing what you're doing. And if you need anything, don't hesitate to ask."

Tim got to his feet. "Thanks. It means a lot to me. Are you stopping by later?"

"Harlan wants us all there, apparently. Maybe we'll finally learn who killed Colonel Mustard in the library. Oh, what can you tell me about the writing on the wall?"

"It's definitely not blood because it's bright red. I think

it's some kind of paint, although there's no odor. Here, I've got pics."

He handed over his phone. Lou scrolled through the half dozen photos. When he got to a closeup of the writing, he enlarged it. Satisfied, he handed the phone back.

"I've already printed those and added them to my report," the young officer said. "Anyway, see you over there."

"Later, Tim."

After he left, the police chief thought about the words written in Latin. What they needed was an exorcist. He wanted to call Fr. Brian to discuss the matter but decided against it. Harlan ran the show, and as long as no actual criminal activity had occurred, Lou's hands were tied.

As his stomach complained, he grabbed his keys and headed out. He hoped The Cracked Pot wasn't too crowded. He had a lot to think about and needed some peace and quiet.

TWENTY-SEVEN

Late for another meeting, Irene gathered her things and left the office. The decision to place the troublesome Grace on administrative leave weighed on her, but the call from Harlan Covington had been persuasive. And after reading the PI's report, she felt compelled to act aggressively. But the caseworker was competent, and with the rising caseload, the program manager needed all the help she could get.

Slinging her large handbag over her shoulder, she strode past the sea of cubicles and out the doors to the elevators. She'd promised the lawyer she'd conduct a thorough investigation into Grace—or as she was now known, Laurel Diamanté. He had committed to providing hard evidence of criminal activity, the thought of which made her cringe.

When the elevator arrived, she stepped in and hit L. She'd never liked Grace. Irene thought she was combative, and sometimes, downright insulting. And she had anger issues. Thinking back, the program manager tried to remember why she'd hired the woman in the first place.

She recalled the glowing recommendation from Mary's Gift in Seattle. What a crock. They were probably glad to be rid of her.

She hurried across the lobby to another set of elevators leading to the parking garage. After pressing the button, she was about to get in when she heard her name. Turning, she saw her assistant hurrying toward her, waving a blue folder.

"You almost forgot this!"

"Oh, my goodness—what a day. Well, that would've been awkward. Thanks so much."

"No problem," the assistant said. "See you tomorrow."

As she hurried away, Irene checked her watch and shook her head. They'd probably start without her, which was fine with her. This was another in a long series of mind-numbing policy review meetings mandated by the archdiocese. In fact, she wondered why she needed to attend at all.

She rode the elevator down to P2. When she got out, the cave-like concrete interior seemed darker than usual. Were her eyes going bad? She could never remember where she parked in this indeterminable circle of hell and decided to go right.

As she made her way down a poorly lit aisle, the clacking of her low heels echoing, she glanced at the upper floor separated by security fencing, where a priest climbed into his car. She recognized him but was unable to recall his name. After several frustrating minutes, she spotted her vehicle and dug out her keys. Someone stepped in front of her.

"Grace?" she laughed with relief. "You startled me. What are you doing here?"

Laurel stood motionless, observing her superior with flat eyes.

"Is everything all right? Look, I had no choice. The archdiocese requires that we—"

Her expression darkening, her attacker moved toward her, holding a curious black object. As she got closer, she pressed on it, and flicking her right hand, revealed a razor-sharp steel blade. Before the woman could scream, her attacker ran the knife through her side. Shuddering, she collapsed, her eyes going glassy, unable to comprehend what had happened.

Though she was short, Laurel towered over her victim, the Warlock knife dripping with fresh blood. *"Enim mihi vindictam ego retribuam."*

"I don't know what you're saying!"

The deranged caseworker smiled like a viper. "Vengeance is mine, I will repay."

As she raised the blade to strike again, a car rounded the corner. The horrified priest stopped short. Glaring at him with contempt, Laurel fled.

He ran to where Irene lay, going into shock. The pool of blood surrounding her spread, forming bright rivulets in the concrete seams. He got out his phone, and his hands shaking badly, dialed 911. While he waited for the operator to pick up, he applied pressure to the wound.

"Be still," he said.

The EMT had finished securing the gurney inside the ambulance when an LAPD officer approached the priest, who he'd watched perform the Anointing of the Sick.

"Where are they taking her?" he said.

"Good Sam, I think."

A pitiful moan came from the gurney, and the cop turned to look. Wrapped in a patient blanket and connected to an IV, the victim lay writhing in the back of the vehicle. He wanted badly to interview her, but he was aware time was of the essence.

He and the cleric moved back as the EMT climbed in and closed the doors from the inside. Soon, the ambulance drove away. Mercifully, they'd left the siren off until they reached the exit.

"You're the one who found her, Father?" the officer said, taking notes.

"Yes."

"Did she say who attacked her?"

"An employee—Grace somebody... Grace Zielinski."

"Do you know her?"

"No."

The cop wrote the name in his notebook. He walked in a circle, careful not to step in the blood.

"Did anyone find a weapon?"

"I don't think so. I'm going to head over to the hospital."

"Okay, Father." The officer handed over the notebook. "Write down your name and a phone number where we can reach you."

The priest scribbled something, and carefully folding his purple stole, returned to his car. The cop watched thoughtfully as he drove off. Why would an employee attack her superior in a parking structure? Now he'd have to cordon off the area. He took a last look around and went to get barrier tape from his cruiser.

Laurel sat in her car staring at the lake in Echo Park. A few people were on the water in white pedal boats shaped like swans. Somewhere, children laughed. The sound sickened her. The bloody Warlock knife lay on the passenger floor mat, its blade exposed.

She'd failed—Irene was alive. If it hadn't been for the damned priest, she would've finished the job. She might die, though. *Shit.* By now, the cops were scouring the parking structure, looking for clues. Even though she'd picked a spot with no security cameras, she was sure the bitch would tell them who attacked her.

The fugitive realized she was finished in Los Angeles. Why had she been so impetuous? She should've continued the way she was going, despite the suspension. There was no evidence that she did anything wrong. Unless...

Had they discovered Grace's body after all these years? Impossible. And yet... Ever since meeting those two psychics, she had the sickening feeling that things were unraveling. She needed to hide until she could figure out what to do next. But where? In no time, they'd have the address of her Mid City apartment.

"I've failed," she said.

As she sat motionless, sobbing, a voice spoke to her. The sound cut through the middle of her brain like a dull, twisting knife.

Protect Ana, it said. *Protect Ana, or I'll bring pain like nothing you've ever felt. I will destroy you.*

A blinding light behind her eyes was followed by a cacophony of vicious dogs fighting. Holding her head in her hands, she gritted her teeth as black waves of agony attacked her skull from the inside, like a hawk's talons clawing their way out of a steel cage.

When the pain subsided, her face went slack. Drool leaked from lips that were numb, and blood dripped from her unfocused eyes. Wiping her face on her sleeve, she put her vehicle into gear and backed out of the parking space.

The first thing she had to do was get rid of the car.

Charlie walked into the library. Harlan was at his desk, sorting through a mass of papers, including the PI's reports and photos from the case. The lawyer looked up as he took a seat opposite him.

"Someone stabbed Irene MacAllister," Charlie said.

"Is she—"

"She's been in surgery for the past two hours. I spoke to the charge nurse, and they're hopeful she'll make it."

"What happened?"

"She was in the parking structure next to her building." He hesitated. "A priest saw the whole thing and identified Laurel Diamanté."

Harlan got to his feet as the PI continued.

"I spoke to the officer who was at the scene. He said if the witness hadn't been there, Irene would most likely be dead."

The lawyer made his way slowly to the doorway, obviously in pain. Mary was busy arranging a vase of camellias on a pedestal in the foyer.

"I need you." He waited for her to walk over. "Call Chief Fiore and ask him to come as quickly as possible. We were supposed to meet at St. Rita's, but things have changed.

Tell him there's a credible threat to the citizens of his town."

She nodded and walked away. Harlan put an arm on Charlie.

"I'm certain Laurel is headed for Dos Santos," the lawyer said. "I'd like you to go to the shelter and wait. There's something I need to attend to."

"Are you all right?"

"I'm fine."

"Sure, like me. What's going on? Are we dealing with a sociopath?"

"This has nothing to do with mental illness. As I told you before, it's about evil, pure and simple."

"Do you think the woman wants to harm Ana Robles?"

"No, I don't," Harlan said. "But Ana is the reason she's coming."

When Lou arrived at Harlan's house, it was after five and already dark. He'd never been to Montecito and marveled at the sheer wealth of the place as he parked. He trotted up to the front door and rang the bell. Almost immediately, he was greeted by a kind-looking, well-dressed woman with tired eyes.

"Chief Fiore?" she said. "Please come in."

Self-conscious, he wiped his feet on the mat and stepped inside. Though overwhelmed by the grandeur of the place, he wasn't envious. He was well aware that most people didn't live this way. And if an attorney had worked hard all his life to afford a place like this, good on him.

"Mr. Covington is in the library. This way."

"I didn't get your name."

"Mary."

She indicated the closed door and left him alone. He knocked softly and entered the room. The interior was like something out of a movie. Hundreds of books lined the walls. The furniture was red leather and rich looking. And the fireplace was lit. Walking in, he'd half-expected a string quartet to be playing in the corner.

"Mr. Covington?"

Harlan looked up from his desk. He seemed much older since the last time Lou had seen him, which had only been a few months ago.

"Don't get up," he said and crossed to the desk. Taking a seat, he gazed at his surroundings. "I have to admit, your message was pretty alarming."

"I appreciate you making the trip. There's a situation. Today, the woman calling herself Grace Zielinski attacked her superior with a knife."

"Is he alive?"

"Ms. MacAllister is indeed alive. She's in intensive care at Good Samaritan Hospital in Los Angeles. The police obtained a statement, a copy of which I have here." He handed the cop three typed pages. "As you can see, she identified her attacker."

Lou read the document, grunting at some of the details. "I appreciate you sharing the information with me. I won't even ask how you got it. But LA is out of my jurisdiction and—"

The lawyer leaned forward, his expression intense. "I have reason to believe this woman is on her way to Dos Santos."

"Why?"

"I'm convinced there's a strong connection between her and Ana Robles. And I'm afraid for the young woman."

"What do we know about the attacker?"

"Her name is Laurel Diamanté, although I'm not sure it's her real name. It's likely she murdered Grace Zielinski in Seattle seven years ago, then came to Los Angeles posing as her victim. I passed along this information to her superior, who suspended Laurel pending an investigation. Apparently, this enraged the woman, and she attacked Irene with the intent to kill her."

The police chief skimmed the statement again, mulling over what Harlan had said. If indeed a cold-blooded killer was on her way to his town, people—innocent people—would be in danger. Though he was a seasoned cop, he had the sense there was something other than normal criminal activity at work. He couldn't fathom what the lawyer's role was in the investigation, and he felt out of his depth.

"What do you need me to do?" he said.

"Put men on the street. Mary will give you flyers with the woman's driver's license photo to distribute. I can't stress enough how important it is that you stop this woman."

"She's probably headed for St. Rita's now."

"I believe that's a safe assumption. Your Tim Whatley is there?"

"He is. I'll send over more cops to watch the building."

"Excellent. Charlie is already there. And Sarah and Carter are on their way."

"Are you sure it's all right for them be there? I mean, if this woman is as dangerous as you say."

"I don't have time to explain. But with your people watching it, the shelter is the safest place they can be right now."

As Lou stood, the old man reached across his desk and took his hand. His was cool, and the cop thought he felt a slight tremble.

"Thank you, Chief Fiore. For everything."

As Lou returned to his vehicle with the flyers, he thought again about Sarah. If anything happened to her on his watch, Rachel would never forgive him.

Not in a million years.

TWENTY-EIGHT

W hen will you be back?" Joe said as Sarah slipped her phone into her purse.

"Couple of hours. What are you going to do?"

"Stay here and worry. I don't see why this is so important. Can't Carter and the others handle it?"

"Harlan insisted we both be there. And besides, why would I leave my friend to deal with this? We'll be fine."

Getting ready earlier, she'd already decided not to tell him about Laurel Diamanté. The lawyer had called her and explained everything. Though she was frightened, she had made up her mind to go, if for no other reason than to support Carter. Besides, Tim would be there, along with the other cops.

She kissed him and squeezed his hand. "I have a couple of minutes. You said you wanted to tell me something?"

"Not now."

"Okay. Hey, I'm looking forward to us getting away." Then on his silence, "Have you thought of anywhere yet? I've always wanted to go to Half Moon Bay."

"I think there's a Ritz-Carlton up there."

She pretended to ignore his lack of enthusiasm. "And once again, you are my hero."

"I love you," he said, brooding.

"I never get tired of hearing you say it. Love you too—later. You might want to break out the Talisker. PTSD be damned."

"Okay. Be safe."

Gary rubbed his back against her ankle. She picked him up and kissed his head. "Stay away from my exercise putty. I mean it."

She pulled the Galaxie out of the garage and backed into the street. Several people stood in a group a long way off. Though they weren't doing anything suspicious, their looks made her nervous. *Stop imagining things, Sarah.*

As she drove past, they turned toward her with wan faces. A police cruiser approached from the opposite direction, and they scattered.

"This town is getting weirder by the minute," she said.

Sarah was unable to park on Myrtle Street and drove around the corner, where she found a spot near Carter's MINI Cooper. It was after five and already dark. But St. Rita's was brightly lit. Several police cruisers were parked outside. Two more from the Santa Barbara PD had passed her as she made her turn. Given the heightened security, she was glad Joe was indoors. Out of habit, she took out her phone. As she did, it vibrated. It was Rachel's office number.

"Hi."

"What's happening?" her sister said. "There are cops everywhere."

"I'm sure it's fine. Why haven't you left the office yet?"

"I'm heading out now. I get the feeling you know what's going on."

"Only that they're looking for a person of interest."

"Well, is he dangerous?"

"It's a she. And yes, she is."

"I don't understand."

"Can I call you later? I have a meeting at the shelter. Promise me you'll go straight home."

"Does this dragnet have anything to do with the Guatemalan woman?"

"Honey, calm down. I have to run."

"Call me, okay?"

"I will—promise."

Sarah didn't like lying to Rachel, but there was nothing to be gained by upsetting her. Laurel would be caught and arrested. Everything would be fine, and Ana would be safe. She trotted up the steps and met a cop guarding the door.

"I'm Sarah Greene," she said. "They're expecting me."

"I recognize you." He opened the door for her. "Go on in."

Though all the lights were on, there was something eerie inside. It felt like a dark presence, though she didn't see anything. A moment later, Carter walked out and led her friend to the conference room.

"How's Ana?" Sarah said.

"She's having dinner with Heidi."

"The town is crawling with cops. Lou even brought some in from Santa Barbara."

"I don't have to tell you I'm more than a little freaked out."

"Just remember—we survived a gray wolf."

When they reached the conference room, Charlie and Tim were already there, eating off paper plates. Someone had set out a tray of sandwiches and chips, along with water and an assortment of sodas. As the women entered, the PI stood. Caught off guard, the young officer did the same.

"Such politeness," Sarah said as they took their seats. "Where's Harlan?"

The sacred room was located in the basement. It was small and spare, with walls painted a warm white. The carpet was a rich brown. A crucifix hung on one wall. Opposite it on the other wall was a crooked staff made of cypress.

A plain wooden chair stood in the center of the room, facing a table with old books lying open. Next to them were small glass bottles of water and oil, candles, and a shofar. Behind the table on the wall hung a portrait of an old man. Affecting a formal pose, he stood in a room filled with books and ancient manuscripts. And he held a staff resembling the one on the wall.

Abramo Levy, the first Guardian.

Harlan sat, his eyes closed, praying silently. As he did, the pages of a book fluttered. When he looked up, he recognized the familiar light coming from behind the books and recited aloud.

> *Lamah hashem, ta'amod berachok; ta'lim,*
> *le'ittot batzarah.*

> *Bega'avat rasha', yidlak ani; yittafesu, bimz-*
> *immot zu chashavu.*
> *Ki-hillel rasha', al-ta'avat nafsho; uvotzea*
> *berech, ni'etz hashem.*

As he continued to pray, the light grew stronger, illuminating the painting. He stopped suddenly. Grabbing his chest, he struggled to breathe. With the other hand, he gripped the arm of the chair.

"Please, God," he said. "Not yet."

Heidi entered the conference room, carrying several rosaries made of plastic beads and string. She distributed them to everyone.

Carter looked up at her. "But I'm not Catholic."

The director patted her hand. "Hold on to it, dear—for safety."

"Harlan wanted us to pray the Rosary?" Sarah said. "But I thought—"

"He's a firm believer in prayer, as am I."

Heidi took a seat next to Tim. His two-way radio crackled with the chatter of the other officers. He turned down the volume. She made the Sign of the Cross, and everyone followed—all except the girl. Clutching her beads, she closed her eyes and lowered her head. As the others prayed aloud, she thought of her best friend.

When they were twelve, she'd attended Franny's bat mitzvah. Carter could still hear her chanting the haftarah, her voice sing-songy as she struggled to pronounce the Hebrew. Her eyes filled with tears as she realized, perhaps for the first time, that she too had wanted the ceremony. More than anything—even now—she wanted to belong.

It was cold outside, and the rain made it hard to see clearly. The cop at the front door squinted at several figures shuffling out of the darkness like ghosts. At first, he thought they might be visitors. But there was something unsettling about them.

Moving as one, they lined the sidewalk, oblivious to the weather. Then, more came. Soon, there were perhaps fifty poorly dressed men and women of various ages standing in a line. All of them stared at the only window on the fourth floor that was lit.

It was Ana's room.

He grabbed his radio and spoke quietly, his voice warbling with fear. "10-66. I repeat, 10-66."

Another voice came back. "More than one?"

"Way more. Forty or fifty."

"What are they doing?"

"Nothing. Just standing there."

"Okay, stay put," the second officer said. "I'm going up to the roof to see if there are more on the other side of the building."

"10-4."

The first cop unholstered his weapon and kept it at his side. "What do you want here?"

They ignored him, their flat eyes focused on the Guatemalan woman's room.

The second officer opened the door to the roof and stepped into the rain. Large puddles lay scattered across the surface. Shining his flashlight beam, he walked out and checked the rear of the building. All clear. As he approached the front, he saw something floating several feet off the edge. Afraid, he inched closer.

Ana Robles hung suspended in midair, high above the ground. She wore a translucent white flowing nightgown. Her hair fell around her shoulders, and she was barefoot.

"What in hell?" he said.

She opened her arms to him, beckoning him to come closer. As he did, his foot slipped on the edge of the building. Regaining his balance, he was about to walk off the ledge when a hand grabbed him by the shoulder and yanked him back. Dazed, he turned to find Tim staring at him.

"It's not real," the young officer said.

When the other cop looked again, he gasped.

Nothing was there but the rain.

Joe sat on the living room sofa, trying to concentrate on the *Dubious* episode he'd been watching. Donnie and Debbie Fisk were investigating a ghost sighting in an old house in Sutter Creek, California. Gary was on his lap, purring and kneading his paws. Joe glanced at his watch. It was after nine.

He had tried calling Sarah several times with no luck. Earlier, he'd had a strong feeling she was holding something back. She hadn't told him the details of her Seattle adventure. And she'd gone quiet after getting a call, which he suspected was from Harlan. He picked up the cat and set him on the floor. Taking out his keys, he walked out the front door and stopped abruptly.

A group of men and women stood in a long line on the sidewalk in the rain, facing the house. Their eyes were distant and lacked emotion. He felt a sharp pain, and when he looked down, he noticed his keys cutting into his hand. He wasn't sure if these people were a threat and ignored them.

His truck was parked in the driveway, and as he walked toward it, he spotted the slashed tires. Then, a familiar sound. A blue plastic ball bounced across the driveway and into the street. His breath caught, and he glared at the strangers. Their stony silence—their sheer indifference—terrified him. He had no weapon. Besides, what would he do if he had? Attack them? Breathing hard, he returned to the house.

After locking the front door, he ignored the meowing cat and hurried into the living room to the French doors, which led to the backyard. The women's shelter wasn't far. If he ran, he'd be there in less than twenty minutes. Gary let out a low howl and hissed.

Two men and a woman stood in the middle of the yard. All wore shabby clothes and looked too thin to be alive. Though they didn't speak, he knew they wanted to hurt him. Grabbing his phone, he dialed 911, but there was no cell service. Frantic, he hurried to the kitchen. Still nothing. He grabbed a large knife and stared at it in his hand. He'd never stabbed anyone. Angry and frustrated, he lowered his arm as the truth of the situation hit him.

"They're everywhere," he said.

Lou had patrolled the streets for two hours and, so far, had seen no one suspicious. As he approached the corner of Dos Santos Boulevard and Cherry, he spotted a lone figure walking past the liquor store—no, gliding. From the size and build, he guessed it was a woman. He slowed to a stop and waited for her to walk under the glow of a streetlamp. When she did, he recognized the suspect and called for backup.

In less than a minute, two Santa Barbara PD cruisers appeared. He pulled forward and flicked on the siren. Glancing back, the suspect broke into a run. He and four other cops got out and pursued her on foot.

"Police! Halt!"

The officers split up, two of them getting ahead of the suspect. Seeing she was trapped, she stopped and raised her arms as the police chief approached her, pointing his weapon.

"Laurel Diamanté, I am arresting you for the attempted murder of Irene MacAllister. You have the right to remain silent. Anything you say can and will be used against you in a court of law."

As he continued to recite the Miranda Warning, he handcuffed her hands behind her back. Surprisingly, she offered no resistance.

"Radio everyone and let them know we got her," he said to a cop.

"10-4," Tim said.

He was in the conference room and put down the radio. Relieved, he looked up at the others. "They got her."

"Oh, thank God!" Heidi said.

Sarah took Carter's hand. "I need to call Joe."

As she stepped away with her phone, the girl approached Tim. "Should we wait for Harlan?"

The young officer glanced at his watch. "I guess he's not coming. Can you stick around until I can check on Ana?"

"Sure." She didn't want to spend another second in this damnable place.

"Charlie?" Tim said. "Can you see if those drifters are still out there?"

As the PI started for the hallway, Sarah and Carter joined him.

"Did you talk to Joe?" the girl said to her friend.

"I can't get through. Where's Whatley?"

"Looking in on Ana."

Opening a blind on the front window, Charlie peeked out. The rain came down steadily, and the street was deserted.

He turned around. "All clear."

"Wait, what's that?" Carter said.

He looked to see where she was pointing. Something lay on the lawn near a hedge, which bordered the front of the building. It wasn't moving. Taking out his weapon, he opened the front door.

"Stay here, both of you," he said. "And lock the door."

Ignoring the pain in his ribs, he made his way across the wet grass toward the dark mass and recognized a police officer. Kneeling, he leaned in. The man's throat had been sliced straight across, the blood washed away in the rain. He felt for a pulse. Getting up stiffly, he made his way back to the building. Sarah let him in and locked the door.

"Is he…"

"Dead," he said.

Tim stepped out of the elevator and saw the body of the officer he'd rescued earlier. It lay just outside Ana's room with a dark gash across the throat. Tim felt for a pulse. There was none, but the body was warm. Drawing his weapon, he wiped the sweat from his brow and entered the darkened room. Empty. He checked the bathroom. Same. He grabbed his radio.

"Code 3. 11-98," he said. "I repeat, 11-98."

Nothing but static. Most likely, the police chief and the others were out of range. He pulled out his phone and dialed the police dispatcher.

"This is Officer Whatley, badge number forty-four," he said. "We have an emergency."

Lou stood near a holding cell at the police station, observing his prisoner. She sat motionless on the bench, meeting his gaze. Something about her eyes wasn't right. The dispatcher hurried toward him, waving a note.

"What is it, Laurie?"

She lowered her voice. "Tim called from St. Rita's. Two officers are dead."

"What about the others?"

"As far as I know, they're fine. Chief, there's something else." She drew him away from the cell. "Ana Robles is missing."

Pivoting, he glowered at Laurel, who grinned at him with unblinking eyes.

"I want all available units over there," he said to Laurie. "And contact EMS."

"Okay." When he looked past him at the cell, she gasped.

"What is it?"

"Where's your prisoner?"

"What? She's right—"

The holding cell was empty. He tried the door—locked.

"No, it can't be!" he said.

Mary descended the stairs quickly, holding her phone. When she reached the bottom, she gasped. Her employer was on his knees in front of the sacred room, its door ajar. His phone lay next to him.

"Harlan!" Kneeling, she lay her hand on his. "I'm calling 911."

"No," he said, gripping her arm firmly with his other hand. "Help me up."

"But—"

"Sarah and Carter are in grave danger."

She got to her feet and placed his arm on her shoulder. With her other hand, she helped him stand. It took two tries, but at last he made it.

"Lock the door," he said.

He handed her the key, and she did as instructed.

"I need you to drive me to Dos Santos."

"You're in no shape."

Fighting the pain in his body, he touched her face. "What have I always told you?"

"*Never underestimate a lawyer,*" she said, shaking her head.

Two EMTs entered the lobby of St. Rita's as Sarah and her friend watched in somber silence.

"This makes no sense," Carter said. "Lou told us they got her."

Sarah rubbed her wrist. "She must've had help." When she saw Heidi and Tim, she said, "I need to get home."

The director turned to the young officer. "Is it safe?"

"I'll escort them to their cars," he said. Then to the other women, "Come on."

The women took turns hugging Heidi.

"I wish there was more we could've done," Sarah said.

Outside, the rain had let up. She looked up to find a moonless sky filled with dark clouds. It was chilly, and as she walked past the police cruisers and ambulance, she thought of Joe. Was he all right? All she wanted was to be in his arms. She thought back to when Rupinder had first told her about the troubles at the women's center. Stupidly, she'd imagined this would be a simple case.

But now, a young woman had committed suicide, a social services manager had been stabbed, and there were two cops with their throats slit. She wasn't cut out for this, despite being able to see beyond the veil. Maybe if she prayed hard enough, God would pity her and take back the gift. Right. *And maybe unicorns are real.* She caught up to Carter and put an arm around her as they walked together.

"I need a vacation," the girl said.

As they turned the corner, Sarah spotted their cars. When she'd reached hers with the others, keys in hand, she touched Tim's arm.

"None of this was your fault," she said.

He looked bewildered. "What's happening to this town? Look, I need to get back. You guys okay?"

"We're fine," she said. "Thanks so much."

She watched as he disappeared around the corner. Moments later, she saw them. A dozen or more badly dressed men and women had been lurking in the shadows and moved swiftly toward them, their eyes menacing.

"Tim!"

There was no time. Taking her friend's hand, Sarah wheeled around, intending to run to the shelter. But it was too late. Another twenty or so had closed in behind them. They were surrounded.

"I wanna scream, but I can barely breathe," Carter said.

"Try to stay calm."

Sarah glanced in both directions. This wasn't like their ghost encounter in the forest. These things were flesh and blood. And worse, there was nowhere to run. By the time the cops showed up, they'd be dead like the two cops. *Pray.* Staring intently at the strangers, she spoke in a quiet, even voice.

"We have to pray the St. Michael prayer. And you need to show them the medal."

Nodding fiercely, the girl held up her shaking hand and, turning, displayed the bracelet to everyone around her. Sarah pulled her St. Michael medal out of her shirt and showed it to them as well. The strangers grunted like animals beaten with crude sticks. As the women chanted aloud, the miscreants cowered and held their hands over their ears, wailing.

They prayed more loudly. One creature dragged herself closer and lunged at Carter. But when she touched the bracelet, her hand burst into flames, the blue fire charring her skin. Shrieking, she stumbled back.

A squeal of tires, then headlights. Sarah turned sharply in time to see Harlan's Mercedes come to a stop at an angle in the middle of the street. The elderly attorney struggled out of the passenger side and made his way toward the demoniacs. When they saw him, they bared their teeth and hissed, their eyes instantly turning black.

Saying something she couldn't make out, he raised his right arm. A brilliant white light poured out of his hand, its rays illuminating the damned creatures and sending them scattering. But some refused to leave and continued to creep toward the women.

Harlan came closer, his arm held high. The light grew stronger. Shielding their eyes, they shrieked, the sound like an impossibly huge metal door scraping against concrete as it closed. The sound was deafening. A powerful ball of white light sent them hurtling back like rag dolls in a hurricane, and they landed far away from the women.

Amazed, the girl watched as they cowered on the ground, whimpering like groveling dogs. Only one—a twenty-something with yellow spiked hair—remained standing.

The Guardian was close now and yanked him by the collar. He tried pressing the ring to the fiend's forehead, but the creature grabbed his hand and violently twisted Harlan's arm until he succumbed with a loud cry and sank to his knees.

Enraged, Carter faced the demoniac. He laughed in a high, grating voice. She slapped his face hard with her right hand. As he wavered, momentarily stunned, she grabbed the back of his greasy neck with her left hand and pulled him close. Then with her right hand, she pressed the St. Benedict medal against his temple.

Putrid gray smoke poured from the creature's head,

accompanied by the acrid smell of burning flesh. Opening his mouth wide, he let out a faint squeak. As his head burst into a holocaust of blue flames, he dropped to his knees on the wet asphalt and collapsed onto his side, dead.

When she looked up again, she saw the others had fled. Only she, Sarah, and Harlan remained. And Mary, cowering next to the Mercedes, her trembling hands clasped in prayer.

"How…" Sarah said to her friend. "How in the world did you do that?"

Tears poured from Carter's eyes. "I don't know!"

Sarah reached out and helped the attorney to his feet.

"Mark, chapter nine," he said. "Remember?"

"The power of prayer. But what she did was…"

He grasped the girl's hands. "You have the gift. Can you see now why they fear you?"

Looking down, she shook her head. "Laurel took Ana."

"I know. Get some rest, both of you. We'll fight another day."

The women embraced him. He seemed so old and frail. What had become of his commanding strength? Sarah watched him leave. Ever so slowly, he walked to his vehicle, then dropped like a rock in the street.

"Harlan!" As she and Carter knelt next to him, the housekeeper came running to assist. "What's wrong with him?"

Mary's eyes brimmed with tears. As she stroked her employer's aged hand, she looked at the other women gravely.

"He's dying," she said.

Laurel pulled the late-model white Lincoln Navigator into the mini-mart parking lot. They'd been driving for more than an hour on the 126 when they arrived in Santa Clarita. She unbuckled her seatbelt and got out. Ana, wearing blue jeans and a hoodie, sat in the passenger seat, her hands folded in her lap. She stared straight ahead.

"Just going to get some supplies," the older woman said.

She walked into the brightly lit store and grabbed a blue plastic handbasket. Quickly, she filled it with water bottles and snacks. As she passed the cleaning supplies aisle, she stopped and picked up plastic gloves, bleach, and paper towels.

The clerk behind the counter looked fifteen, with dyed black hair, tattoos up and down both arms, and acne scars. As she placed the items on the counter, he rang them up, looking past her at the vehicle parked out in front.

"Sweet ride," he said without enthusiasm.

She handed him a one-hundred-dollar bill. He frowned at it.

"You don't have anything smaller?"

"If I had, I would've given it to you."

Rolling his eyes, he took the bill and examined the purple stripe down the middle, moving it back and forth to see if the color changed. He grabbed a flashlight and shone it behind the bill toward him, revealing a hidden image of Benjamin Franklin.

"Are you finished?" she said, ignoring his gap-toothed grin.

"Had to make sure it's not a fake. Don't wanna get fired."

He put the money in the cash register and gave her the

change. Without another word, she walked out with her bags and got into the vehicle as the clerk watched.

She pulled out onto the main highway, heading toward the entrance to the I-5. She would go a little farther north to Bakersfield. Then she'd stop at one of the hundreds of abandoned oil wells and dump the body of the driver whose vehicle she had stolen. He'd hardly put up a fight.

"Easy peasy," Laurel said.

TWENTY-NINE

It was almost midnight when the women arrived. Carter parked on the street and followed her friend to the front door. Joe had been watching from the window and flung open the door as they approached. When Sarah saw him, she opened her arms and let his arms envelop her.

"I was so worried," he said, kissing the top of her head. "Hey, Carter."

Sarah looked up at him, her eyes misty. "I hope you don't mind, but she's going to crash here tonight."

"It's fine."

Hiding his irritation, he moved aside. He was desperate to talk to her about what had happened. But he wanted to do it when they were alone—another thing he was forced to put off.

"Are you guys hungry?" he said.

Sarah shook her head. "I'm not. Carter?"

"I just wanna go to bed."

"The guest bedroom is already made up. Let me know if you need a toothbrush."

"Thanks. Night."

Joe and Sarah watched as the girl wandered off. He took his ex-wife's face in his hands and kissed her.

"We really need to talk," he said.

She patted his hand. "We will."

"Want a drink?"

"Okay, maybe one."

She followed him into the kitchen, where Gary was eating from his bowl. Beyond exhausted, she took a seat at the counter as he poured them each a shot of Talisker. Unenthusiastically, she clinked glasses with him and threw back the whiskey.

"Hit me again," she said.

He touched her hand, wondering if now was a good time to bring up the hostile strangers. Tomorrow—it was obvious things had gone badly tonight for her. As he sipped his drink in silence, she grabbed the bottle and headed for the living room. He looked down and found the cat staring at him.

"I'm going," he said.

When they were comfortable on the sofa, he placed his arm around her shoulders. She rested her head against his chest.

"Two police officers died tonight," she said.

He sat up straight. "How did it happen?"

"The cops were looking for a suspect. We think it was her."

She hadn't planned on telling him anything tonight, but the words came pouring out. She told him about Laurel's arrest and how she'd somehow vanished from the holding cell. Then she mentioned Ana, who had gone missing, and Charlie and Tim discovering the dead officers.

But what she didn't say was how she and Carter had

almost died at the hands of demoniacs acting on the orders of someone unseen. And how her friend had saved them. Because telling him would inevitably lead to Harlan.

"I tried going over there tonight," he said.

"What?"

"I couldn't. These weird strangers showed up out of nowhere. And they prevented me from leaving."

"Prevented how?"

"For starters, they slashed my tires. And there was something about them."

"Their eyes, right?"

"I can't believe I'm saying this, but I was terrified."

She took his hand. "You should be. Something's happening to this town. And these strangers are a part of it. I'm so glad you're safe. Oh my God, Rachel! I promised to call her."

He finished his drink as she ended the call with her sister. "I don't like this."

"Neither do I." Getting up, she offered him her hand. "Come on, let's go to bed."

They left the bottle and glasses on the coffee table and wandered toward her bedroom.

After she'd finished in the bathroom, she climbed into bed. Joe wore a T-shirt and boxers. She wanted to make love, but she was too exhausted. Instead, she slipped under the covers and lay her head on his chest. As he gently stroked her hair, she fell into a peaceful, dreamless sleep.

"I love you," she said.

Mary sat in the darkened private room at Santa Barbara Cottage Hospital, praying the Rosary as Harlan slept fitfully. The doctors had determined that the stress if his disease had affected his heart. She'd asked the doctor why he passed out, and the young man with the beard stubble and thick glasses said it was probably nervous exhaustion.

She was aware there wasn't much time left and wondered what would happen after he was gone. He'd provided her with a generous pension, and she would be free to do whatever she wanted. But what did she want? After leaving the convent, she'd thought she would end up in business and had signed up for classes at the community college. But she needed money and had decided to register at an employment agency.

As soon as she met with the recruiter, she was offered the position as housekeeper to a local attorney. Why her? She had no experience running a household, yet they claimed she was perfect for the job. That was twenty years ago. She'd asked Harlan about it on her ten-year anniversary, and he assured her it was merely a case of good timing, as he'd just posted the position the same week.

Since then, she'd been devoted to him, as she had been to Christ when she was a nun. It would be five years before she learned who her employer really was. And another five until she witnessed his awesome power. A drifter had wandered onto the property, intent on killing Harlan. She was outside in the garden, tending the rose bushes, which always relaxed her.

The demoniac with the flat eyes approached her, not speaking. Terrified, she screamed. Then the Guardian appeared. Raising his hand, he drove the miscreant back. Holding his head, the cursed thing howled like an animal in pain. She recalled his eyes, which were spinning in their sockets until, at last, they rolled up into his head. Recovering, he fled.

Still on her knees, she trembled, with no idea what had happened. All she wanted was to retreat to her room to pray. Harlan helped her up and, touching her shoulder, spoke in a gentle voice.

"Now you know what I am," he said. "And don't worry. This power doesn't come from the Evil One. I will always protect you."

Mary looked over at the bed and realized his eyes were open. She went to him and took his hand.

"What time is it?" he said.

"Almost morning."

"I had the strangest dream. I saw Ana. She was free."

"I don't understand."

"Free of the demon."

He sat up, wincing at the pain in his chest. Lovingly, she adjusted his pillows.

"But that wasn't all. You were there, looking after her."

She laughed. "What nonsense."

"What about Sarah and Carter?"

"They're fine."

He took her hand. "We have a lot of work ahead of us, you know."

"But now you must rest."

Tired, he lay down and closed his eyes. She adjusted his blanket.

"It's gaining strength," he said. "And it knows I'm getting weaker."

He was quiet for a time, and she thought he'd fallen asleep. She was about to get up when he spoke, his eyes closed.

"I've already left you written instructions. Carry them out as soon as you get back. Then burn them."

"Don't worry," she said, patting his hand. "Go to sleep."

Carter had risen before dawn and returned to her apartment. She recalled the dream of her standing outside her apartment building. A man was there—straight blond hair and wearing an expensive black suit. He wasn't threatening, so she said hello to him. But instead of saying hello back, he repeated the words Harlan had told her the night before, only now in a cultured English accent. *You have the gift. Can you see now why they fear you?* Though the dream wasn't disturbing, it left her with questions. She knew no such man. Clearly, he was a stand-in for the Guardian, but why English?

She wasn't due at The Cracked Pot until eleven. Desperate for a cigarette, she was disappointed to find there were none left in her purse. A smoke, a shower, and breakfast sounded good. She still didn't understand what she'd done—how she saved Sarah and herself. It had all seemed so...what? *Natural.* Despite what Harlan had told her, though, she clung to the idea that it was the St. Benedict medal all along and not her.

After finding a parking spot at the end of her street, she jogged toward her building and climbed the familiar stairs. She let herself in and went into the kitchen. In a cupboard, she discovered an open carton of Dunhill cigarettes. She took down the familiar red-and-silver box and set it on the counter. These were expensive and hard to get. After coming into her money, she'd happily switched from Marlboro.

She took out a fresh pack and was about to unwrap it when she remembered running away from those ghosts in Mt. Rainier National Park with Sarah. Her lungs had hurt so badly, and she'd nearly passed out trying to catch her breath. But her friend had sprinted away like a kid on the playground. Carter recalled the demoniacs the previous night. What if the medal hadn't worked, and they'd had to flee? Would she have been able to?

Instead of smoking, she decided to change shoes and go for a run—but only a short one. No use going all crazy. Outside, the air was crisp and smelled wonderful. Adjusting her hoodie, she trotted down the stairs and crossed to the street, which was deserted. At first, she hacked repeatedly and felt her lungs burning. She slowed to a walk until the spasm passed.

She resumed jogging at a slower pace, this time ignoring the urge to cough. After fifteen minutes, she realized she'd gone farther than she thought she would. But rather than push her luck, she turned around and headed back to her apartment.

It was after seven by the time she'd showered and dressed. She was about to head out to grab breakfast when she noticed her laptop sitting on the desk by the window. Excited, she went over and sat.

The story she had written, "The Girl in the Mirror," was on her MacBook desktop. She checked her watch. Seven-thirty. She could always show up at The Cracked Pot early and eat breakfast there. She wasn't sure what she would call this one, but she knew she had to write everything down—all except the Guardian's involvement.

As Carter typed furiously, she realized she'd never been so happy to be alive. And she continued, the words pouring out of her like nectar from a honey bear.

THIRTY

The trip to Half Moon Bay would take six-and-a-half hours. Though they could've saved more than an hour using the 101 instead of Highway 1, Sarah had wanted to see the coast, and Joe obliged. There was plenty of daylight as they approached Monterey. She thought they might have lunch and visit the aquarium.

It had been two days since the horrible night. She'd had an emergency session with Roxanne, which made her feel better. When they first met, the therapist had assured her patient that she was a strong woman. Now, after having survived a harrowing day in a haunted forest and demoniacs who threatened to kill her, she began to believe it.

Carter had changed too in so many ways. She'd found a new strength in herself. And it thrilled Sarah to learn her friend was trying to quit smoking and had taken up running. When they returned from their mini vacation, she planned to go on regular runs with Carter, partly to encourage her. But mostly because she loved the girl and enjoyed her company.

The sky was bright blue. Though Sarah was in the passenger seat, on her left she saw the waves crashing against the shore. She looked at her ex-husband. Damn, even his profile was perfect. And she told herself, despite everything, God must have put him in her path for a reason.

The aquarium was beautiful and not very crowded. Among the attractions, she had especially liked the bigfin reef squid and the jellyfish. For reasons she didn't understand, they reminded her of underwater fairies.

It was almost evening when they arrived at the Ritz-Carlton in Half Moon Bay. The majestic property sat on a bluff overlooking the ocean. Though she'd wanted to walk on the beach, by the time they checked in and went to their room, it was dark. So instead, they decided to shower and change, then have dinner at Navio, one of the hotel restaurants.

"I feel pretty great," she said as she took another sip of her Chardonnay.

"I'm glad."

He'd been unusually quiet, and she wondered if he was still upset about what happened at the house. Better to let it go for now. Knowing him, she believed he'd open up when he was ready. All she wanted now was to enjoy their time together. After the ahi tuna ribbons, she'd settled on the diver scallops for an entrée. Everything was incredible. When the dessert menu came, she wanted nothing more than a thirty-year-old scotch and the arms of the man she loved surrounding her.

The two days had gone by much too quickly, and it was time to return to Dos Santos. Before getting on the road, Sarah thought it would be nice to have breakfast in town and walk its streets a little. She'd never been to Half Moon Bay and was eager to explore. Ever accommodating, Joe agreed.

After breakfast, they made their way leisurely down Main Street when they passed a small art gallery.

"Hey, I'm going to pop in there for a sec," she said.

An attractive middle-aged woman wearing wool pants and a silk shirt approached them. "Is there something I can show you?"

Sarah took it all in. It had been a long time since she'd been to a gallery. "I'm looking for a gift for a friend."

"Any particular style?"

"I remember attending a Gwen John exhibit years ago. And I can still see those images. Solitary women sitting at tables and reading."

"I know what you mean—I love her work." The gallery owner smiled. "Come on back. I'd like to show you something."

As Joe perused the small space, Sarah followed the woman to her office.

"I don't hang everything I own," the owner said. "There just isn't room."

She sat at her desk and brought up a catalog of paintings on her computer. "Let me see... Ah, yes, here it is."

Sarah came around the desk and was struck immediately by the image of a young woman with short, dark hair sitting at a table, reading by candlelight. Behind her was a tall window. And outside in the darkness, watching the girl, was the pale, ghostly image of another woman. She was the same age.

"Oh my God!" Sarah said, squinting at the title—*The Lost Friend.*

"Would you like to see it?"

"I'm not leaving until I do."

"Okay, wait here."

Soon, the woman returned, carrying an unframed canvas. She stood it up on the desk as Sarah moved back to look at it properly. The work was wonderful and seemed so much like Gwen John.

"Was the artist copying her?" she said.

"Let's just say she was inspired."

Before coming here, Sarah had no idea what she would buy Carter for her new house. And now, here was the perfect painting. Bending down, she examined the artist's signature in the lower right-hand corner, trying to decipher it. She thought the name started with an "F."

"I can't make out the last name," she said.

"Jacobson."

"F. Jacobson. I'll take it." She laughed. "I suppose I should've asked the price first."

"Fifty-five hundred. She's a young artist who's starting out. But she's very talented, as you can see. I'm expecting great things from her."

Sarah knitted her brow. "Well, I'd better check with my husband."

"You know what? You seem like a nice couple. I can offer you a twenty percent discount."

"Thank you," Sarah said, hugging the owner. "I'll leave it to you to choose the frame. Let me write down my address."

"You should have it in about a week."

"I was wondering. Does the artist live around here?"

"Yes."

"I'd love to meet her."

"I'm afraid she's rather a private person."

"Well, at least let me know the next time she has a show."

"I will."

As they left the gallery, Joe shook his head. *"Husband?"*

"It got us the discount, didn't it?"

"I can't believe you found the perfect gift for Carter three hundred miles from home."

"It was meant to be, my friend," she said. "Do you think she'll love it as much as I do?"

It was late when Sarah and Joe walked into her house. Before leaving, she had boarded Gary. As a result, the place seemed oddly quiet. He carried in the bags, and she brought the Papa Pepito pizza to the kitchen. As she poured two glasses of a pinot noir they'd picked up in Los Olivos, he took a seat. Though they were starved, he didn't reach for a slice.

"I feel like there's something on your mind," she said. "Is it what you mentioned before?"

He set down his wineglass. "I didn't tell you everything about the other night. And I really don't know if I was imagining it or not."

"What is it?"

He took her hand and kissed it. "When those weird strangers showed up, something else happened. I saw..." He choked on the words. "It was a blue plastic ball bouncing across the driveway. Just like the one..."

Sensing something bad, she scooted her chair closer

and took both his hands. He didn't make eye contact. Then he drained his glass.

"Whatever it is you need to tell me, it's okay," she said. "I promise I'll understand."

"I don't think you will."

"We've been through too much together—you have to trust me."

His eyes pleaded with her. Sniffling, he brushed away the hair from her face and kissed her forehead. After everything that had happened, she wasn't sure she was ready and braced herself.

"When I was sixteen, I killed a little girl." Her hands tensed. "It was an accident. She ran out into the road, and before I could stop the car, I hit her. But it was the ball—a warning. It bounced into the street in front of me, before she— Just before I ran her over."

He squeezed his eyes shut, willing the tears to stop. But it was no use.

"There weren't any witnesses. My mother was with me. She told me when the police came, I was to say it was she who was driving—not me. No one else knows the truth— not even my father. Now you know what kind of person I am. I don't deserve you."

Overcome, she felt unable to breathe. When he tried getting but she held him firmly. "You were a kid."

"That's no excuse."

"Joe, look at me. I know you. And I know in my heart if there was any way to save her, you would have."

"I love you so much, Sarah. I don't know why I ever—"
"Shh."

Taking his hand, she led him to her bedroom. They lay on top of the duvet, both in torment, and held onto each other as if their own existence depended on the other.

"I will never stop loving you," she said.

As they lay there, she felt something coming to rest on them like an invisible cloak. It was warm and comforting. And then she felt something on her cheek.

It was a playful puff of air, made by a laughing child.

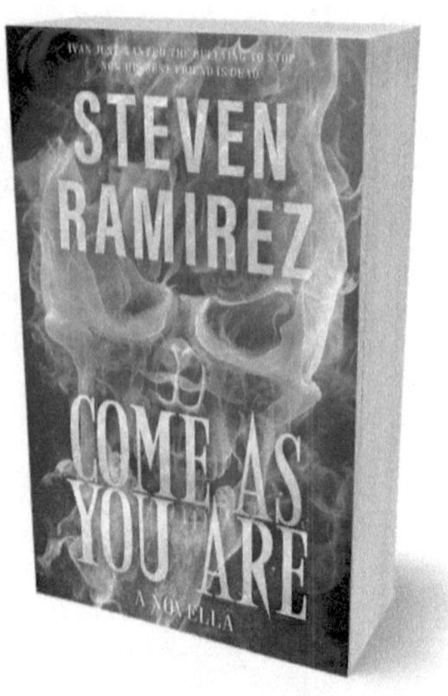

YOUR FREE BOOK IS WAITING

Ivan just wanted the bullying to stop. Now his best friend is dead.

Download your free copy of the novella *Come As You Are*. Then, turn on all the lights.

BOOKS.STEVENRAMIREZ.COM/GET-HORROR

ABOUT THE AUTHOR

Steven Ramirez is the award-winning American author of thriller, supernatural, and literary fiction. A former screenwriter, he's written about man-made plagues and idyllic towns infested with ghosts and demons. His latest novel is *Let's Get Lost*, a modern fairy tale. Steven lives in Los Angeles.

AUTHOR WEBSITE
stevenramirez.com

instagram.com/byStevenRamirez
goodreads.com/byStevenRamirez
bookbub.com/authors/steven-ramirez